HIGHLAND LEGEND

KATHRYN LeVEQUE

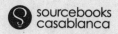

sourcebooks
casablanca

Published by Sourcebooks Casablanca, an imprint of Sourcebooks
P.O. Box 4410, Naperville, Illinois 60567-4410
(630) 961-3900
sourcebooks.com

Printed and bound in Canada.
MBP 10 9 8 7 6 5 4 3 2 1

Cum Gratiarum Actione (with thanks)

With thanks to the very first romance reader I ever knew—my grandmother, Hester. Though she has long since left us, I can still see her, sitting in her living room with a dog-eared Harlequin or Dorothy Garlock novel in her hands. She sure loved those books. Little did she know what she would inspire in her eldest granddaughter.

Thank you, Gramma, for giving me a glimpse of what joy a romance novel can give. I'll imagine you with a dog-eared Kathryn Le Veque novel in your hands from now on...

IT IS THE YEAR OF OUR LORD 1453, AND SIR CLEGG DE LAVE, A battle-scarred English knight, begins his search for a life that will bring him glory and riches…

After years as a mercenary in France, Spain, and the Holy Roman Empire, Clegg returns to Scotland to establish the most powerful and profitable gambling guild the world had ever seen, modeled on the gladiatorial schools of ancient Rome.

The Ludus Caledonia quickly becomes the center of battles for entertainment, but also for opportunity—if a warrior wins, a lord may offer him a lucrative military position.

The lure of money and position makes men from all walks of life into fighters and some into winners, and only a rare few find something beyond the love of a fight.

The love of a good woman.

This rare few who will know their happily ever after.

This is the world of the Ludus Caledonia…and business is booming.

THE SACRAMENTUM

I faithfully swear to do all that is commanded of me,
All that is required of me,
And all that is asked of me.
May I live both to fight and to protect my brethren.
May God smile upon me and grant me courage
So that I may not fail myself nor those around me.
Thus it is spoken, thus it shall be done.

—*Fionnadh Fuil (Blood Oath)*
of the Ludus Caledonia

PART ONE

VADE AD VICTOR SPOLIA

(TO THE VICTOR GO THE SPOILS)

CHAPTER ONE

Edinburgh, Scotland—The Ludus Caledonia
The Month of August
Year of Our Lord 1488

HE COULD SEE HIS OPPONENT ACROSS THE ARENA FLOOR, through a haze of dust that seemed to conceal just how badly injured his opponent was.

But no amount of dust could dampen his bloodlust.

It was time to go in for the kill.

His heart always started pumping in a moment like this. It had been a long, drawn-out fight with a hairy brute from Saxony known as *der Bär*, or the Bear. He'd been brought to the Ludus Caledonia, the premier fight guild of Scotland, by an arrogant Saxon lord who was positive he could make a wagonful of money on the fights.

His warrior against a *tertiarius*—the Cal's top warrior.

Magnus Stewart was that warrior. Known as the Eagle, he watched the Bear pace on the other side of the arena known as the Fields of Mars. He could hear the roar of the crowd, men who also had bloodlust now that they knew the Bear was wounded. A wounded bear could be a dangerous thing, but Magnus was confident he could deliver a blow that would end this match.

Truth be told, he was becoming weary.

But not weary enough.

He was going to skin that bear.

The field marshals had checked upon the condition of the Bear to ensure he could continue and were satisfied that the man could withstand more pounding. On the opposite side of the arena, Magnus was pacing, anxious to move, anxious to win yet one more fight in a long line of fights that had seen him emerge the victor.

And to the victor went the spoils.

He was ready.

The field marshals signaled for the bout to continue. It was a surprisingly warm August afternoon. As the last vestiges of golden rays beat upon Magnus's bronzed skin, he approached his injured opponent. He began to circle the man, preparing to deliver what was his signature move.

A kick to the side of the head.

One blow to the Bear's already damaged skull and the man would be no more.

The Bear, however, wasn't stupid. He tracked Magnus as the man skirted him, walking circles around him, then reversing course in an attempt to disorient him. Magnus had the ability to block out the world around him when focused on a target, one of the gifts that made him such a great warrior. He was a true hunter. Even now, all he could see in this vast arena full of people was the man in front of him.

It was time to end this.

The Bear roared and the crowd roared along with him. Magnus used that moment to make his charge, knowing that the Bear would hear the roar of the crowd and more than likely be distracted by it. He rushed the man as fast as he could run, and that was very fast, indeed. His feet were light, his muscular legs pumping, and as he got within about ten feet of the Bear, he suddenly went airborne.

The Bear, who had been expecting a head-on charge, was unprepared when Magnus used the man's own chest as leverage against a vicious kick to the skull.

The Bear fell like a stone.

The crowd in the arena went mad. They cheered their champion as Magnus threw up his arms, signifying his victory. Money began to rain down into the arena as people threw coins to signify their appreciation. Since this happened frequently, Magnus had two servants he trusted who would run out onto the field and collect the money that had been thrown at him. They would collect every last coin for him and he would give them a cut.

Tonight's haul would be a big one.

The crowd screamed and cheered for him for at least five minutes, which only fed his indomitable pride. His record for the longest cheering was twelve minutes, but tonight he didn't feel like soaking up their adoration for too long. He had already had three bouts today, ending with the Bear, so he was ready for some good food, some good wine, and hopefully some good companionship.

He knew that particular kind of companionship, the female kind, was already clamoring for him at the gates that led from the public area into the staging area because that was where the wealthy matrons gathered.

He expected a long line and much bidding tonight.

Waving to the crowd one last time, he made his way to the exit of the arena floor, where other fight-guild warriors were applauding him. He did not acknowledge them because, frankly, they were not of his class. The only ones he really respected were men he considered his equal, and those were few. But he could see those men standing just inside the staging area, and they were not cheering.

They were laughing at him.

Lor Careston, a *doctores*, or trainer, was the first one Magnus made eye contact with. Big, blond, and a brilliant tactical fighter, Lor simply stood there and shook his head.

"Do ye ever do anything different?" he asked drolly. "Is it always yer finishing move tae kick a man where he thinks?"

"Of course it is," Magnus said, untying the leather gloves on his hands. "By the time I kick him there, he is thinking about kicking *me*, so I must deliver the death blow."

Lor was a quiet one for the most part, but he loved to poke holes in Magnus's pride. It was in good-natured fun, however. Magnus knew he had Lor's admiration and friendship. The man standing next to Lor was another matter because at one time, Magnus and the man were both colleagues and opponents.

Magnus made eye contact with Bane Morgan. Muscular, handsome Bane used to be competition for the ladies' attention until he married last year. Women still looked at him and cheered for him, but there was no woman for Bane except his wife, which made Magnus appreciate him all the more.

Less competition for women's attention.

"And what does the great Highland Defender have tae say about my bout?" Magnus demanded. "Did ye not see how perfect it was?"

Bane, whose fight-guild nickname was the Highland Defender, knew the man was looking to have his ego stroked.

He would not oblige.

"It was decent," he said.

Magnus was insulted. "Better than anything ye've fought in yer life," he said. "'Tis understandable for ye tae be envious of me. 'Tis all right, lad. Someday, ye may fight as well as I do."

Bane started laughing, looking to Lor and rolling his eyes. Bane and Magnus had been on many tandem teams because, surprisingly, they worked well together and they were undefeated before Bane retired to become a *doctores*. Still, Magnus liked to poke at Bane, as brothers would roast each other.

And it was most definitely a brotherhood.

The last of the trio of men was another *doctores* who had Magnus's respect, although he'd rather die than admit it. Galan de Lara and Magnus had suffered their share of bouts with each other, and Magnus had the edge on victories. Unlike Lor and Bane, Galan was English. That meant he was the butt of insults, more than most, and he greatly frustrated Magnus from time to time.

Even so, their bond was strong.

"And ye, *Sassenach*," he said to Galan. "Tell me how great I am. I would hear yer praise."

Galan sighed heavily. Like Lor and Bane, he found great annoyance with Magnus, but the man was pure greatness. They all knew it. Magnus knew it. It was a game between them after nearly every bout, with Magnus demanding recognition and the *doctores* refusing to give it to him.

But tonight was different.

They had a little surprise for him.

"You were magnificent," Galan said. "In fact, you were so magnificent that Lor and Bane and I have chosen the most beautiful woman in the arena for you tonight."

Magnus looked at them in surprise. "Is this true?" he asked. "Where is she?"

Galan pointed into the holding area, where a three-story structure comprised the north wall of the area. The bottom levels were for the competitors, while the very top level, complete with a large stone balcony, was the private viewing apartment of the owner of the Ludus Caledonia, Clegg de Lave.

Clegg, however, was away from the Ludus Caledonia this night. He and one of his senior *doctores*, Luther Eddleston, were off visiting other fight guilds. That left his private rooms empty, but not for long.

That's where the *doctores* had the surprise waiting.

"There," Galan said. "In Clegg's apartment. Take the private stairs so the women waiting at the gates overlooking the holding area do not see you."

Magnus's emerald gaze looked up at the third floor of the building, envisioning the beauty who would surely be waiting for him. A seductive smile crossed his lips, but he refused to heed their advice about taking the private stairs.

He paraded across the holding-area floor for all to see.

Women were screaming at him from above, since the holding area was down below, sunk into the same hillside that the arena had been carved out of. Magnus looked up at the throng, blowing kisses, flexing his biceps, and he had women fainting at the sight.

Behind him, Lor and Bane and Galan followed, watching the spectacle with the greatest amusement. Magnus was great; he *knew* he was great. He wanted to make sure everyone else knew that he was great, so the man never did anything subtly or secretively.

It was part of his charm.

And then came the garments.

It was usual every time Magnus pranced around after a bout. Women started throwing pieces of clothing over the iron fence that separated them from the holding area. Scarves would come raining down in a flutter of perfumed material. They almost always smelled heavily of perfume.

Next came the hose—fine silk hose would hit the floor of the holding area with a thud because women had stuffed coins into them. Magnus pointed to some of the warriors standing around to pick up the hose, snapping at them when they wanted to keep the money. He would snatch the hose and the money away from them.

Holding his booty of coin-filled hose, Magnus looked up at the women lining the fence to see that half were screaming and half were crying. That was usual. He paused, blowing more kisses up to the crowd, and one young woman was so overcome that she vomited. Chunks of the stuff fell through the fence and landed near Magnus, who eyed it with some disgust and decided to end his cavalcade of worship. If the crowd was beginning to spew in excitement, it was time for him to exit.

Until the next time.

He decided to take the private stairs after all.

Leaving his friends down in the holding area, Magnus took the steps two at a time. He was sweaty and dirty from his bouts in the arena, but he knew that Clegg's private apartment had a bathing area. The viewing rooms had floor-to-ceiling doors that opened to a private balcony, the same balcony that the stairs led up to. As he hit the balcony, he was quite curious to see the woman his friends had chosen.

Beautiful, they'd said.

He might even permit her to bathe him.

When he reached the top of the steps, the door into the private rooms was open. He stepped in, his dirty sandals slapping against the tile floor that Clegg had brought all the way from Rome. In fact, everything at the Ludus Caledonia reflected the Romans and their architecture, all the way down to the beautiful robes that Clegg wore, like a great patriarch.

Even the chamber itself reflected that love of ancient Rome— beautiful columns, tile, glass. It was lovely. There were tapestries on the walls, silks on the cushioned couches, and great bowls of incense that burned all day and all night. Magnus expected that the woman would be waiting for him, but he didn't see anyone as he entered. He was halfway into the chamber when he saw movement on one of the couches.

"Ye must be Magnus."

Magnus froze. The voice was low and raspy, not at all sweet and delicate-sounding, and he turned his head to see a pile of silk moving on one of the couches. A delicate, age-worn hand came up, removing the veil from a head that was covered in soft, white hair.

The woman revealed herself fully. She wasn't simply old; she was ancient. He could see that she'd been lovely in her day, but that had been long ago. She wasn't exactly the raging young beauty that his friends had lauded.

And they'd known it all along.

Magnus knew in an instant that he'd been fooled.

"So ye're tae be my companion this evening?" he asked evenly. "Ye must have paid a high price."

The woman nodded as she sat up. She was well dressed, in

velvet and perfume, and he could smell the sweet scent where he stood. There was something graceful about her, in fact, in the way she moved. In her time, she must have been most alluring.

But it didn't change the fact that she was old enough to be his grandmother.

"I did," she said. "I paid the *ianista* handsomely. I can see it was worth every penny."

Had Magnus not been so shocked at his rather ancient company, the situation would have been laughable. His gaze drifted over the woman, her fine clothing and surprisingly shapely figure for her age. But her statement made him realize that not only were his friends in on the joke, but so was the manager of the Ludus Caledonia, Axel von Rossau.

Magnus was certain they'd done it to teach him a lesson in humility.

"Of course I'm worth every penny," he said after a moment, moving in her direction. "Let us come tae know each other, sweetheart. What's yer name?"

"Mary," the woman said, her features lighting up with joy. "Lady MacMerry of Whitekirk Castle. My dead husband was lord of Whitekirk Castle. Surely ye've heard of Harry MacMerry."

Magnus had. He might present the image of a man only interested in money and victory, but he was much deeper than that. It was a trait he kept well hidden. His father, Hugh Stewart, Duke of Kintyre and Lorne, was the king's youngest brother and a prince of the Scottish royal family. Magnus had been born out of wedlock to a lady-in-waiting to the duke's wife.

But being a royal bastard wasn't information that Magnus spread around.

Royal blood had been a curse in Magnus's case, but it also meant he kept abreast of the politics of Scotland. He was a sharp and astute man, and he knew who the enemies of the crown were. MacMerry had most definitely been an enemy.

Therefore, he was careful in his reply.

"What does it matter if I have or have not?" he asked, a twinkle in his eyes. "All that matters is that ye have the money and I have the time. Let's have a drink before I wash the grime from my body."

He was already moving for Clegg's elaborate sideboard, brought all the way from Constantinople. Upon it sat a full pitcher of wine and cut-glass cups. Magnus set down the coin-filled hose he'd been carrying, the stockings he'd collected from the staging-area floor, and poured two full measures. He handed one cup to the old woman, who was gulping it down before he even took the first sip of his own.

He watched her drink, wondering what he was going to do with her. He wasn't one to bed anything other than young and beautiful women, but he supposed a good lay was a good lay. Maybe a woman of Mary MacMerry's age would have more experience than most.

Perhaps he'd even learn something.

"More, love?" he asked, picking up the pitcher again. "Let's drink tae our good health and tae the sovereignty of Scotland."

Mary eagerly took another drink. "'Tis fine wine, indeed."

Magnus refilled her cup even though it wasn't quite empty. "It is," he said. "The finest wine for the finest women. Tell me, Mary. How did ye come here? I've not seen ye before."

Mary was nervous. Magnus hadn't noticed that before. He could see that her hands were trembling as she downed her wine.

"I've been here before," she said. "I've seen ye fight many a time. Ye're the prettiest man I've ever seen. A beauteous lad, ye are."

Magnus grinned, flashing straight and white teeth. "And ye've never wanted tae meet me before now?"

Mary shrugged. "There are a hundred women waiting for ye every time I come," she said. "I paid well tae have ye tae myself tonight because I've come with a purpose."

"Oh?" he said, sipping his wine. "What is that?"

Mary took another gulp of wine that drained her cup. Oddly, she wasn't as confident as she had been when he'd first entered the chamber. She seemed nervous and…forlorn. It was difficult to describe, but he was starting to feel some pity for her.

He filled her cup again.

"Tell me, Mary," he said. "Why did ye come?"

She took another big drink before looking at him. "I came tae be with ye," she said. "And I'll give ye something in exchange."

"Of course ye will. Money."

She shook her head. "Something better," she said. "I have no heirs. When I pass, Whitekirk Castle will return tae the king and I dunna want him tae have it."

"I canna help ye, lady."

She nodded eagerly. "Ye can," she said. "Instead of money, I'll make ye my heir. I'd rather have Whitekirk go tae a fighter than go tae the bastard on the throne. Will ye take the castle instead of money?"

Magnus almost started laughing. If the woman knew who he really was, she would not have made such an offer. It certainly wasn't an offer he had expected.

At first, he wasn't sure what to say, but the royal bastard in him who had been denied everything from birth wasn't afraid to speak up. It was the entire reason Magnus had become a fighter for profit. He had to work for everything he ever had and ever would have. He'd been born illegitimate, held captive for years with the understanding that his father wanted nothing to do with him, before finally being released and having nowhere to go. Therefore, he'd learned to take money where he could get it.

Including accepting a castle from an old woman with no heirs.

"Are ye certain about that?" he said. "It seems like a high price tae pay, even tae me."

"I've no one else. Will ye accept?"

He eyed her a moment as if deliberating, but it was all an act. If she was serious, then he'd be foolish to pass it up.

"Of course," he said. "I wouldna want ye tae go tae yer grave fearful of leaving yer property behind. But tell me again so there are no misunderstandings. Are ye *sure* ye want me tae have it?"

The old woman nodded. "I do," she said, downing most of her second cup of wine. "And dunna worry, I've no relatives tae contest my wishes. I'll find a serjeant-at-law and have him witness my signature on my will. But I only know ye as the Eagle, love. What's yer name?"

"Magnus Alexander Albert Hugh Stewart."

The long name sank into her wine-soaked mind and she gave him a startled expression. "Stewart?" she repeated. "Like the king?"

"Not like the king."

It was a lie, but she didn't question it. She accepted his answer and settled down quickly, finishing off her cup of wine. She was well on her way to becoming drunk, and with the next measure of drink, Magnus watered down the wine significantly. He didn't need a drunken old woman on his hands.

"Well and good ye're not related tae the king," she said. "I dunna want Whitekirk tae fall tae a relation."

"Ye worry too much," he said, avoiding a direct answer to her statement. "Tell me about yer family. Where do ye come from?"

It was a distraction. He wanted to get her talking, hoping she might forget that she'd come to bed him. In fact, the wine was making her chatty and Magnus feigned interest when she spoke of her childhood as a lass in Blackness and how Harry MacMerry came courting.

After her third full cup of wine, Mary lay her head back on the couch and stared up at the ceiling. She'd stopped talking and was now simply staring up into space. Magnus watched her carefully, wondering if she was about to pass out, when she quietly spoke.

"I like ye, Magnus," she said. "Ye listened tae an old woman talk about herself, and most men wouldna do such a thing."

Magnus propped his elbows on his knees, folding his hands and resting his chin upon them as he watched her.

"I want tae know about the woman who is tae give me her castle," he said. "If ye truly want tae make me yer heir, then I should know about ye."

She didn't reply for a moment. She just kept staring up to the ceiling. But then, her head came up and she looked at him.

"Ye know that yer friends put me in this chamber as a joke, don't ye?" she asked softly.

It was a strange change in subject, but not entirely unexpected in hindsight. She was sharp for her age, and even she saw the irony of their situation. As if a man of Magnus's stature would really want a woman of her advanced years.

He didn't hesitate in his reply.

"I know."

"And ye still are willing tae go through with it?"

"Are ye still willing tae give me yer castle?"

She cocked her head thoughtfully. "I've a suspicion that yer friends like tae play jokes on ye," she said, avoiding his question. "I got that sense from them because they were quite gleeful tae put me here. Am I wrong?"

"Ye're not wrong."

"Then they've done this kind of thing before?"

He fought off a grin. "We've done many things tae each other all in the name of the friendship."

"They dunna sound like good friends."

"They're the best I've ever had."

"Do ye want tae seek revenge on them?"

He was intrigued at the suggestion. "Always," he said. "What did ye have in mind?"

"Give me one of those coin purses ye were carrying when ye entered the chamber and I'll tell ye."

He snorted; he couldn't help it. "Are ye saying ye'll help me for a price?"

She nodded, a smug grin on her face. "I'm sure ye have no

intention of bedding me. But I'll help ye get revenge on yer friends just the same."

"Why?"

"I told ye. Because ye've been kind tae me and I like ye. And this was a nasty little joke they wanted tae play on ye."

She may have been tipsy, but she wasn't stupid. In fact, her dark eyes were glittering with surprising lucidity. He snorted.

"Very well, Mary MacMerry," he said. "What did ye have in mind?"

"Money first. Then I'll tell ye."

Magnus stood up, going to the table with the wine on it, and collected one of the coin-filled hose. He weighed a couple of them and, selecting the lighter one, handed it over to Mary. She snatched it, feeling the weight, before tucking it into the purse on her belt.

"Follow me," she said.

Up she came from the couch, moving with surprising agility considering the wine she'd ingested. There was a sleeping area in a sectioned-off corner of the apartment, back behind a massive screen with a scene depicting ancient Rome painted upon it. Mary headed straight to the bed.

It was a big piece of furniture, with a carved wooden frame, and she braced her hands on the end of the bed. She silently gestured, making quick motions as if to shove the bed right into the wall, but she was doing it in a rhythmic motion. Magnus quickly understood what she meant, and with a grin, he put his hands on one of the four end posts.

If his friends thought they'd pulled a joke on him, they were about to learn differently.

He was about to turn the tables on them.

Magnus and Mary started ramming the bed into the wall with a regular rhythm, as a man would when making love to a woman. The banging bed was accompanied by loud grunts on his part, as if he were genuinely bedding the woman and having a good time doing it. His grunts were peppered with high-pitched gasps from Mary, mimicking cries of pleasure.

They went on for an hour.

A solid hour of the bed bumping, of his loud growls of pleasure, and of her female shrieks. It was the performance of a lifetime. They only stopped because Magnus was becoming weary, especially after having fought three bouts that night, so he ended the spectacle with rapid thumps against the wall and then a high-pitched scream from Mary.

After that, there was dead silence.

At least, silence to anyone listening in from the outside, but by then, he and Mary were nearly doubled over with laughter. Magnus could just see the shocked faces of Lor and Bane and Galan as they realized their arrogant friend had not only taken the bait but had used it. By the sounds emitting from the apartment, he'd had a good time of it, too.

After he and Mary rested a few minutes, they went on to bed bump for another half hour that would certainly impress his friends. They were going to know that their trick on him had failed spectacularly. But soon, Magnus's exhaustion got the better of him and they ended their brilliant performance for the night.

It had been glorious.

In the quiet of pseudo afterglow that followed, Magnus went to bathe as Mary ate the food that had been brought up earlier. Magnus joined her once he was clean, taking the time to eat and chat with the clever old woman he was genuinely coming to like. They passed the hours until it neared dawn and the Ludus Caledonia was shutting down for the night. Patrons were leaving on horseback or in fine carriages, and warriors were retreating to their cottages, so Magnus finished his food and stood up from the table.

"Time tae leave, m'dear," he said. "'Ye've been a grand companion this night, but 'tis time for ye tae go home."

Mary was groggy. She had been sitting at the table for the last hour, her eyes half-lidded from wine, food, and exhaustion. She stood up, weaving dangerously, as Magnus draped her with the shawl that was tossed over a chair. She smoothed at her white hair, but he ruffled it, making it a wild mass of silver. Mary looked as if she'd spent all night being pleasured by a virile warrior, and when she realized why he'd done it, she cast him a reproachful look.

Naughty lad.

He simply smiled.

Magnus wanted to make sure her disheveled appearance matched the screaming she'd done earlier, and once he was satisfied that she appeared properly pleasured, he directed her toward the entry that led out into the common areas of the Ludus Caledonia.

"Ye have a carriage, I assume?" he asked as he escorted her to the door.

Mary nodded. "Aye."

"Good," he said. Then he lowered his voice and leaned down to her. "If ye dunna look as if I've taken advantage of ye all night, no one will believe the performance we just gave, so look properly weary, will ye?"

Mary nodded quickly, leaning against him as if she could hardly stand. Magnus threw open the door and began walking her out to the area where the carriages usually waited. His gaze scanned the area, immediately spying Galan and Axel, the enormous Saxon manager of the Ludus Caledonia. He could see that they were trying to stay out of sight, but everyone made eye contact, so there was no use in trying to hide.

He could see the pair smirking in the torchlight.

That only made Magnus give the old woman a squeeze.

"There, now, m'lady," he said for all to hear. "Ye had quite a night. Go home and rest and I will see ye another time."

Mary was pretending to have difficulty with her balance, but she managed to spy her carriage. She pointed to it and Magnus turned her in that direction.

"Did we have a good time, then?" she asked loudly.

Magnus nodded confidently. "The best time ye've ever had."

"Was I good?"

"Ye were excellent. And so was I."

That was enough for the nosy ears around them. Magnus took her right up to the carriage. The driver was there, an old man who took Mary from Magnus and practically lifted her into the open carriage. When the driver returned to his seat, Mary crooked a finger at Magnus.

He moved closer.

"I'm sorry for ye, my beauteous lad," she said. "But there's something ye must know."

"What?"

"Yer friends will have the last laugh, after all."

He frowned. "What do ye mean?"

"I mean that I never paid them for the chance tae be with ye," she said. "They paid *me*. It was all part of the joke. When ye paid me tae help ye get revenge upon them, I was paid twice. Dunna be angry, lad, there's not much opportunity for a woman my age tae make good money."

A creeping sense of realization filled him. "I see," he said. "They paid ye tae trick me."

"They did."

"And Whitekirk?"

She sighed heavily. "It willna belong tae ye, sorry tae say," she said, reaching out to pat his cheek. "And my name isn't Mary MacMerry. That's what I meant by yer friends having the last laugh. Ye did well, but in the end, the victory is theirs. Better luck next time, Magnus."

The carriage pulled away, leaving Magnus standing there with his mouth open. A split second of shock was followed by the acute awareness that he'd been duped all the way around. He loved his friends at the Ludus Caledonia, the only real friends he'd ever had, and they'd spent the past year playing pranks on one another as part of the bond of their brotherhood, but this one…this one was a master stroke.

He had to admit, it had been brilliant.

A crafty old woman in need of money and their plan had been perfect.

As more carriages began to pull away beneath the pewter skies of the breaking dawn, he turned to see Galan and Axel waving at him, rejoicing in his humiliation. Lor and Bane had probably already gone to bed, with wives who were waiting for them, but Galan and Axel didn't have any female baggage.

They had the freedom to stay up all night, reveling in the Eagle's humiliation.

It had been the biggest one yet.

Even Magnus appreciated the very clever prank. To prove how unhumiliated he was, he waved back at them and even bowed, as if to acknowledge that they'd wholly tricked him. It was a gesture of respect, but beneath it, he was already calculating his revenge.

Surely, they had to know he would come for them, and he would.

When they least expected it.

CHAPTER TWO

Edinburgh

"I WANT SOMETHING THAT WILL MAKE THEM THINK THEIR guts are all coming out through the one small hole in their arses, but I dunna want tae truly hurt them. I just want them tae think they're dying."

Two days after his bout with the faux Mary MacMerry, Magnus was bent on revenge more than ever. He was completely serious as he delivered his request to a wool-swathed apothecary who was the most reputable one in all of Edinburgh. The shop was called the Seed, run by two brothers who were nearly as old as Scotland herself.

At least, that was the rumor. They were quite old, and identical twins, and some said they'd found the very secret to immortality. But Magnus didn't want their secret of life.

He simply wanted something to make his friends ill.

The old apothecary tried not to look too shocked or too confused.

"Ye want tae make them…*ill*?" he asked.

Magnus nodded. "For a day or two," he said. "As a joke, ye see. They saddled me with a… Well, it doesna matter. I need tae punish them but not hurt them. I want everything they've eaten tae come out from the top and the bottom. What can ye sell me that will do that but not harm them?"

"Ye want a cleanse?"

"If that will expel everything from their innards, I do."

The old man with the yellow beard was beginning to

understand. He didn't seem confused any longer, but rather disapproving of what he was being asked for and the purpose for which it would be used. However, given that he'd seen this man before, once in the company of the owner of the Ludus Caledonia and a few other times on his own, the apothecary didn't press him further. He wanted to get through this without any trouble from the muscular warrior, so he turned back to his shelves of glass phials.

Each little bottle held something different, mysterious or expensive ingredients. There had to be hundreds of the phials lining the shelves of the shop. Most contained what was called "simple" ingredients, meaning that each was only one element. But others had multiple ingredients, or "compounds," which were mixed for a specific purpose.

The old man went to a particular area of the shop, peering up toward the top shelf, lined with dusty glass bottles. Pulling forth a small ladder, he climbed the rickety rungs and plucked one of the bottles from the top shelf. With the glass carefully cradled in one hand, he returned to Magnus.

The phial was filled with silver pellets. Removing the stopper, he plucked one of the pellets and held it up to Magnus.

"Steep this in wine a few hours," he said. "Have yer...friends drink the wine without the pellet in it. It will have the desired effect without injuring them."

Magnus took the silver bit out of his hand, holding it up to the dim light of the shop to get a better look at it.

"What is it?" he asked.

The old man was already turning away from him, returning the bottle to its proper place.

"It is called tartar emetic," he said. "It is used tae purge foul humors. Careful ye dunna give yer friends too much or it will kill them."

Magnus didn't want to do that. He just wanted to get back at them for the old-whore trick.

"I let it soak just a few hours?" he clarified.

"Just a few and no longer."

"And it willna kill them?"

"If ye use it properly, it shouldna."

That was good enough for Magnus. He inspected the silver pellet a moment longer before tucking it into his purse and pulling forth two silver coins. Handing those over to the appreciative apothecary, he was just turning for the door when a group of women blew in.

Magnus couldn't see them very well because of the bright sunlight coming in through the doorway behind them, but he could see their shapes. He could smell the perfume. As they came deeper into the shop, he realized that he recognized the woman in the lead.

A bolt of shock ran through him.

The woman was well dressed and elegant, and Magnus knew her well, but she reminded him of a time in his life he'd rather forget. For a moment, he wasn't sure what to do, and his moment of indecision cost him, for the woman locked gazes with him and she, too, registered great surprise.

"Magnus?" she gasped. "Magnus, is that you?"

Magnus nodded, realizing that he could not run now. He took a deep breath to steady himself as his heart began to pound.

"Aye," he said. "Greetings, Lady Ayr."

The woman shuffled over to him in a flurry of fine fabric and strong perfume, her expression filled with delight.

"Oh, it *is* you," she said in her clipped English accent. "What a magnificent stroke of luck to find you here, Magnus. I've not seen you in years."

That was very true. Not since he'd had been her husband's hostage. He'd spent most of his life in captivity before being released, cast off into the world to fend for himself. Those were the years that Magnus tried to pretend never happened, but seeing Agnes

Stewart, Duchess of Ayr, brought back that which he hadn't thought of in quite some time.

Seeing her face brought back the old, familiar hatred.

"It has been many years, m'lady," he said, feeling uncomfortable. "If ye will excuse me, I've business elsewhere."

"Magnus, wait," she said, putting her hand on his arm to stop him. Her gaze looked him over appraisingly. "Do you not have a moment to spare me? My, you *have* grown. When I last saw you, you had only just become a man and my husband had finally found peace with your father. What a glorious day that was, your release. To tell you the truth, I had begun to look at you as one of the family. You had been with us for so long, I felt as if I had raised you and I was sorry to see you go."

I doubt that raising your children means keeping them locked up and punished at the slightest infraction, he thought bitterly. Lady Ayr wasn't a terrible person, at least not as terrible as her husband, but she had been guilty of ignorance. She was slightly daft, and silly, and hardly noticed the things that went on around her. The more Magnus looked at her, the more those terrible memories filled him.

The more he was bombarded by things he had tried hard to forget.

He had been so young when he'd been taken hostage by Ambrose Stewart, Duke of Ayr. The man was a cousin to his father, the youngest brother of the King of Scotland, James. Hugh Stewart, Duke of Kintyre and Lorne, was a man with a rebellious streak in him. At least, that was the general consensus from the royals when others called him a true loyalist to Scotland. When Hugh had fallen afoul of his brother in a sloppy coup attempt, Ambrose had stepped in to take Hugh's bastard son hostage to ensure Hugh's good behavior.

And that's how Magnus had spent his entire life up until his release seven years ago. He had been treated adequately or poorly within the household of the Duke of Ayr, depending on his father's behavior.

It had been a horrible way to live.

"Aye, it was a long time," he said. It was all he could manage. "Please excuse me, m'lady. I do have pressing business elsewhere."

This time, Agnes let him go. "Of course, Magnus," she said, watching him head for the door. "I shall tell my husband that I have seen you and that you look well. We are staying at Trinity House in town. You remember the place? To the north, near the sea. Please visit us when you have the time to do so."

Her last words were called out to him as he quit the shop, a shouted invitation he would never accept. But just as he rushed through the doorway and onto the street, he plowed into a small body in his path. He hadn't been watching where he was going, and he heard a feminine yelp as he knocked a woman into the gutter.

Magnus would have kept going, leaving the woman on her backside, had she not been in his way. But she was, and if he took another step, he would have stepped on her. Therefore, he was forced to stop out of necessity, annoyed that she was blocking his exit. He sidestepped her and reached down to pull her to her feet, purely as a courtesy.

He didn't know why he should show any courtesy because he wasn't the courteous type. Or polite when it came to women in general. Other than natural male urges or a way to make money, he'd never had any use for them. But the moment he pulled the woman to her feet and looked into her eyes, something changed.

Magnus found himself looking into a face that could only be described as angelic. The startled eyes gazing at him were large and bottomless, a pale shade of brown he'd never seen before. Her nose was pert, her mouth lush and generous, now popped open in surprise. There was a strange magic to the moment, a buzzing in his ears that shut out everything else around him.

Suddenly, he didn't feel like running off.

"My apologies, m'lady," he said. "I dinna see ye."

She was trying to brush off her beautiful dress. It was pale green, perhaps silk because it was so fine, with yellow edges around the neckline and at the bottom of her belled sleeves. Now, it had the addition of dirt from the gutter, and Magnus took his eyes from her long enough to realize that she was quite dirty as the result of his handiwork.

"No wonder," she said in an accent that was not Scots. "You were moving so quickly, it is a wonder you waited for the door to open at all. Why not take it right from the hinges?"

She was scolding him.

He deserved it.

"Had it not moved aside fast enough, I would have," he said defensively, crouching down to brush the dirt from the bottom of her hem. "If I've ruined yer dress, I'll pay for it."

She continued shaking out the dress, looking for any real damage. "It is not my dress," she said. "It belongs to the Duchess of Ayr. She will not be pleased if you've ruined it."

She was shaking the dress around so much that he stopped trying to brush the dirt from it. Standing up, he studied her for a moment, coming to think there was something oddly familiar about her now that he'd had a good look.

It began to occur to him that he'd seen those eyes somewhere before.

"Are ye a lady for the duchess?" he asked.

She nodded, now brushing her left sleeve. "I am," she said, taking more time to look at him than at her dress. "No harm done, I suppose. But be careful the next time. The next lady you shove into the gutter may not be as gracious as I am."

"What's yer name?"

She stopped brushing, incensed at the question. "That is none of your affair," she said. "Go on with you or I shall call for a guard."

He shook his head. "Ye misunderstand," he said. "I–I think I've seen ye before."

She cocked a disbelieving eyebrow. "Nay, you have not," she said. "Go on, now."

"Will ye at least tell me where ye're from? Ye dunna speak like a Scots."

"That is because I am not Scots."

"What are ye?"

"I am from Navarre, if you must know."

She turned away from him, brushing him off. Magnus could hardly believe it. Was there really a woman in Scotland that would brush *him* off? He was embarrassed, but more than that, he was incensed. Now, it was becoming a matter of pride.

He wanted to know who she was.

Without another word, he pushed past her into the shop where the duchess was examining several phials with her women. They were smelling, touching, examining. Magnus walked up to her.

"M'lady," he said. "I have a question tae ask ye."

Lady Ayr was instantly attentive. "Of course, Magnus," she said. "What is it?"

At that moment, the woman in the pale-green dress was just coming in through the door and Magnus pointed to her.

"That woman," he said. "Who is she?"

All eyes turned to the diminutive woman in the doorway, including Lady Ayr's. When she saw who Magnus was referring to, she smiled.

"Do you not recognize her?" she said. "That is our own Diantha."

The name meant nothing to him. "Diantha?" he repeated as if it might help him remember. "I dunna know her."

Lady Ayr laughed softly, putting her hand on his arm. "Of course you do," she said. "She came to us right before you left us. Her father is a great Spanish warlord from Navarre. She is meant for my son, Conan. Do you recall her now?"

He was starting to. He knew he'd seen her before, but he simply couldn't place her. Now, it was starting to come back to him.

Years ago, a young and frightened Spanish lass had been brought into the fold at Culroy Castle, seat of the Dukes of Ayr, on a dark and stormy night. Magnus remembered because the lass had screamed until Lady Ayr took charge of her and whisked her away. Everyone thought she was injured or dying, but it turned out she was simply terrified.

Diantha…*dee-ON-tha*…

He rolled the name around in his mind a few times.

That's not what she'd been called at the time, however. Everyone referred to her as Flaca, a girl on the cusp of womanhood who was all arms and legs. Skinny and pale, with a boyish body.

She certainly didn't look like that now.

"It's not Flaca, is it?" he asked hesitantly.

Lady Ayr nodded. "Aye, 'tis Flaca," she said. "Only we do not call her that any longer. She is Lady Diantha Marabella Silva y de Mora, a lady of fine Spanish breeding. She will make Conan a fine wife, very soon."

Magnus found himself staring at Diantha, who was standing by the door with an anxious look on her face. Her gaze darted between Lady Ayr and Magnus, hearing what was being said about her.

But Lady Ayr didn't give Magnus a chance to respond. She took him by the arm and led him over to Diantha.

"Diantha, do you remember Magnus?" she asked. "This is our very own Magnus, a cousin to my husband. His father is the Duke of Kintyre and Lorne."

Diantha never had a chance to reply. The other women who knew Magnus, or at least knew *of* him, crowded around to greet him. Magnus was looking at Diantha when she was pushed out of the way by overeager women. Women who wanted to closely inspect the handsome, muscular man Lady Ayr was flaunting.

They pressed forward.

"Tell us what activities you have been engaged in since you left Culroy," Lady Ayr said for the benefit of her ladies. "We have often spoken of you with fondness and hoped you had fared well."

Magnus didn't think that was quite the truth. There had been no love lost for him at Culroy. He recognized most of the women with Lady Ayr, now that he'd gotten a chance to look them over, but he didn't know them well. Normally, he wouldn't have given them the benefit of his attention, but something prompted him to respond.

Diantha, who had been pushed to the rear of the group, was watching him.

Maybe he simply wanted her to know how great he was.

"I am a professional warrior, m'lady," he said, tearing his gaze away from Diantha to focus on the duchess. "Ye can tell the duke that I've learned tae fight and I am well paid for it."

Lady Ayr's gaze moved over his well-muscled and quite perfect body. "I can see that you have grown quite…strong," she said. "Are you a mercenary, then?"

He shook his head. "Nay," he said. "I am a warrior who fights for my living."

"I do not understand."

"I live and fight at a fight guild. I am a professional warrior, paid to entertain."

"What fight guild?"

Magnus paused before answering. The Ludus Caledonia wasn't spoken of openly. Because of the nature of the business and the vast amounts of money exchanged there on a nightly basis, the location wasn't openly shared so opportunist armies and thieves wouldn't converge on them.

It wasn't supposed to be public knowledge.

However, it was probably one of the worst-kept secrets in Scotland because it was a gambling guild that depended on the money of visitors, a mysterious place where men fought for money, but nonetheless, those who were part of the guild did not share the secret freely.

Not even bold, brash Magnus.

He was careful in his reply.

"The greatest fight guild in all of Scotland," he finally said. "If ye dunna know what I mean, ask yer husband. Ask him if he knows of the greatest fight guild in Scotland, and ye can tell him that is where I have thrived. All of those years at Culroy Castle taught me how tae survive…and I have learned well."

There was an insult there, something that dampened Lady Ayr's enthusiasm a little, though she wasn't quite sure how to respond.

The smile on her lips faded.

"Are you at least happy, Magnus?" she asked. "I would hope you have found some joy in your new life."

He couldn't decide if she was being sincere or patronizing. With Lady Ayr, it was difficult to know. But he knew one thing—he wouldn't waste any further time on her. He had better things to do than reminisce about something he wanted to forget.

"Aye," he said. "I am happy. Thank ye for yer concern, Lady Ayr."

With that, he simply dipped his head and excused himself, but his gaze lingered on Diantha as he quit the shop. She was watching him, her expression almost…*anxious*. There was an odd shadow of anxiety there that he hadn't seen before. A look of curiosity, of concern…

Of desperation?

He wondered if it was the same expression he'd had all of those years at Culroy. Maybe it was something all wards at Culroy had at one time or another, an expression that suggested they would rather be anywhere but in that damnable castle commanded by an unpredictable duke and his spoiled son. Try as he might to shake the thought, he knew he couldn't. It would haunt him.

She would haunt him.

With a final glance at the beautiful young woman, he quit the shop and headed out into the cloudy Scottish day.

CHAPTER THREE

Magnus Stewart.

It had been a distinct surprise to run into him at the apothecary's shop. Even now, as Agnes and her ladies headed to the Street of the Merchants, their destination being a broker in fine silks from across the sea, Agnes couldn't help but think of the young boy who had grown into a fine, strong, and beautiful man.

It was a shocking realization.

It had been one for him, too. She hadn't been oblivious to the expression on his face when he first saw her. There was pain among the surprise from the man who had spent years at Culroy.

Unfortunately for him, they hadn't been good years.

Magnus hadn't been a normal ward. He'd been a hostage and he'd been treated like one, no matter how Agnes had tried to put a spin on the years he'd spent there. She'd tried to make it sound as if he'd been a welcome resident when that had been far from the truth.

He'd been at Culroy for a purpose.

Magnus knew the purpose, but he didn't know all of it.

He didn't know that the very root of his presence had been built on lies.

Lies perpetrated by Agnes's husband, meant to keep Magnus apart from his father. Ambrose had fed Magnus lies from a young age, insisting that his father wanted nothing to do with him. It kept Magnus confused and defeated, unwilling to escape because he had no one to escape *to*. It had been a control measure that Agnes had known about but had done nothing to prevent.

The truth was that Hugh Stewart was very concerned for his son.

A son he was told hated the very mention of his name.

And all of it had been orchestrated by Ambrose. Father and son had been told that they hated one another, that there was no love lost between them. Hugh never tried to see the son he was told hated him, and Magnus never tried to see the father who didn't want him.

Ambrose's scheme had worked beautifully.

But Agnes knew it had all been a lie. There had been times when she had wanted to tell Magnus the truth, but she was afraid to go against her husband. He was a man who always had to dominate those around him, finding the manipulations of others as pleasurable as some men found joy in happy pursuits. Being in control *was* Ambrose's happy pursuit and he did it with anyone he could, especially a cousin he hated and the man's bastard son.

Magnus had never questioned his father's apathy toward him. Being illegitimate, he never demanded that he be recognized. He accepted that he was unwanted. Even today, when Agnes saw Magnus for the first time in years, she could see that old acceptance in his eyes. That child hostage was still in there somewhere.

The boy who just wanted to be loved, no matter how successful he became.

As the carriage bumped over the uneven street, heading to the fabric broker, Agnes tried to put the sight of that sad little boy from her mind. There was nothing she could do about it. Nothing she could say. It had been going on for so long that she would not interfere. She knew what would happen if she did.

Therefore, Magnus would have to go on thinking his father hated him.

And Hugh would have to go on believing his son wanted nothing to do with him.

It was a sad lot in life for them both.

And Agnes had to live with the guilt.

⚭ ⚭ ⚭

She remembered him.

Even after he departed from the dingy little apothecary shop, Diantha's thoughts lingered on Magnus Stewart. Like the other women in Lady Ayr's adoring throng, she recognized him vaguely. But the young man she had known those years ago was not the same man she had just witnessed.

The man she had just witnessed was magnificent in every sense of the word.

From her youth, she remembered Magnus to be a short, dark, and sullen young creature. She remembered him as keeping to himself. Someone had told her that he was a hostage, the son of an enemy of Lord Ayr, but she didn't know anything more about him. During her first years at Culroy Castle, she had only seen him on occasion, and she had never exchanged more than a couple of words with him.

Magnus Stewart had been a loner.

Diantha had been little more than a child when she had come to Culroy. Those had been dark and turbulent days, and she had lived in fear with people who spoke a language she did not understand. But she was sharp and learned English quickly, and as the weeks and months passed, she had come to know the people in her environment, and that included the young men who were squires and wards of the Duke of Ayr.

Magnus had been among a group of younger men who squired for some of the older warriors. She remembered seeing him with the duke's son, Conan, a man everyone at the castle despised to varying degrees. Conan Stewart was brash, rude, spoiled, and intolerable at times, but he was the duke's one and only son, and he was treated as if he were the Christ child reborn.

Now, he was a man she was expected to marry.

But she had no intention of doing it.

In the appearance of Magnus, she saw her way out. If he had

been released from the hellish fortress that was her prison, then perhaps he could help her find a way out as well.

She had to find a way.

This wasn't a spur-of-the-moment decision. She'd been planning to flee Culroy as long as she'd been a captive. That big, dirty, salty castle sat by the sea, where the heavy fog rolled in from the ocean and smothered everything it touched. It was hell.

It always had been.

For as long as she could recall, her intention had been to flee, but it wasn't so easy. Both Culroy and the Edinburgh town home of Trinity House were heavily guarded. Several times, Diantha thought she might be able to slip out, but she'd lost her nerve because there was no one to help her. If she was caught, she would always be watched, so she didn't try.

She bided her time.

The time had finally come.

God, is it possible I've finally found a way to escape?

It all started when Lady Ayr and her women stopped at a merchant that supplied beautiful fabric after they'd left the apothecary's stall. Lady Ayr made several purchases of lovely fabric, and when they departed the shop for home, Diantha pretended to have left something behind.

She made a show of being greatly concerned by her forgetfulness, and the carriage she was riding in came to a halt. She assured the annoyed driver that she could find her way back to Trinity House and that he need not wait for her, but the man balked. The streets of Edinburgh were not safe for ladies to travel alone. But there were several impatient women in the carriage, and eventually he had no choice but to continue on, leaving Diantha on the street.

It was exactly what she had wanted.

She rushed back to the apothecary shop. It was empty now and she could see both brothers in a corner, counting something in one of those glass phials.

Quickly, she made her way toward them.

"My lords?" she said, politely catching their attention. When the old men turned to look at her, she smiled hesitantly. "I was wondering… The man who was here, called Magnus… Do you know where he lives?"

The apothecary who had been assisting Magnus cocked his head curiously. "Yer lady knew him," he said. "Why not ask her?"

Diantha scrambled for an answer. "She does not know," she said. "She asked me to… She wanted me to find out where he lives. He would not tell her, but she…she has something to give him. Will you tell me?"

She was stumbling over her words because they were spur-of-the-moment lies. She had never been very good at lying. The old apothecary scratched his head.

"He comes in with Sir Clegg at times," he said.

"Who is Sir Clegg?"

"He owns the Ludus Caledonia."

"What's that?"

"A great place," the old man said. "It is where men fight. Sometimes they come here afterward tae find something tae cure an aching head or an aching belly so their wives willna know they have been eating and drinking like gluttons."

Diantha was trying not to look bewildered. "They…they eat and drink at the Ludus Caledonia?"

The old man nodded and so did his brother. "It is a place where men fight while still other men wager on them," he said. "I've never been, but I hear they provide their guests with the finest food and drink. It is a place of great entertainment and great debauchery. But if ye are thinking of going there, it is no fitting place for a woman."

She cocked her head curiously. "Women do not go there?"

"Decent women dunna. Tell yer mistress that, if she's thinking on going."

Diantha's next question was going to be for directions but she suspected they might not tell her after warning her away from it. Therefore, she tried to be clever.

"She did not say that she wanted to go, only that she wanted to send him something," she said. "She will probably send a soldier. Where is this place?"

The brothers looked at each other, since neither one really knew. "South," the old apothecary said. "In the hills south of Edinburgh, I think."

His brother, ever silent, simply nodded and turned back to his ingredients and glass vessels as Diantha sought more definite directions.

"South," she repeated. "The lands are wild and there are many hills to the south."

The old man nodded. "I heard someone say once that it was south of the church in Morningside," he said. "St. Eustace's Church is down there. So are the Bonaly hills. But if ye want tae know for certain, they'll tell ye at the Sticky Wick. Those from the Ludus Caledonia haunt the tavern, but it's no place for a lady. Send a man there tae do the asking."

He turned back to his task, and Diantha could see that the conversation was over. But she had what she wanted.

She could make it south of Morningside.

Over the course of the past several years, Diantha had been to Edinburgh many times and she had traveled the streets with Lady Ayr, a mistress who liked to experience taverns and shops and entertainment. Diantha knew the city fairly well, so surely a place like this fight guild would not be difficult to find. Strange how she'd never heard of it in all that time. But no matter. She would find Magnus and beg him to help her.

Finally, that time had come.

Tonight was the night.

CHAPTER FOUR

The Ludus Caledonia

"WHAT DID YE PUT IN MY DRINK?"

The question came from Lor.

It was evening, a hush having fallen over the land as the night birds chattered and brooks through the glens sang their gentle song. In the complex of the Ludus Caledonia, it was time for the evening meal and although each competitor had his own stone cottage where he ate and slept, there was a small communal hall where men could gather and socialize.

Friendly gatherings weren't widely encouraged because friends tended not to want to fight, and defeat, other friends. Isolation when not in the arena was urged, but sometimes on the nights when the Ludus Caledonia had no fights, the *doctores* and the senior warriors would gather and share a meal.

Tonight was one of those times.

It had been a perfect opportunity for Magnus to slip his friends the wine that had been steeped all afternoon with the silver pellet, but Lor was already on to him. Therefore, he replied confidently to the man's question.

"What makes ye think I put anything in it?" he asked.

Lor pointed to one of the *doctores*, an Englishman named Wendell Stanhope. Wendell was bent over near the exit of the hall, vomiting onto the dirt floor. Magnus looked at him, unconcerned.

"What is wrong with him?" he asked.

Lor lifted a blond eyebrow. "He took my wine by mistake. *What* did ye put in it?"

Across the table, Bane was about to take a drink of his wine, but when he saw Wendell doubled over, his eyes widened and he quickly set the cup down.

"Idiot," he hissed at Magnus. "Ye almost caught me with whatever ye've poisoned Wendell with."

Sitting next to Bane, Galan looked at his half-empty cup of wine, realizing he'd been made a victim in Magnus's nasty game. "Great bleeding Christ," he hissed. "Did you just poison me, Chicken?"

The *Chicken* nickname was a running joke among them. It was actually an affectionate term, with Magnus's moniker being the Eagle, and his friends would tease him by calling him the Chicken.

But this was no teasing matter.

Magnus smiled smugly.

"Do ye not have more faith in me than that?" he said. "Ye may be English, but I wouldna poison ye. Not much, anyway."

Galan could already feel something going to work in his belly. "Damn you," he muttered. "What did you do, you Scottish bastard?"

"Ye'll soon find out."

Galan was beginning to sweat. "I'll get you for this, Chicken. You'll be very sorry."

Magnus snorted. "Not as sorry as ye'll be in a little while," he said. "But have no fear. Ye'll be fine on the morrow. But it's going tae be a long night."

As Galan grunted and grasped his belly, horrified, Bane and Lor were looking at him as if waiting for him to explode in all directions. Realizing Magnus may have gotten the upper hand on them wasn't acceptable to Bane. Wanting to create trouble for his smug friend, he lifted his cup and called out to one of the newer warriors at the Cal.

"Tay," he shouted across the hall. "Tay MacNaughton! Attend me!"

At the far end of the hall, a mountain of a man stood up and headed in their direction. Tay MacNaughton was not new to the Ludus Caledonia, but he hadn't fought there in quite some time. Like Magnus, he was a professional fighter, having been in the fight guild system for several years. He and Magnus were old friends. They'd fought with, and against, each other.

Tay was one of the most formidable men at the fight guild, purely from his size. His father was Scots but his mother was from Constantinople, and Tay had the dark eyes and hair from the land of the Turks and a fluid, almost poetic manner about him, but his temper and size were purely Scots. When Magnus saw the man heading over, the smirk vanished from his face.

"Dunna give it tae him, Bane," he said seriously. "A joke is a joke, but Tay will rip yer arms from their sockets if he's angry enough."

Bane wasn't intimidated. "I'll tell him the wine is from ye."

"But ye're the one giving it tae him. Do ye want tae take that chance?"

He had a point. Bane had a wife and a child he would very much like to see grow up. With a sigh of resignation, he set the wine down and purposely tipped it over.

"Och," he said as Tay drew near. "I was going tae offer ye a drink, but it looks like I've been clumsy. Sit with us, man. I'll send for more food and drink."

Galan picked that moment to bolt up from the bench and make his way from the hall, hunched over as he walked. Everyone, including Tay, watched him go.

"What is wrong with him?" Tay asked in his deep baritone.

Magnus started chuckling. "Wine with a purge in it," he said. Then he pointed to the spilled wine. "Bane has been giving it tae everyone. Now he wanted tae give it tae ye."

Tay looked accusingly at Bane, whose eyes widened at the fact that he had been implicated as the culprit in Magnus's vile scheme. He sighed heavily.

"Magnus," he said deliberately. "Tell the man ye're only jesting.

I want tae see my child live tae be a man, and if Tay thinks I'm going around poisoning people, that mayna happen."

Magnus was still laughing, but he waved Tay off. "'Tis true," he said. "I lied. 'Tis what we do around here—play very bad jokes on one another. But I can tell ye that I would die for every man at this table because they are honorable and worthy. Playing tricks on each other is how we show our love and devotion."

A smile tugged at Tay's lips. "Ye always were a twisted lad, Magnus."

"Some things never change."

Tay's grin bloomed as he sat down, and Bane sat down next to him, convinced Tay wouldn't try to throttle him. They made Magnus give up the wine he'd been giving everyone, however, as he'd kept it tucked under his legs beneath the table. It was Axel, the Ludus Caledonia's manager, who finally took the pitcher from him and tossed the contents out the door.

Once the wine was disposed of, it was forgotten, and they were back to laughing and jesting with one another, wondering how Galan and Wendell were faring. Both men had run into the privy and had yet to come out.

The apothecary had been true to his word about the purge.

The meal that night was a stew with beef and lamb in it, rich with root vegetables. Men who fought as viciously as these men did required good food, and the offerings at the Ludus Caledonia were the best. In addition to the stew, there were copious amounts of bread and butter, stewed fruit, and a baked egg dish called a daryol. It was full of cheese and herbs, and was quite delicious.

Magnus was deep into his daryol when a sentry came through the entry. The sentries at the Ludus Caledonia were all highly trained men, mostly mercenaries, and they were extremely well paid. This man was the commander of the night watch. When he spied Magnus, he headed in his direction.

"M'lord," he said. "We've captured a trespasser. She has asked for ye."

Magnus's mouth was full as he looked at the man. "*She?*" he repeated. He chewed a couple of times before swallowing what was in his mouth. "Who is it?"

The sentry shook his head. "She refuses tae give us her name."

The other men at the table were listening. "It is probably one of yer past conquests," Bane muttered. "She's come back for more."

Magnus cocked a dark eyebrow. "And why shouldna she?" he said. "Once a woman has a taste of me, I ruin all other men for her."

The men snorted as Magnus returned his attention to the sentry. "No name?" he said. "Then I'm not interested."

The sentry grinned. "Ye should be," he said. "She's beautiful. She fought like a banshee when we captured her and screamed at us in a language not English or Gaelic. One of my men said it was Spanish."

A Spanish banshee…

Somewhere in the back of Magnus's mind, the flame of recognition sparked. The first and only Spaniard who screamed like a banshee that he knew of was the very one he'd seen earlier in the day. Literally, the only one. He'd not seen the woman in over seven years and he never expected to see her again.

Did he?

His curiosity had the better of him. Puzzled, he set his spoon down and stood up.

"Where is she?" he asked.

The sentry jerked his head in the direction of the entry to the Ludus Caledonia. "The gatehouse," he said.

Magnus followed him out into the night, ignoring the inquisitive stares of his friends. It was a warm evening as far as evenings in Scotland went, a symptom of a summer that had been unusually warm and dry.

Magnus was dressed for the weather, in only linen breeches, boots, and a tunic that he didn't even have laced up. It was open in the front, down to his waist, baring his broad tanned chest. He followed the sentry through the north section of the warriors' encampment with its dozens of tiny cottages, passing by Caelian Hill, which was the name given to the keep of the Ludus Caledonia, the crown jewel of the complex.

Caelian Hill was surrounded by an enormous curtain wall, circular in shape, with a gatehouse and portcullis built into it. The sentry took him straight to the gatehouse, a two-storied structure, and as he approached, he could hear a woman shouting angrily.

Only they were words he could not understand.

Spanish.

Magnus eyed the sentry curiously when the man paused by the door to the guardroom built into the gatehouse, but the sentry simply indicated for him to enter the room.

Warily, he did.

Immediately, his gaze fell on Diantha as she sat in a corner, surrounded by three heavily armed guards. No one was touching her, at least at the moment, but that beautiful green brocade dress with the yellow border that he'd seen her wearing earlier was dirty and disheveled. One sleeve was torn. Baffled, Magnus walked up between the guards, shocked at what he was seeing.

"Great bleeding Christ," he muttered. "What are ye doing here, lass?"

Diantha's expression went from frightened to relieved in a split second. "Do you remember me from today?" she asked, her voice suddenly quiet and trembling. "I was with Lady Ayr and we saw you at the apothecary in Edinburgh, and…"

He cut her off, though it wasn't harsh. "Of course I remember ye," he said. "Ye're Flaca… I mean, Dian…Dianca…"

"Diantha," she said helpfully. "I came to find you but these *tontos* grabbed me and tore my dress. I told them I wanted to speak with you, but they thought it better to drag me here and humiliate me. I—"

She suddenly stopped speaking, looking at the guards standing around her and evidently unwilling or unable to speak further in front of them. After a moment, she lowered her gaze and Magnus swore he saw her lower lip tremble.

He didn't know why she was here, but he was going to find out.

"Back away," he told the guards. "Get out. I will speak with the lady."

The guards obeyed. They backed out of the little chamber, and Magnus shut the door behind them so he and the lady would have some privacy. With the door shut, he stood there a moment, looking her over. It only confirmed what he'd seen this afternoon, that she was as fine a beauty as he'd ever seen.

And she looked very lost.

Scratching his ear, he stepped in her direction.

"They're gone," he said. "Now…what are ye doing here? Did Lady Ayr send ye?"

Diantha lifted her eyes, looking at him. "Nay," she said. "She did not send me. I came because I need your help."

"What help?"

"I want you to help me escape and go home."

He eyed her with some confusion. "Escape? Go home?" he repeated. "I dunna understand. Where is home?"

Diantha's big eyes were filling with tears, which she was quickly flicking away. "Navarre," she said softly. "I want to go home."

"Then why come tae me? Why not simply tell Lady Ayr?"

She shook her head. "You misunderstand," she said. "I am not a guest or a ward of the duchess, as she has told everyone."

"Ye're not?"

"Nay," she said. "I am a hostage. Someone told me once that you were also a hostage. You were able to escape and I want to escape, too. Won't you help me?"

Magnus hadn't known that she was a hostage. He'd always thought she was simply a ward, as she said. That was the story the duke and duchess had made known, but he wasn't surprised to hear it wasn't true.

"Then Lady Ayr doesna know ye're here?" he asked.

"Nay."

"Did ye run away?"

"Aye."

"Does *anyone* know ye're here?"

"The apothecary might."

"Where I saw ye today?"

"Aye. I returned to ask him where the Ludus Caledonia was."

Magnus sighed faintly. "If the duchess sends men tae look for ye, they'll go tae the shop, dunna ye think? The apothecary will tell them what he told ye, and that will lead them here."

Diantha shook her head. "I never told anyone I was going to the apothecary's shop," she said. "I am sure they will not discover where I have gone. I will pay you for your assistance, I swear it, but please…please help me."

Magnus didn't know what to make of any of it. There was another chair in the guardroom and he pulled it up so that he could sit next to her. In truth, he was quite curious about her, and whether or not he wanted to be, he found himself swept up in the situation.

Unusual for a man who rarely showed regard for someone other than himself.

"I think ye'd better start from the beginning," he said. "Ye say ye are a hostage of Ayr?"

Diantha nodded solemnly. "Aye."

"But why?"

She sighed faintly. "It is a complicated situation, as complicated as the situation between the Scottish and the English."

"I understand the politics of such things. Tell me."

She pondered his question a moment, perhaps thinking of the most concise way of telling him the situation that had consumed her entire life.

"There is much civil war in Navarre right now," she said after a moment. "Castillo de Santacara is my family's home. We have always supported the kings and queens of Navarre, but the queen has been dead these past years and her husband, who is not the rightful heir to the throne, has assumed power. My father sent word to the Scottish court for assistance to fight the usurper, and the Duke of Ayr answered. He told my father to send money and one of his children as a hostage in good faith, and he would send him an army. But the army was never sent."

Magnus's eyebrows lifted. It was indeed complicated and complex, as politics and wars often were.

"I see," he said. "Then the duke betrayed yer father."

"Aye, he did. The duke took his only child and his money."

"Does the duke know ye're the only child?"

She nodded sadly. "That is why he wants to marry me to Conan," he said. "Then Conan will inherit Santacara, through me. He will also inherit the County of Mélida—my father is the Conde de Mélida."

That was the Spanish equivalent of an earl. It was quite a mess, but Magnus wasn't surprised by any of it. Ambrose Stewart was an ambition, greedy, and callous bastard, but he'd learned that from the rest of the Scottish royal family, who were all cut from the same fabric. Even Magnus's own father was calculating and ambitious, because in a den of jackals, one had to learn to survive...or one did not.

But it still didn't excuse the betrayal. Magnus thought that there had to be more to it than what she was telling him.

"What would make yer father send his young daughter tae a faraway land, tae people he dinna even know?" he said. "The man sent money *and* his only child?"

Diantha shrugged her slender shoulders. "Desperation will make a man do things he would not normally do," she said. "My father has a large fortress and a big army, but that was not enough against the usurper. At least, that was what I was told. One of my father's men took me from the convent where I had been living and brought me to Scotland. He told me many things I had not known since I had been away."

Magnus eyed her strangely. "Ye were in a convent?"

She nodded. "Since I was very young," she said. "Iglesia de Santa Brigida. It was a school in the province that every noble family sent their young girls to. We learned to read, to write, to dance, to paint. My father's man came and took me away from it when I was eleven years of age, escorting me across the sea to a place where I did not know the language. He was supposed to return with the army promised by the duke, but he did not."

"How do ye know?"

She snorted ironically. "Mayhap I did not speak the language, but I did not need to in order to see that my father's man and the escort with him were killed," she said. "The next morning, their horses were still in the stable yard and I saw men taking away something in a cart, out into the fields. They were bodies covered with straw because I saw a foot sticking out. My father's men were killed because the duke had no intention of honoring his part of the bargain."

Magnus was coming to feel the slightest bit guilty. Guilty because he thought he'd had it the worst of anyone at Culroy Castle, but clearly there was someone else with a more tragic story to tell. He leaned back in the chair, pondering what he'd been told.

"Why did yer father never come for ye, then?" he asked. "If he had a large army, surely he could bring it tae Scotland and retrieve ye."

Her eyes started to fill with tears again, but she blinked them back furiously. "I do not know," she said honestly. "It has been nine years since I last saw my father, and I have received no word from him during that time. When his men were killed and did not return to Santacara, I thought he would come for me, but he did not. It is my fear that he is dead, but even so, I must go home. I must discover for myself what has become of him, and I have waited these many years to escape Culroy. When I saw you, I knew the time was right. Please, my lord. Please...help me."

Magnus looked at her. In his world, Magnus only helped Magnus. That was the only thing of importance to him. He'd long bred the emotion out of himself, the ability to feel anything, the ability to show and to accept compassion. That process began as a young lad when he'd first been taken hostage at Culroy, and it continued to this day. It wasn't selfishness.

It was self-preservation.

He stood up from the chair.

"Why me?" he asked. "Ye are presuming a great deal by coming here tae ask me such things. I'm not responsible for ye."

Her expression fell and Magnus resisted the urge to recant everything he'd just said. But something held him back, perhaps that young lad who had refused to make friends or grant favors. He wasn't willing to risk himself for this woman. The only risks he ever took were for himself, for his greater gain. As he wrestled with his thoughts, Diantha lowered her gaze.

"I know you are not responsible for me," she said. "I understand that completely. And I do realize that I am asking a great deal of someone I do not know, but given that you were a hostage at Culroy, surely you can understand my desperation. Did you not wish to escape the entire time you were there?"

He had. Every day of those long years he'd spent at that horrible place. "I was released, eventually," he said. "If ye go back, mayhap they'll release ye eventually, too."

Her features hardened. "After what I just told you?" she said. "Ridiculous. They want me for that barbarian of a son so he will inherit my lands. They will never release me because I am of great value to them."

Magnus knew that bunch enough to know that she spoke the truth. Greed flowed through their veins instead of blood. He saw that during his time spent there, something that had rubbed off on him because he was greedy, too. He was a professional fighter and he'd earned a great deal of money over the years because, according to the Duke of Ayr, money was the most important thing in the world. He'd learned that lesson well. But as he looked at her, a thought occurred to him.

He had spent the past seven years forgetting what his captors had done to him. Seven years of pushing hate from his heart, seven years of struggling to find a place in a world where he didn't fit in. There were many to blame for this, including his own father, but his worthlessness as a human being had never been so pressed upon him as it had during those captive years.

It began to occur to him that if he helped Diantha, he would obtain some satisfaction against those who had persecuted him for so long. In helping her escape, he would be ruining their plans for Conan. Anything he could ruin for that wretch, he would. It would be a small victory against people who had treated him so poorly, a chance to seek some satisfaction.

With that in mind, why *wouldn't* he help her?

Certainly, there would be risks involved. He would be bringing someone into the Ludus Caledonia who did not belong, someone viewed as a possession by the Duke of Ayr. It was, in essence, stealing.

But no one needed to know that.

"Very well, m'lady," he said slowly. "What help did ye have in mind?"

Diantha straightened in her chair, shocked that he would suddenly be receptive to her request. From the expression on her face, she had been positive he was about to turn her out.

Now, he was asking her how he could help her.

"I–I will need to earn passage to Navarre," she said. "I had money at Culroy that I had earned, but it was stolen, so I need to find a way to earn money to pay for my passage. I was taught to read and write Spanish, Catalan, and French in the convent, and the duchess's ladies taught me how to read and write English. I can teach others for a small price."

"Do ye want tae teach me, then? I already know how tae read and write, lass."

She looked over his shoulder to the complex of the Ludus Caledonia outside the door. "Then mayhap you can help me find others who will pay for my tutelage," she said. "Though I've not really seen it, this looks like a big place. Surely there are people here who want to learn to read and write."

He shrugged. "Mayhap there are, but if ye go about it that way, it will take ye a long time tae earn passage," he said. "If I give ye the money, ye can go now."

There was something in her surprised expression that suggested she very much wanted to take him up on his offer. But the excitement in her eyes quickly faded.

"Your offer is very generous, but I do not know when I would be able to pay it back," she said. "I could not take your money with that knowledge. It would be better if I earned it for myself."

"Ye asked me for help. I'm offering."

"That is not the kind of help I was asking for. I am not afraid of hard work to earn my money."

He lifted his eyebrows. "Is that so?" he said. "Other than teach men tae read and write, what else can ye do?"

She cocked her head thoughtfully. "I know how to cook and sew," she said. "I could tend your cottage and it would cost you very little. I am only asking for your help in finding ways to earn money so I can return home. Mayhap there are others I can tend house for, too?"

She was eager and, if Magnus was honest with himself, very brave. She wasn't looking for something to be given to her. She wanted to work for it, and that impressed him. He'd dealt with so many women who were pampered and perfumed and probably hadn't worked an honest day in their lives. Those were soulless chits, women he used and tossed aside.

But not Diantha.

Already, he could see she was different. There had been a day not long ago when Clegg would not permit women at the Ludus Caledonia other than those who serviced the warriors, but those times were over. Now, women were permitted. There were even families, as evidenced by Lor and Bane's wives and children. Women were an integral part of the Ludus Caledonia these days.

It seemed as if Magnus might have one of his very own.

"That is possible," he said after a moment. "Get up and come with me."

Diantha stood up right away. "Where are we going?"

He reached out and grasped her by the arm. "Back tae my cottage unless ye plan tae remain here all night," he said. "Let's both sleep on this and discuss it further in the morning."

Diantha went along with him without hesitation. "I knew you would help me," she said gratefully. "When I saw you this afternoon, I could feel it."

He glanced at her. "Even when ye were refusing tae tell me yer name?"

She was properly contrite. "I did not know who you were then," she said. "For all I knew, you were a brute and a masher."

He snorted, pulling her out of the guardroom and waving away the sentries who started to come near. He pulled her through the crowd of men, casting her a long glance.

"Who says I'm not?"

Diantha eyed him, but she didn't reply. She was certain he was jesting—at least, she was hoping he was—and she didn't want to say anything that might break whatever spell of cooperation had fallen upon him. Masher or not, for tonight, she was willing to go along with him.

Tomorrow would tell the tale of whether her decision had been a wise one.

CHAPTER FIVE

Edinburgh—Trinity House

IT WAS THE EVENING MEAL AT THE GREAT BARONIAL MANSE on the north side of Edinburgh known as Trinity House. The town home of the Dukes of Ayr, it was built from sandstone that had hues of pink and gold, a masterful example of architectural design that soared four stories into the sky. The north side of the manse had turned darker and pitted because of the salt that blew off the sea, but the south side was still a fresh and lovely shade of pink.

Locals called it *taigh pinc*.

The pink house.

In the dining hall with its carved-paneled walls and an elegant stone hearth, the Duke and Duchess of Ayr sat at a feasting table that could easily seat thirty people. Ambrose Stewart, Duke of Ayr, was double-fisting his good beef dinner into his mouth as his wife sat silently by, drinking her fine Spanish wine and hardly touching her food.

The hall was quiet on this evening but for the couple and their servants, who were moving about in silence to ensure the lord and lady were not disturbed. Not even the duchess's women were in attendance because the opportunities for Lady Ayr to dine alone with her husband were few and far between.

He was a man who hadn't much time for his wife.

Usually, her only companion at supper was her cup of wine.

But tonight, she had her husband to herself and she wanted to be amusing, or at least pleasing. There had been a time when he had appreciated her conversation. As he slurped his meal, she tried to think of things to discuss with him, things he might respond to. She thought back on her day, remembering her brief encounter with Magnus. That would be of interest to him. It would also be of interest to him to know that Diantha de Mora, the future Lady Ayr, had gone off looking for lost ribbons from the fabric shop and had not returned. Soldiers were currently out searching for her.

No, she wouldn't mention *that*.

"You will never guess who I saw today," she said brightly.

He was more interested in his meal. "I couldna imagine," he said. "Tell me."

Lady Ayr heard the apathy in his tone, watching as he shoveled bread into his mouth. Still, she missed those days when he had been more interested in her than his food.

"I saw our dear Magnus," she said.

He chewed a few times before finally looking at her, puzzled. "Magnus?"

"Hugh's lad," she said. "*Our* Magnus, Ambrose. Surely you remember the lad who spent all of those years with us."

Surprised, he stopped chewing. Before he could reply, however, the door to the hall shoved open and a young man appeared.

The cozy supper, just the two of them, was over.

At the table, both Agnes and her husband turned to watch the new addition to the hall. He was well-dressed, with heavy and expensive boots thumping loudly against scrubbed wooden floors.

Thump, thump, thump.

He sounded as if he were marching.

Conan Stewart had made an appearance.

"Conan," she said evenly. "Where have you been? We waited supper as long as we could, darling."

Conan didn't look at his mother, nor did he pay any attention to her. He ignored her as if she hadn't spoken to him at all, but that was usual. He had never had much respect for his mother, a woman he considered useless and stupid.

He looked straight at his father.

"Sorry I'm late, Da," he said. "I had tae go down tae the horse dealer near Chalmers. Ye know the one—the man missing fingers because horses have bitten them off over the years? *That* dealer. Do ye know the bastard tried to cheat me? I specifically told him I wanted a young jennet from Andalusia, but he tried tae give me an Arabian instead. They are beautiful horses, but that wasna what I wanted. So I had tae take the horse back."

Ambrose lifted his eyebrows. "Is that so?" he said. "Ye should have let me take a look at it. I might have wanted it."

But Conan shook his head as he sat down at his father's right hand. "Not *this* horse," he said. "It was older than I am. I felt sorry for the beast, but I have no place for it here in our stables."

"I hope ye forced him tae give ye excellent concessions on the jennet."

"Of course I did. I am my father's son."

The two of them grinned at each other as if they shared the same despicable secret. As Ambrose returned to his meal, the servants were already emerging from the shadows, bringing Conan copious amounts of food and drink. He was the young lord, the future duke, and they treated him carefully because Conan had a dark streak in him that no one wished to tempt.

Not servants, not lying horse dealers.

He dug in to his food with gusto, slurping the succulent beef and washing it down with the same fine wine his mother was drinking. Like his father, he was a glutton. As he continued to wolf down his food, Ambrose spoke.

"Yer mother was telling me that she saw Magnus today," he said. "I havena heard of Magnus since he left us."

Conan had much the same reaction to Magnus's name as his father had. He stopped chewing and looked at his mother in surprise.

"Ye saw him?" he asked. "Where?"

Agnes considered it a distinct privilege that her son was actually speaking to her, so she answered him eagerly.

"My ladies and I visited the Seed today," she said. "You know the shop—the apothecary brothers. Magnus was just leaving as I was entering. I have not seen him in so long that I hardly recognized him. He has…grown."

There was something in her tone that her son and husband missed, an inflection suggesting that she liked what she had seen in the strong, young stud. Oblivious to his mother's lusty thoughts, Conan snorted as he turned back to his food.

"Of course he has grown," he said, spearing a piece of stringy beef with his fine knife. "He has tae be nearing thirty years in age now. I would assume that he is living in the streets like the bastard that he is. Amuse us with a humorous tale of what Magnus is now doing with his life, Agnes. I want tae laugh."

He had never been able to bring himself to call her "mother." It was yet another indignity he heaped upon Agnes in a long line of indignities. She could hear the condescending tone in his voice, a tone he so often used when speaking to her or about her. The only respect Conan had for anyone in the family was for his father, and that was because the man would give him his inheritance upon his death. Conan was smart enough to know not to anger him.

But he held no such caution for his mother.

Agnes had long resigned herself to her son's hurtful manner. But Conan did as he pleased, and there was no stopping his arrogance or his ambition, much like his father. Therefore, she took some satisfaction in delivering the news about Magnus. She wanted her son to know that the boy Conan had been so intensely jealous of had made something of himself.

"He has thrived since his departure from Culroy," she said, drinking more wine and feeling the fortification flooding her veins. "He told me that he is a professional fighter at the greatest fight guild in all of Scotland. He told me to ask if you knew of it."

Both Ambrose and Conan stopped chewing. Shocked, they looked at each other, processing what Agnes had just told them.

Or perhaps they had misunderstood.

Ambrose swallowed the bite in his mouth.

"There is only one fight guild in Edinburgh," he said, incredulous. "It is called the Ludus Caledonia. Is that the one he meant?"

Agnes paused, pouring herself more wine. "He would not say the name of the place. He would only say that it was the greatest fight guild in all of Scotland," she said. "Do you know of it?"

Ambrose stared at her a moment before setting his spoon and knife down. Sitting back in his chair, he continued to stare at his wife as he wiped his mouth with the back of his hand.

"I do," he said. "He *truly* told ye that?"

"Is it someplace terrible?"

Ambrose shook his head. "Nay," he said. "Or mayhap it is tae some. I suppose it depends on yer point of view. I visited the place once, though that was several years ago. I've not been back since. A professional fighter, ye say?"

Agnes took a long drink of her wine, smacking her lips. "He looked like one, too," she said. "He is built like a warrior now, muscular and broad. If he says he is a professional fighter, I believe him because he has the outward appearance of one. I suspect Conan would not be able to best him again now."

Conan's expression tensed. "I can still thrash him like I always have," he said. "I will always be able tae defeat him."

Agnes was feeling her wine. She looked at her son, a man she tried hard not to hate at times. "You always hated him," she said. "He is the son of the king's brother while you are only the son of a duke."

"He's a bastard."

"His bloodlines are better than yours."

Furious, Conan smashed his fists on the table. "Shut yer yap, woman," he hissed. "I wouldna speak of bloodlines if I were ye, considering ye're a Sassenach wench."

"And you are half-Sassenach. It is a shame you will always have to bear."

It genuinely infuriated Conan when she said things like that. Before he could throw a fork at her, as he'd done before, Ambrose turned to his wife.

"Leave us," he said in a low voice. "I will speak with my son alone."

With a smile playing on her lips at the victory over her snobbish son, Agnes graciously dipped her head and rose from the table, quitting the hall in silence. Only when she was gone did Ambrose turn to his son.

"I've told ye not tae speak tae yer mother like that," he said quietly. "Ye may not like it, but she's the only mother ye have, sorry tae say."

It was as close to a rebuke as he could get, but Conan received the message. The young man had pushed his food away and was now well into his wine, much as his mother had been.

"She shouldna speak tae me so," he grumbled. "When I am the duke, I'll—"

Ambrose cut him off. "When ye're the duke, ye'll tolerate her just as I've tolerated her all these years," he said pointedly. "But forget about her for now. We have other things tae discuss."

"What?"

Ambrose scratched his cheek, trying to determine where to begin. "It's so strange that she has seen Magnus," he muttered. "Do ye remember what we were speaking of only yesterday? About Magnus's father?"

Conan was still angry, but he forced himself off the subject of Agnes and onto a subject that was common between him and his father—Hugh Stewart, the youngest brother of the king. He was a man who hadn't been far from Ambrose's thoughts for many years, mostly because there had always been contention between them. Hugh resisted his brother, the king, and Ambrose was supplicant to the king.

It made for interesting dynamics.

"Aye," he said after a moment. "I remember."

"Do ye remember the *whole* conversation, Connie?"

His father only called him Connie when he wanted something, or was trying to be manipulative or affectionate, or both. Conan took a swallow of wine before answering.

"I remember," he said. "One conversation about Hugh as the latest of several we've had about the man. It seems we've been speaking of him quite a bit recently. Seems very coincidental that Agnes would see Magnus today."

Ambrose shook his head as he collected his own cup of wine. "Mayhap not so coincidental, after all," he said. "Mayhap it is a sign."

"What sign?"

Ambrose settled back in his chair. "We've discussed the rumors that Hugh Stewart is allying himself with the Earl of Ross, the Laird of the Isles," he said. "Do ye remember men from Clan MacKay telling us that Hugh had allied himself with the Laird of the Isles, who has himself allied with the exiled English king? 'Tis a dangerous thing tae do, allying with an exiled *Sassenach* king."

Conan had calmed down sufficiently from his run-in with his mother as he focused on what his father was saying.

"Hugh has run afoul of our king before," he said. "'Tis why we held Magnus for so long, tae ensure the man's good behavior. Seems as if we should never have let him go."

Ambrose's gaze glittered on his son. "There was no reason tae hold the lad any longer than we had tae," he said. "Besides...Hugh behaved himself for a time, but he's gone back tae his old ways, siding against his brother in all things. Now he sides with the Laird of the Isles and they have as much power in Scotland as the king has. Ye know what this means, dunna ye?"

Conan shook his head. "What?"

Ambrose leaned forward in his chair. "*Think*, lad," he said quietly. "There's been no armies raised as of yet, but that will come. We know it will and we will be expected tae take up arms for the king."

"And?"

Ambrose snorted. "Ye have sawdust for brains," he said. "Magnus, Hugh's son, is now a professional fighter, so he says."

Conan tried not to look shocked. "Do ye plan tae take him hostage against his father again?" he said. "How would we do it, Da? If he truly fights at the Ludus Caledonia, then..."

Ambrose waved him off. "Not take him hostage," he said. "Have ye been tae the Cal, lad?"

Conan shook his head. "Nay," he said. "But I've heard tales of it. Betting on men fighting isna something that interests me. I'd rather wager on horses."

Ambrose held up a finger to beg patience while he explained his idea. "At the Ludus Caledonia, a man can buy himself an excellent warrior," he said. "'Tis why they train men there. They train them tae become the greatest warriors in the world. The last time I was there, I saw a man from Vilnius purchase a warrior who had won several bloody bouts. Everyone knows that the greatest warriors in the world come from the Ludus Caledonia, and if Magnus fights there now as yer mother says he does, then he has a price."

He said it as if it were a great revelation, but Conan still wasn't following his father's train of thought. He'd never been particularly bright, at least not when it came to scheming.

"What will ye do, then?" he asked.

Ambrose was disappointed that Conan didn't understand his enthusiasm. "We go tae the Cal and we buy him," he said. "We buy him and we make him fight against Hugh when we raise our armies."

Now, Conan finally caught on and his eyes widened. "Do ye think he'll do it?"

Ambrose was quite titillated with the possibilities. "If he doesna, then we throw him in the vault and tell Hugh that we'll kill him if he continues his alliance with the Laird of the Isles. Either way, we must go tae the Cal and purchase Magnus. Yer mother sighting him today is the answer we've been looking for, dunna ye see? When I said it was a sign, that's what I meant."

Conan wasn't sure it was a sign, but it was certainly a welcome coincidence. "I hear the warriors there cost a good deal of money," he said. "Will ye pay it?"

"I'll pay whatever the cost," Ambrose said firmly. "Magnus could very well be crucial tae his father's submission. God is show- ing us the way...tae the Ludus Caledonia."

Conan digested his father's plan, which wasn't an unreasonable one, but he saw one problem with it.

"When ye released Magnus, we told him that his father wanted nothing tae do with him," he said. "Ye seem tae be neglecting the fact that we've driven a wedge between the pair. How do ye expect Hugh's submission when we told him that his son hated him?"

That thought had crossed Ambrose's mind, too. Since Magnus had been a young lad, Ambrose had convinced both Magnus and Hugh that neither wanted anything to do with the other. It was a ploy to keep them apart, to control the situation, because deep down, that's what Ambrose wanted to do—control Hugh. There was no better way of doing that than by turning father against son. But deep down, the true reason was something more than control.

It was jealousy.

The brother of a king had more power than Ambrose could ever hope to have, and Ambrose hated him for it.

But he couldn't think on that now. He was too focused on the possibility of reuniting with Magnus Stewart and using him against his father.

"No father could refuse tae save his son if given the chance," he said. "But think on it—what vengeance Magnus must have in his heart for his father because he believes his father hates him. Hatred I put there. We'll give Magnus the opportunity tae seek revenge for Hugh's wrongs."

That made perfect sense to Conan. Vengeance and other primitive emotions were something he completely understood. He smiled at his father and lifted his cup.

"Tae the wounded heart of a bastard son," he said. "May it play in our favor."

Ambrose lifted his cup as well. Already, he could taste victory.

As father and son toasted the future, Agnes had been listening. She often lurked in the shadows when the two were speaking simply because she wanted to know what fresh new hell she could be expecting from them. With Ambrose, something was always afoot, and with Conan… Her son was always trying to ruin someone.

She'd failed as a mother when it came to him.

But tonight, the plans they were making were for Magnus, someone they'd not spoken of since the moment he'd left Culroy. But now…

Once again, Magnus Stewart would be a pawn.

That didn't sit well with Agnes. She never interfered in her husband's affairs because she usually had no emotional investment in them. But with Magnus, it was different. She felt guilty because of what she knew—that hatred and jealousy had driven her husband to manipulate the relationship between Magnus and his father. It had been selfishness on their parts, something that had condemned a young boy, now a young man, to a lonely and detached life.

Now that they were going to use him again, she wondered what would happen if Hugh Stewart knew all about their plans for Magnus, and the fact that Magnus never hated his father after all.

Perhaps she couldn't do anything to help Magnus, but perhaps his father could.

It would certainly be a way to ruin Ambrose and Conan's plans.

For the first time since the situation with Magnus and Hugh started, Agnes pushed her guilt aside. She was finally going to do something about it.

What mistreated wife wouldn't be agreeable to a little revenge…

PART TWO

VITA NOVUM

(A NEW LIFE)

CHAPTER SIX

The Ludus Caledonia

WAS IT ALL A DREAM?

That was the first thought on Diantha's mind when she opened her eyes. For a moment, she simply stared at the ceiling, a pitched roof covered in sod in a chamber that she didn't recognize.

It took her a moment to remember where she was.

Rays of golden light were streaming in between the closed shutters on the windows and from underneath the door. Slowly sitting up, Diantha looked around the room, orienting herself. This was the first day of the freedom she sought.

She could hardly believe it.

But her path to the Ludus Caledonia had not been without difficulty.

After the apothecary brothers had directed her to the church in Morningside, it had taken her several hours to walk there on a road that was well traveled. She wasn't convinced that Lady Ayr's soldiers weren't somehow tracking her, so she hid from every sound, every traveler.

The priests at St. Eustace knew of the fight guild but, surprisingly, had no hesitation in telling her how to find it. She was instructed to continue to follow the road south until she found a pile of rocks with a rusted shackle embedded in it. The road to the Ludus Caledonia would be in the range of rocky hills south of that marker. Diantha had faithfully followed their advice. She'd made her way up into the hillside and found a road in the trees.

But that was where the problems started.

Just as she was making her way up the road, men in cloaks bearing nasty crossbows surrounded her. Even when she explained her purpose, they tried to chase her away, but she insisted that she had come to see Magnus Stewart. That name seemed to have an impact, for she was escorted to a castle on the top of a hill where she spent several hours being interrogated by the mercenaries who protected the Ludus Caledonia.

After hours of frustration, someone finally sent for Magnus. Diantha would never forget the moment their eyes met. He looked shocked, but there was also something else there. Something curious...interested, even.

Somewhere inside of him, a spark burned deep.

She could see it.

After a brief conversation, Magnus had taken her back to his cottage in a rather large village at the base of the fortress where there were dozens of cottages constructed in neat rows. He'd given her some blankets and told her to go sleep on the floor.

And that was where she found herself now.

The cottage had two rooms and she was in the larger of the two, a chamber with chairs, a table, a few chests, and other personal possessions. There was a second, smaller room that Magnus had disappeared into the night before, and she noted that the door was open. Rising to her feet, she timidly made her way over to the open panel.

"My lord?" she called softly. "My lord, are you awake?"

Receiving no answer, she stuck her head into the open doorway to see that the only thing in the chamber was, in fact, a very messy bed. Linens were strewn about and pillows were on the floor. Clothing was also tossed all over the chamber as if a tempest wind had blown through.

Since she had told Magnus that she would keep house for him, she thought she might as well start. The entire place was a mess, so she went right to work.

She very much wanted to earn her keep.

The first order of business was the laundry. Clothing was all over the place, so Diantha collected everything she could find, including the bed linens, and put them into a big pile next to the door. Once she had it neatly organized, she realized that she had no idea where to wash anything. A further inspection of the cottage failed to turn up a broom or anything to clean with, not even a tub. Once the laundry was wrangled, she was stuck.

But she wasn't stopped.

Timidly, she opened the door to the cottage, revealing a bright morning and the warriors' village. Magnus's cottage was on the fringe, on an elevated position, looking down into the collection of rock cottages. Taking a few steps out of the cottage, she was awed by what she was seeing—the vast complex of cottages and stone outbuildings, plus the castle on the rise.

The property itself was nestled on the top of the hill range with a view to the south that went on for miles. The castle, with its circular curtain wall and enormous gatehouse, was at the crest of the hill with the village spread out below it. She could also see a large structure off to the east, or at least part of it. It was built into the hillside, but she couldn't quite see what it was. As she held her hand up to shield her eyes from the sun, she heard a female voice.

"We were wondering when ye would come out. Good morn tae ye."

Diantha turned to see two women in front of a neighboring cottage. One woman was tall and lovely, with red curls, while a second woman with beautiful brown hair was seated. Both women had infants in their arms as a tow-haired toddler played in the dirt at their feet.

Diantha smiled timidly.

"*Saludos,*" she said. "Greetings."

Both women smiled in return, but the redhead spoke.

"My name is Isabail," she said. She indicated her companion.

"This is Lucia. Magnus told us tae watch for ye and help ye find yer way."

Diantha made her way over to them. "I am Diantha de Mora," she said. "Where *is* Magnus?"

"At the Fields of Mars," Lucia said, rocking the sleeping infant. "That is the big arena over there, cut into the hill. Ye can only see the top of it from here, but it goes all the way down to the bottom of a glen."

Diantha looked over at the structure in the distance. "I see," she said. "I thought it looked strange. I could not tell what it was."

"That is where the men spend most of their time," Isabail said. "On fight nights, the entire arena is lit up with a thousand torches. Ye've never seen anything so bright."

Diantha's gaze lingered on the distant arena a moment longer before turning to Isabail and Lucia. At closer range, they were both quite lovely and seemed friendly enough. But she sensed unspoken questions for all their politeness simply from the way they were looking at her, so it was better to get everything out in the open.

"Did Magnus tell you why I am here?" she asked. "If he did not, I am happy to tell you."

Isabail shook her head. "He dinna tell us anything," she said. "He simply asked if we'd keep watch for ye and help ye along if ye needed it."

Diantha nodded in understanding, but she realized that speaking about her situation wasn't easy. It was complicated. Moreover, she'd never been one to speak of herself much, mostly because she'd never had any real friends at Culroy. The women there had been disparaging and shunned her because she wasn't Scottish, so opening up was difficult.

A new life, she reminded herself.

Perhaps with these women of the Ludus Caledonia, things would be different.

"'Tis all quite innocent, I assure ye," she said. "Magnus is simply...helping me."

Isabail began to sway back and forth as the infant in her arms grew fussy. "Magnus helping someone other than himself?" she said, grinning. "I dinna know he was capable of such a thing."

Diantha wasn't sure what to say to that, so she simply continued. "Like Magnus was in the past, I am a ward of the Duke of Ayr," she began, but then she stopped herself. "Nay, that is not entirely true. I am a hostage and Magnus was, too. But Magnus escaped his predicament, and when I saw him in Edinburgh yesterday, I knew he could help me escape and return home, so I sought him out. That is why I am here—because I need his help. I must earn money for passage back to Navarre."

She held her breath, waiting for a reaction, but there was no judgment from the women gazing back at her. At least, not outwardly. They only seemed politely curious.

"I thought ye sounded different," Isabail said. "Ye dunna speak like a Scot. Ye're from Navarre?"

Diantha nodded. "I am from Navarre," she said. "Do you know of it?"

Isabail grinned, shaking her head. "I wish I did," she said. "Ye said ye were a hostage of the Duke of...of...?"

"Ayr."

"Aye, Ayr. Why were ye a hostage?"

Diantha debated how much to tell her. Not knowing the woman, she didn't want to tell her everything. She'd learned over the years to be cautious with the truth.

"Political reasons," she said. "Suffice it to say that the duke betrayed my father, and my only chance to return home is to escape. That is why I am here. I have asked Magnus to help me."

"What kind of help do ye need?"

Diantha was honest. "Money," she said. "As I said, I must earn it to pay for my passage. I can sew and I can read and write. I told

Magnus that I could help anyone who wanted to learn to read or write. I can do it in four languages."

That drew a reaction. Isabail's eyebrows lifted. "Impressive," she said. "So ye want tae teach?"

Diantha nodded. "If I can," she said. "Magnus can help me find men to teach, but I can also tend house. In fact, I was just tidying up Magnus's cottage and I've collected his dirty clothing. Men need someone to do things like that, things a wife would do. I could do that for a price."

"Things a wife can do?" Isabail repeated hesitantly. "Eh...what more would ye do?"

Diantha was oblivious to what Isabail was thinking. Lucia, too. They were both looking at Diantha strangely.

Things a wife would do...

"As I said, I can sew," Diantha said. "I can also cook, just a little. I worked in the kitchens sometimes at Culroy Castle and I learned a great deal. I can ensure there is firewood and a fire in the hearth, and the floors are swept. Everything a wife can do."

Isabail's brow furrowed further. "*Everything?*"

It was in that moment that Diantha realized what had Isabail's focus. *Everything a wife can do.* Diantha suddenly realized how it sounded.

Her cheeks flushed a bright red.

"Almost everything," she said quickly. "Everything but...*that.* I'll tend a man's house, but I'll not tend his bed."

Both Isabail and Lucia appeared visibly relieved. "Not tae disparage ye, lass, but it sounded as if ye meant more than tending his house. Ye said ye needed money, so..." Isabail said, her voice trailing off.

She couldn't finish the statement, inferring the obvious, and Diantha shook her head emphatically. Deeply embarrassed, she lowered her head.

"I am not that kind of a woman, I assure you," she said. "I

simply wish to earn money so I can return home. Home, away from women who think I would…"

She couldn't even finish. She was too ashamed. Turning away quickly, she headed toward Magnus's cottage, verging on tears. But a soft hand on her arm stopped her.

"Nay, lass," Isabail said softly. "Dunna go. I'm sorry if we hurt yer feelings. But what ye said sounded as if… Well, I'll not repeat it. And given that Magnus has more female companionship than he needs, it was easy tae think…but it was wrong of us. Forgive us."

Diantha didn't try to pull away. In truth, she was surprised at the apology. "I am the one who made the mistake," she said, sniffling. "I can see how I sounded as if I were willing to do anything at all, but that's not the truth. I've never even been kissed, to be completely honest. I only came to Magnus because I thought he could help me. I do not even really know the man."

Isabail was pulling her back over to where Lucia was now standing up with an infant in her arms who was starting to wake up. The towheaded toddler in the dirt was also on his feet, running to Isabail and grabbing hold of her skirts as she walked.

"Any friend of Magnus's is a friend of ours," Isabail assured her. At her feet, the toddler was whining, and she grasped the boy's hand. "Ye may as well meet everyone. This is my son, Nikolaus, but we call him Nikki. The babes belong to Lucia."

Diantha could see that Isabail was trying to make her feel welcome. She also noticed when the woman shifted the baby in her arms that she was pregnant. She smiled weakly.

"It looks as if you have another babe on the way, too," she said. "Your husband fights for the Ludus Caledonia also?"

When Nikki yanked his hand away and ran back for his toys in the dirt, Isabail put a hand on her gently swollen midsection. "He is a *doctores*," she said. When Diantha looked at her curiously, she explained. "That means he trains men. Did ye not know that?"

Diantha shook her head. "I do not know anything about this place," she said. "Until yesterday, I'd never heard of it."

"Ah," Isabail said, leading her over to a stool that was next to Lucia. "Sit down, then. Let us tell ye about this place."

Diantha gladly did as she was told, eager to hear about this vast complex that was tucked away in the hills.

"How long have you been here?" she asked.

Isabail began to sway back and forth, soothing the irritable baby. "Three years," she said. "Welcome tae the Ludus Caledonia, Diantha de Mora. Think of it as a crown. The castle, called Caelian Hill, is the jewel at the top of the crown. Everything surrounding it is the rest of the crown—the smaller jewels, the gold. It is owned and operated by Sir Clegg de Lave, who was a great Sassenach knight once. King James granted him the property in payment for his services. The Ludus Caledonia is the term for everything ye see."

From her perch on the stool, Diantha was looking around. "It looks very big."

"It is," Lucia said, next to her. "The arena is called the Fields of Mars, and that's where all of the fighting and training take place. It's the heart of the Cal."

Diantha looked at her. "The Cal?"

Lucia snorted softly. "'Tis what everyone calls it," she said. "If ye hear anyone speaking of the Cal, now ye know. Sir Clegg modeled it after the gladiator schools of ancient Rome, where men would train tae fight tae the death for their ancient kings."

Diantha nodded, but she was still looking around. "There are so many cottages," she said. "Are there so many warriors?"

Lucia shrugged. "Sometimes," she said. "But all of the cottages aren't occupied. Most of them, though. Men in training must have a good roof over their heads and a good bed tae sleep in. That is what Clegg says."

Diantha looked at her. "I was told that men fight here and

still other men place wagers on them," she said. "This is all for entertainment?"

Lucia shook her head. "Not all," she said. "Men are trained tae fight and they are taught by the best, men like our husbands. They swear fealty tae Clegg for seven years, and they are housed and fed and trained. They become highly skilled warriors and sometimes great lords pay a good deal of money for their services. That is the greatest honor of all—being bought by a great lord. I've seen dukes and princes and earls here, paying well for a fine warrior. When a man's service is bought, he is given a *gladius*, a sword, with a red sash tied around it as a symbol of release from the Cal. That is always exciting tae see."

It was a lot of information to absorb, but Diantha was sharp. She understood quickly what they were telling her.

"You said that your husband is a trainer?" she asked, looking at Isabail. "But Magnus told me he is a fighter. Does that mean he is still in training?"

The conversation shifted back to Isabail. "Nay," she said. "Magnus is a professional fighter, the very top the Cal has tae offer. He fights for purses."

"Not for his freedom?"

Isabail shrugged. "Many a lord has made an offer for him, but he always declines," she said. "He likes the opportunity tae make money, I suppose, but I also think that he doesna like taking orders. Here at the Cal, he doesna have tae. Here, he *is* the king."

Diantha shook her head, both surprised and impressed by what she was hearing. "It is a big change from when he was held hostage by the Duke of Ayr," she said. "I did not know him at all, really, but I knew *of* him. He spent his time alone because the other lads did not like him. He always seemed so...lonely."

Isabail was still swaying back and forth, now with a sleeping baby on her shoulder. "We've known Magnus for a while and dinna know he was a hostage of Ayr," she said. "He never speaks about himself."

Diantha realized that she might have divulged information that Magnus didn't want known. "Then do not tell him I told you," she said. "He should tell you himself."

"Dunna worry, lass," Isabail assured her. "The secret is safe. Now, ye said ye wanted tae earn money for yer passage back tae Navarre."

"Aye, very much. I do not want to be a burden on Magnus any longer than I must."

Isabail cocked her head thoughtfully. "I think there are a few men around here who might like tae learn how tae read and write," she said. "I will ask my husband tonight. Meanwhile, ye asked about washing Magnus's clothing. We'll put the bairns down tae sleep and show ye the way. Ye might want tae change intae something not so fanciful tae wash with."

A tip of her head in Diantha's direction had the woman looking down at her clothing. It was the green silk with the yellow trim, such a beautiful dress that was now dirty and wrinkled.

"I do not have anything else," she admitted. "I came to the Ludus Caledonia with only the clothing I was wearing."

Lucia was out of her chair now, looking over the pale-green dress. "No comb or soap?" she asked. "Do ye have a cloak or blanket at least?"

Diantha shook her head. "Nothing."

Lucia shrugged. "We can find ye clothing to wear," she said. "And a few other things."

That worried Diantha. "It is not necessary for you to go to the trouble, truly," she said. "I cannot pay for such things now, but I will be happy to buy them when I have a few coins."

Lucia paused, a smile on her lovely face. "Ye dunna have tae pay for anything," she said quietly. "Ye need clothing tae work in, lass. That silk dress willna hold together much longer if ye wear it constantly."

Diantha struggled not to argue. "You are most generous, but I do not wish to start my life here at the Ludus Caledonia by accepting charity," she said. "I told you that I intend to work. When I can pay for it, I shall be happy to buy what I need."

Lucia laughed softly. "Ye dunna understand, Diantha," she said. "'Tis not charity. Call it…a loan. When ye gather enough things of yer own, ye can give it back tae me."

Diantha wasn't sure what to say. She didn't want to offend the women, but taking charity, or a loan, was all the same to her.

She wasn't accustomed to such kindness.

They were all herding toward the cottage, with Isabail taking hold of her toddler son and dragging the whining child along. As the babies were put to bed by doting mothers, Diantha remained outside of the cottage, trying to figure out what, exactly, she was feeling.

Much had happened in a short time.

Isabail and Lucia seemed to be kind and understanding, and Diantha appreciated that. They had been thoughtful enough to explain the world of the Ludus Caledonia to her and patient enough to work through the misunderstandings of her awkward social behavior. Given that Diantha hadn't had any friends at Culroy Castle, her interaction with other women had been limited out of sheer self-protection.

But she didn't feel like that with Isabail and Lucia.

Were there really women like that in the world, thoughtful and genuine?

Out of the world of Culroy Castle, perhaps such things *were* possible.

CHAPTER SEVEN

WHAT WAS I THINKING?

As Magnus went through drills with several top-tiered warriors on the arena floor, his mind wasn't on his task.

It was on Diantha.

Try as he might, he couldn't seem to get her out of his mind. A chance meeting yesterday had created something that was greatly impacting his life, and now he was questioning his decision to help her. He tried to tell himself that it was to seek some measure of satisfaction against Ambrose and Conan, but that wasn't all of it.

That beautiful, serene face had done something to him.

He was a man who saw beautiful women on a regular basis, so he had no idea why Diantha affected him so. All he knew was that her lovely face kept coming back to him, flashing in his mind's eye, causing his concentration to fracture. He was out here, beneath the August sun, swinging a sword at opponents who were looking for any chance to clip the Eagle's wings.

He needed to pay more attention.

But he couldn't seem to do it.

What was it about Diantha that was so memorable? She was the daughter of a Spanish count, with a lineage probably a mile long. That made her special. Magnus understood Ambrose's reasons for wanting to keep her. Perhaps her blood made her special, but her beauty was what had branded him.

Last night when she had come to the Ludus Caledonia, he realized that he could not have sent her away. It had been dark by the time he was notified of her arrival, and sending the woman back out into the night simply wasn't safe.

But it was more than that.

He remembered crashing into her at the apothecary's shop and how entranced he had been with her from the very start. But she had refused to tell him her name and he very well remembered his outrage at that. Perhaps her refusal had also intrigued him. He had grown complacent with women throwing themselves at his feet, so a challenge was refreshing.

Wasn't it?

Now, that intriguing, frustrating creature had taken up residence in his cottage. When he had departed that morning before dawn, he had passed her on the floor of his common room, curled up on the blankets he had practically thrown at her the night before. She was a little thing, petite and curvy, and there was something about her that brought out his male instincts.

He had told her that they would speak further on her predicament this morning, and he found himself both wanting to speak to her and not wanting to speak to her. When the woman looked at him a certain way, he could feel himself willing to do anything for her.

Last night, he had.

Whack!

Something hit him from behind, nearly knocking him to his knees, and he turned to see one of the other fighters standing behind him, shield in one hand and a *gladius*, or wooden practice sword, in the other.

He found himself looking at Tay.

"What is wrong with ye, Eagle?" Tay demanded. "Ye're in another world."

Magnus turned to him, rubbing the spot on his back where Tay had smacked him. "I'm in this world long enough tae send ye tae yer knees," he said, shaking a finger at Tay. "Dunna test me. Ye willna like the results."

Tay grinned big, showing white teeth against his tanned skin. "Probably not," he said. "But something has ye distracted. What is it, sweetheart? Is yer womb troubling ye again?"

Everyone in earshot burst out laughing, including Magnus. "Tay, my friend," he said, "I think I've kicked ye in the head one too many times. Ye've clearly lost yer mind."

Tay closed the gap between them as the group began to disband so they could move on to something else. While the others were walking away, Tay and Magnus remained.

"What is it?" Tay asked more seriously. "I've not seen ye like this before. There has never been a time when I could come up behind ye and smack ye on the backside without ye trying tae throttle me first."

Magnus wasn't sure he could tell him. It wasn't like him to let his guard down to anyone. Everyone saw what Magnus wanted them to see, which was a man who was always and forever in control.

He had no weaknesses.

But then again, he'd never really had to deal with a woman on his mind.

He didn't feel as if he could tell Tay that, however. It was true that he and Tay were old friends, for he had known the man even longer than he'd known Lor and Bane and Galan. They had never been terribly close, but all things considered, closer than most of the professional warriors were. Magnus knew that Tay would always have his back and that he would always have Tay's.

But it was greatly humiliating to have to confess the reasons for his distraction.

Therefore, he didn't try.

"'Tis nothing," he finally said. "I dinna sleep well last night. I'm thinking of returning tae my cottage and trying tae sleep before tonight's event."

Great bleeding Christ, now I'm making excuses to go home and see her!

As Magnus realized the true reason for wanting to return to his cottage, Tay put a big hand on his shoulder.

"Go," he said. "I hear the Bear will be fighting again. If he is, he'll want revenge on ye."

Magnus smiled weakly but before he could speak, he caught sight of something over near the mouth of the arena. Men were emerging from the holding area. The smile faded from his face.

"It looks as if he's already here."

Tay turned to see the enormous warrior known as the Bear making his way out onto the arena floor. The man was with his manager and two other men to train against, but Magnus knew immediately that the Bear was there to send Magnus a message. As he stood there and watched, he heard a voice behind him.

"He's come tae intimidate ye," Lor said, looking over Magnus's shoulder to the Bear in the distance. "Axel tried tae convince him tae leave this morning, but he wouldna. Seems he has a score tae settle with ye and he made it clear that he means tae destroy ye."

Magnus's smile was back, a confident gesture that told everyone around him that he wasn't worried in the least.

"I've beaten him before," he said. "I shall do it again."

They all watched as the Bear took one of his training partners out by the knees, throwing the man so violently to the ground that he broke his arm when he fell. It was a testament to the anger in the Bear, an anger that heightened his sense of revenge. He knew the Eagle was watching.

He wanted to show the man what was in store for him.

"Be cautious tonight," Lor muttered. "He knows yer tricks. He'll be expecting a kick tae the head. Mind that he doesna break yer leg."

Magnus looked at the man. Almost more than any of the others, Lor had a sense of concern and compassion for his friends. He didn't come from a warring background, which meant that the inherent cruelty that men could so often commit against each other in battle wasn't ingrained in him. He was genuinely concerned for Magnus.

But Magnus couldn't let Lor know that he was a wee bit concerned, too.

He patted Lor on the cheek.

"Ye worry like an old woman," he said. "But I wouldna have it any other way."

As Lor smirked and shook his head at his cocky friend, Magnus handed his *gladius* off to one of the servants who tended the field and the armory. They were everywhere on the arena floor, making sure the men were properly armed and that everything was in good condition.

Without another word, and without a hind glance to the Bear, who was trying very hard to impress upon Magnus the beating he was in for that evening, Magnus headed out of the arena. He wasn't thinking about the Bear.

There was a certain Spanish lass he intended to see.

⚜ ⚜ ⚜

It had been a busy morning.

It had all started after the infants had been put to bed. Diantha had returned to Magnus's cottage to collect his laundry, and by the time she had emerged with it, Isabail and Lucia were heading in her direction, their arms heavy with garments. Isabail was even carrying a big basket loaded with more items like hose and slippers and combs.

Diantha was pushed back into the cottage by her well-meaning new friends. She set Magnus's laundry aside as Isabail and Lucia went to work on her. They had brought her so many things that it was difficult to know where to start, but they began by pulling out a clean and serviceable broadcloth dress.

Lady Ayr's fine green silk came off.

The broadcloth was a little worn, but still very nice. It belonged to Lucia, who was about the same size as Diantha. They had also brought soap and linens with them, and they helped Diantha wash before pulling a shift over her head. The broadcloth dress followed. The sleeves were long, and the bodice was made snug with a tie in the back. Isabail tied so tightly that Diantha joked she must have been used to saddling horses.

In truth, Diantha was touched that they should go through so much trouble. She had never been around women who were so willing to help. All of the women she had known since coming to Scotland had been self-absorbed and not particularly compassionate to a young woman who did not fit in. Therefore, to meet two young women who were so willing to be kind to her was surprising.

But it was also wonderful.

Finding them, in all places, at a fight guild.

When Diantha was finally dressed, Lucia stayed with the children while Isabail gave her a tour of the complex. Among the many hidden attributes of the place, Diantha discovered that there was a community garden where women tended vegetables to serve to their men. Both Isabail and Lucia had their own little plots, and Isabail explained that not long ago, women weren't even allowed at the Ludus Caledonia.

But times had changed. Entire families were at the Ludus Caledonia, and it was as self-sufficient as any city. Some women liked to grow their own food even though two massive kitchens provided meals twice a day, and a butcher provided cuts of meat from the herds of cow and sheep that belonged to the Ludus Caledonia.

In addition to the butcher and garden, there was a washhouse where the laundry was done, a big stone structure built around a well and a trough, and there were already a dozen women inside tending to their washing. There was much gossip and laughter, and Isabail introduced Diantha to the women. She braced herself for more cattiness but was surprised, yet again, by their polite and genuine interest in a morning that had been full of such surprises.

In fact, it had been a day of unexpected pleasantness.

The tour took about an hour, and when it was all done, Diantha could see that the Ludus Caledonia was a city unto itself, completely self-sustaining. The only difference with this city was that the source of revenue came from the fighting games, which took place four nights a week. The nights were not consecutive, most of the time, so the warriors would have a rest in between their bouts, and not all warriors fought every night.

She also learned that the warrior classes were tiered. They ranged from novices all the way up to the professional fighters, like Magnus. Since Magnus was such a popular fighter, he had his choice of the nights he wanted to fight. Diantha was told that he generally fought at least three nights a week, depending on how big the purses were. There was speculation that Magnus was the wealthiest fighter at the Ludus Caledonia because since he had arrived, he had never lost a fight.

It had been a very enlightening morning.

Once they returned home, Isabail set up the wash area in the trees behind the cottages. As it turned out, neither she nor Lucia used the common washhouse, and Diantha washed every bit of clothing she had found in Magnus's cottage with perfectionist zeal. It had taken her most of the morning to do six tunics, three pairs of linen breeches, and the linens off his bed.

It was hard physical labor, but Diantha didn't mind. She enjoyed doing something useful, so different from her days of idleness at Culroy. When she was finally finished washing all of Magnus's items, she hung them on the branches of trees. She was just hanging the last of the bed linens when she caught sight of Magnus.

Her heart skipped a beat.

He was naked from the waist up as he approached, his broad chest a beautiful shade of bronze. After all she'd heard that morning about him, she was coming to realize that he was a very important person. At the Ludus Caledonia, he'd earned himself quite a reputation and there was a part of her that thought perhaps she was unworthy of such a man. It had been presumptuous of her to have asked for his help.

She was suddenly nervous.

In her haste to greet Magnus, Diantha accidentally yanked down one of the big bed linens that she had so carefully washed. As it came down over her head, her foot caught in it and down she went into the dirt.

Hands were reaching down to untangle her.

"Are ye in there?" Magnus asked.

Horribly embarrassed, Diantha growled in frustration as she yanked the damp linen off her head. Hair askew, she looked up at him and Isabail to see that they were both smiling down at her. Magnus started to laugh.

"Ye look as if ye fought the linen and the linen won," he said.

Diantha made a face, but Magnus's laughter made her feel not quite so embarrassed. "I was going to surprise you with clean bed linens and clean clothing," she said, looking at the dirty linen with disappointment. "It looks as if I must wash this again."

Magnus reached down and pulled her to her feet. "What compelled ye tae do such a thing?" he said. "I dinna tell ye tae."

Before Diantha could reply, Isabail spoke. "Magnus, they needed a wash," she said frankly. "They were dirty and smelly."

He lifted his chin. "They smelled like me."

"As I said—smelly."

Magnus curled his lip at her. "I'll tell yer husband ye insulted me. He'll take a hand tae ye, ye insolent woman."

Isabail burst out laughing. "Ye think so, do ye? He'll tell ye that ye stink, too," she said, turning away. "Ye think ye're the only man in Scotland without a stench."

"I am."

Isabail continued to laugh and walk away as Diantha stood

there, trying very hard not to smile. When Magnus looked at her, incensed, she bit her lip.

"And ye?" he said. "I suppose ye think I stink, too. Ye've been listening tae that bold wench Isabail."

Diantha shook her head quickly. "I do not think that," she said. "I washed the linens because it seemed like a good way to thank you for taking me in last night and giving me a place to sleep. I washed your tunics and breeches, too."

Magnus looked at the tree strewn with his drying clothing. The offended expression on his face faded as he looked at everything she'd done for him. Realizing that she'd gone to a great deal of trouble, his focus returned to her face.

"Ye dinna have tae do all of this," he said, quieter now. "I dunna recall giving ye permission."

Diantha's brow furrowed. "I told you last night that I would tend your cottage," she said. "I do not expect to have shelter given to me without working for it."

"I never told ye I expected this."

She was growing increasingly confused. "You did not, but I hope you do not think I would accept your help and not do something for you in return."

He looked around again at all of her efforts and finally motioned to her.

"Come with me," he said.

Diantha followed him back into his cottage. Entering the larger chamber, he nearly tripped over a big copper tub, dented and used, as well as a broom, a bucket, and other items meant for cleaning. Diantha came in behind him, and as soon as she shut the door, he turned to her.

"I'm going tae give ye the money for passage tae Navarre," he said quietly. "If ye want tae go home, I'll send ye home. I know ye're worried that ye canna pay me in return, but I dunna want ye tae worry so. The money will be my gift tae ye."

Diantha looked at him, wide-eyed. "I cannot take money I have not earned. I told you that last night."

"It is a gift. Ye canna refuse a gift."

"I can and I will."

"Take it and *go*."

The way he said it made it sound like he wanted her out, so she didn't argue. In fact, she felt ashamed and wounded. There was a chair behind her and she sank into it, slowly.

"Did I do wrong by washing your clothing?" she asked. "My lord, I could not accept your shelter and your help without paying you in return or at least working for my keep, and I will not take your money without earning it. I am sorry if you cannot accept that, but that is the way of things. I will not take anything that does not belong to me."

Magnus looked at her—hard. He wasn't quite sure why she made him nervous, or why he was offering to pay for her way to Navarre when the truth was that he very much liked her presence here. The woman was trying to be honorable by working for her keep and, God knew, he respected that. He admired a woman of honor.

So what was the problem?

He wasn't sure, but it had something to do with the fact that even now, as he stood before her, his heart was racing a mile a minute. Looking at her made him feel...*giddy*. He wanted her to go, but he wanted her to stay. He wanted to talk to her, but he didn't want to talk to her. He didn't know *what* he wanted. All he knew was his carefully held control, the wall that he always had up around himself, was beginning to show signs of stress when she was around.

Weakening.

And he couldn't explain it.

"Ye dinna do wrong by washing my things," he said after a moment. "But ye...ye're the daughter of a *conde*. Ye're from Spanish nobility and ye shouldna be working like a common wench. Ye're a fine and beautiful woman and ye should be living a life of leisure, and…where in the world did ye get that ugly dress?"

The subject shifted to the brown broadcloth she was wearing, and Diantha looked down at herself.

"Lucia loaned it to me," she said. "Lady Ayr's fine silk was coming apart at the seams, so she gave me this to work in."

"Ye're too beautiful tae wear such things."

"But I have nothing else."

That stopped him, at least momentarily. "Then I'll buy ye what ye need, but ye're not tae wear things like that," he said. "I dunna like tae see ye in them."

It was clear by the expression on Diantha's face that she thought she had offended him somehow. She had no idea what to make of his statement, but she knew that he was displeased. That was the last thing she wanted.

She stood up from her chair and nodded quickly, moving to the door.

"I…I must retrieve my dress from Lucia," she said tightly. "She was going to clean the dirt from it, but I will take it back right away."

Magnus could see that she was close to tears. That hadn't been his intention, and he stopped her before she could get to the door.

"Wait," he said, watching her pause with her hand on the latch. "I meant that ye're not meant tae be wearing a peasant's dress."

Diantha was losing the battle against her tears. "But it is *all* that I have."

Magnus could see that he wasn't communicating well with her. This was an entirely new situation for him. Usually when he was alone with a woman, she was doing all the speaking. And all of the work. He just lay there and let her do it.

But this was different. It wasn't that he *had* to communicate with her; it was that he wanted to.

He didn't want to make her cry.

"Come back here," he said quietly. "Sit down. I dinna mean tae upset ye."

Diantha turned away from the door slowly, but that wasn't fast enough for him. Magnus reached out and took her by the arm, directing her back into the chair where she'd been sitting. She plopped down, keeping her gaze lowered as she wiped at her nose with the back of her hand.

He just stood there and watched her, feeling a good deal of remorse.

"I dinna do a very good job of telling ye that I think ye're too beautiful tae wear such plain clothing," he said. "That's what I meant."

She nodded, sniffling. "I did not mean to displease you," she said. "I do not want you to regret agreeing to help me, so I was trying to make myself useful."

"I realize that."

She didn't reply, but simply sat there and continued to wipe at her eyes as the silent tears fell. With a sigh, Magnus sought out the nearest chair and sat down heavily, weary from his morning of training and wandering thoughts.

The object of those thoughts was sitting a few feet away, and he took a moment to stare at her, unimpeded. He could see her long, dark lashes when she blinked, and he noticed that her eyes were beautiful and expressive. He liked that. She was the most enchanting creature he'd ever seen but he literally couldn't figure out why.

What *was* it about her that had his attention?

Any regrets or second thoughts he had about helping her evaporated. He was sorry he had even suggested giving her the money to return to Navarre.

He didn't want to see her go.

"So…ye willna take my money."

It wasn't a question, but a statement. Diantha lifted her gaze, looking at him as she shook her head.

"I will not take anything that I do not earn," she said quietly.

"Not even a gift?"

She sighed heavily. "If you do not want to help me any longer, then please say so," she said. "I am free of Lady Ayr now. I can go south and find an English castle and find work there as a maid or a nurse. All you need to do is tell me and I shall be on my way."

He shook his head. "I told ye that I would help ye and I will," he said. "I've just never met a lass like ye, Diantha. I'm trying tae understand ye."

She stiffened. "That is because I am not like the women in Scotland," she said with a hint of rage. "*No soy débil y sin sentido como esas morenas tontas.*"

She was off speaking her language again, angrily. "What does that mean?" he asked calmly.

There was fire in her eyes. "It means that I am not weak and mindless like those foolish wenches."

He grinned. "Even Isabail and Lucia? They are Scottish."

She backed down a little. "Not them," she said. "They were very kind to me."

"Ye had a chance tae know them a little?"

She nodded. "They were very helpful."

"Good," he said, his eyes glimmering at her. "But I suspect ye've not known many kind Scotswomen."

Diantha cast him a long look. "My only experience with them has been at Culroy Castle," she said. "They are a self-centered lot with little time for a woman who is not of Scottish blood. In fact, they are why I need to earn money."

"What do ye mean?"

She was starting to calm down a little, the fire in her eyes fading. "Because they stole my money," she said. "When I came to Culroy, I had a purse with a good deal of coinage that my father gave me. I kept close watch on it, always making sure it was safe. One of Lady Ayr's wards was friendly to me and I trusted her, but she only wanted my money. She stole it from me and then denied it."

"How do ye know it was her?"

"Because she was the only one who knew where I hid it," she said, pain in her voice. "A week after it disappeared, Lady Ayr moved her household to Trinity House and this lass showed up one day with a new emerald brooch. She said it was a gift, but I heard her tell the other ladies that she bought it. When I told Lady Ayr, she made the lass give me the brooch, but it turned up missing a couple of days later. No one seemed to know anything about it."

Magnus wasn't surprised to hear any of that, especially not from Culroy Castle. "Let me guess... Lady Ayr did nothing."

Diantha shook her head. "She refused to get involved," she said. "She told me that she'd done as much as she intended to do about it. And that is why I must earn money for my passage, my lord."

He snorted in disapproval. "I'm sorry for ye," he said. "But not surprised. It seems that villainy and wickedness runs rampant through the ranks of the Duke and Duchess of Ayr."

She was watching him closely. "You have experienced it, too?"

He almost told her some of his experiences but thought better of it. He just wasn't the kind of man to open up about himself. He wasn't comfortable doing it. But something told him it wouldn't be long before he was opening himself up to Diantha. She was easy to talk to, open and honest.

It was just a feeling he had.

"Aye," he said, rising out of his chair. "Now, promise me ye willna run off while I sleep."

He was changing the subject and Diantha went with it. He didn't want to talk about himself and she respected that.

"I promise," she said. "Are you feeling poorly?"

He shook his head. "Nay," he said. "But I intend to sleep for a few hours before the bouts tonight. Unless the cottage is burning down or the barbarians are at the door, dunna disturb me."

She nodded seriously. "I will not," she said. "But…but may I continue my chores?"

He was in the process of turning for his bedchamber door when she asked. He paused to look at her.

"Do ye *really* want tae work?" he asked.

She nodded. "I do. May I?"

"I've not even told ye if I'll pay ye for it."

She shrugged. "It does not matter if you do," she said. "I will do it because you are allowing me to stay in your cottage. I will do it to earn my keep."

It seemed as if she had an answer for everything, and he was coming to see that for her, working to earn her keep was a way of maintaining her honor. The woman wouldn't take anything she hadn't worked for.

He'd fussed at her enough for it.

"I'll pay ye two shillings a day, then," he said, moving for the bedchamber door again. "But only if ye dunna disturb me."

It was a very generous daily wage. "I promise that I shall not disturb you."

"If ye do, I'll throw ye out on yer arse."

"Then I shall make doubly sure not to disturb you."

Magnus didn't say anything further. He entered the bedchamber, shutting the door and realizing he had a silly smile on his lips. His bed was stripped, his clothing missing, and a woman was determined to take over his house and hold.

But he didn't care.

The thought of it made him smile.

What he didn't know was that on the other side of the door, Diantha was smiling, too.

CHAPTER EIGHT

The Bear was pacing again.

It was another warm night in the Highlands as Magnus stood at one end of the arena and the Bear stood at the other. It was the *ultimus* bout, the last one of the night, and the crowd had been prepared for it.

They were on their feet now because Magnus had entered the arena after the Bear, a privilege reserved for the Ludus Caledonia's elite warriors. There wasn't a man or woman in the stands who wasn't somewhat drunk because they had been drinking all evening, betting on fights, and waiting with great anticipation for the very last one.

It had finally arrived.

Magnus soaked up the adoration of the crowd like he always did. It was something that fed him, nurtured him, and gave him the very foundation of the arrogance for which he was known. The spectators knew he was great, *he* knew he was great, and everyone was in agreement. Magnus looked up to the crowd, acknowledging them with a mere glance, and it drove them mad.

Already, coins were raining down on the arena floor and the two servants that Magnus employed to collect that money were running out onto the field, grabbing at the money. At the edge of the arena where it joined up with the staging area, Magnus could see his friends and supporters standing there—Lor, Bane, Galan, Axel, Wendell, and another *doctores* named Milo Linton. Even Tay was with them, watching the crowd, watching the Bear, and feeling some trepidation just like the rest of them.

This was the bout that everyone, including those who ran the Ludus Caledonia, had been waiting for.

The Bear was pacing in circles now, beating his chest and roaring, going through some kind of ritual meant to work himself into a frenzy. Magnus was busy pulling on what amounted to fingerless leather gloves, meant to protect his hands yet leave his fingers free to work. He bent down and scooped up some of the dirt of the arena floor, sprinkling it onto the gloves to give them better traction. He was pretending to be busy when what he was really doing was watching the Bear in his periphery.

He was watching every move the man made.

As he busied himself, he caught sight of Axel as the man made his way out onto the arena floor. As the manager of the Ludus Caledonia, he was permitted everywhere at any time, even in the arena before a bout started. Axel von Rossau was an enormous man, Saxon by birth, with skin as dark as tanned leather and bright-blue eyes. He was a ferocious fighter, as Magnus had seen on occasion, and he was greatly respected by all as a fair and just man, if not quite hard. As he came near, Magnus continued busying himself.

"Eagle," Axel said in his heavy Germanic accent, "I came to give you some advice."

Magnus didn't look up from his gloves. "I am listening."

Axel's gaze drifted to the opponent across the arena. "He is going to try to kill you," he said. "I have not been told this, it is simply a feeling I have. I have seen enough men to know what is in his heart and on his mind. He will kill you if he can."

Magnus nodded his head as he finished with the gloves. "I trust ye," he said. "It is my intention tae take him out immediately. I willna toy with this one. He smells my blood."

"He does indeed," Axel said. "If you do not disable him at the first, it will go badly for you. A wounded bear is a dangerous thing."

"I know."

Axel paused. "You should also know something else," he said. "Your friends have decided that if the Bear harms you in any way, they will swarm the field and destroy him."

Magnus's head snapped up. "Tell them that if they do, I'll never speak tae them again," he said. "This is *my* fight. I'm not a weakling who needs others tae fight my battles."

Axel smiled faintly. "You need to learn the difference between men believing you to be weak and men wanting to protect their friend," he said. "They know you are not weak."

"Then tell them to stay away."

Axel cocked his head. "Let me ask you a question," he said. "If it was Lor or Bane lying on the ground, about to be murdered by a man three times his size, would you stand by and let it happen?"

Magnus knew what he meant. He backed down a little, looking back to his gloves. "Of course not," he said. "I would kill any man who threatened my friends. But tell those nervous women tae stay out of my fight."

Axel chuckled. "As you wish."

He started to walk away, but Magnus stopped him. "And...and tell them that I love them for their concern, but I'll break the neck of the first man who sets foot in the arena while I'm fighting."

Axel paused, his eyes glimmering with mirth. "*Glück*, Eagle."

Magnus had heard that word from him before. It meant good luck or good fortune. As Axel walked away, Magnus stole a glance at the Bear. The man had worked himself up into a froth, and the field marshals were looking to Magnus to see if he was ready. Once he signaled that he was, the bout would begin.

Magnus turned fully to look at the Bear, observing the man as he formulated a plan. Axel was right. He would have to strike first and make it count. If he didn't, his life would be in danger.

He knew that as surely as he breathed.

He'd faced big men before. Since he wasn't particularly tall, that happened all of the time. Tall men weren't much of a challenge because they usually couldn't move very quickly, certainly not as quickly as Magnus could. That was one of his greatest strengths— his ability to move swiftly.

His ability to go airborne and kick a man in the head.

But that wasn't going to work this time.

This time, he was going to have to be smarter, and more deadly, than the Bear.

Fortunately, he had an idea that he was certain would work. He just had to be fast enough to execute it. In the arena, men were limited to clubs as weapons, but Magnus never used one. He used his legs and feet as a club. However, this was an exception. If the Bear was expecting his feet to come up, then he would have to do something different.

An array of clubs was stacked on the sidelines of the arena, and he kept his gaze on the Bear as he made his way over to the big iron racks that held all shapes and sizes of clubs. When the Bear saw him moving for a weapon, he too moved quickly to claim a club. Even from across the arena, Magnus could hear the Bear laughing, thinking he would have it easy in hand-to-hand combat with clubs.

That only served to infuriate Magnus.

This time, he was going to skin the Bear for good.

The roar of the crowd was growing louder as the spectators became restless. The Bear and the Eagle were delaying the inevitable, and the crowd began to get rowdy. Magnus glanced up into the stands, and that was his mistake. On the left side where the wives of the gladiators usually sat, he caught a glimpse of Isabail, Lucia, and…Diantha.

Great bleeding Christ!

It had been a grave error. Now he knew Diantha was watching him, his entire balance was thrown off. Why it should be, he had no idea, but it was. He felt…edgy. Uncertain. It was performance anxiety, something he never experienced because he'd never performed in front of someone whose thoughts actually mattered to him. He knew that he could no longer delay. Suddenly, he was running for the Bear, club raised, bellowing at the top of his lungs.

His unexpected charge caught the crowd, the Bear, and the field marshals off guard. The crowd screamed to earsplitting proportions as the Bear, startled by the Eagle's move, simply lifted his club. Magnus was nearly to him by the time he raised it, unable to react any faster. Magnus drew near and the Bear roared, preparing to bring his club down with ferocious strength, but an odd thing happened.

Magnus abruptly fell to his knees, although it wasn't an accident. It was by design. He went down, sliding across the dirt as the Bear swung his club and missed, but he'd swung so hard that it threw him off-balance. It was enough of a stumble that Magnus, on his knees as he slid into the Bear's feet, was able to bring up his club and smash it into the man's groin as hard as he could.

The crowd gasped.

The Bear, immediately disabled, toppled onto the dust as Magnus leapt to his feet. Lifting his club once more, he hit the Bear in the head so hard that he split the man's skull. He hit him again, full of battle lust, and ended up crushing the Bear's head. Blood and brain matter stuck to the club, but he tossed it aside as the Bear bled out into the dust of the Fields of Mars.

And with that, the fight was over.

The spectators, who had gasped loudly when Magnus hit the Bear in the groin, were stunned into shocked silence when they saw Magnus break the Bear's skull. But that silence was only momentary. As soon as they realized Magnus was victorious and the Bear would no longer rise against their champion, they began screaming even louder than before.

Magnus turned away from the Bear without a hind glance, heading toward the arena exit as Axel, Milo, and Wendell spilled into the arena, moving straight for the Bear. Magnus didn't even look at them. He kept going until he came to Lor, Bane, Galan, and Tay, who had come out to meet him.

It was Lor who reached out and grasped him around the shoulders.

"Easy, Magnus," Lor said quietly. "Ye had no choice. If ye dinna kill him, he was going tae kill ye. It wasna a clean victory, but a necessary one."

Magnus knew that. His sense of self-preservation had been in overdrive. He also knew that if a gladiator killed an opponent in a match, the gladiator was usually suspended for the next several games. There was punishment in the event of a death. But Magnus honestly didn't care if he was suspended. He was alive, and he had won, and that was all that mattered to him.

"The man wanted my blood," Magnus said as he forced himself to calm. "We could all see it. It was either me or him."

"Ye did what ye had tae do," Bane said, agreeing with Lor. "I dunna believe Axel will punish ye for it."

Magnus looked at him. "He was the one who told me the Bear intended tae kill me," he said. "He all but gave me his permission tae do what needed tae be done."

No one disagreed with him. Galan, with whom Magnus sometimes had a contentious relationship, put his hand on Magnus's shoulder.

"Sometimes men come to the Cal with the scent of blood in their nostrils," he said. "They are not here to fight a clean fight for the money. They are here simply for the thrill of a kill. I believe that is what the Bear came for—death. From what I've heard of the man, he has killed many an opponent before."

The crowd was still screaming for Magnus even as the Bear was put on a stretcher and hauled off alongside his wailing trainer. While Milo and Wendell went with him, Axel headed over to Magnus as he stood with the others. Magnus could feel himself tensing up, preparing to take a scolding, or worse, and he fully intended to defend himself.

But Axel never gave him the chance.

"Go," he said, gesturing to the arena. "You will be the last memory of this battle, not the dead man being taken away. Go out there and acknowledge those who love you, those who would have probably stormed the arena had you fallen to the Bear."

It was a surprising reaction given the seriousness of what had happened, but Magnus didn't argue. He simply nodded and headed back out into the arena and the roar of the crowd lifted when they saw him. Money began to rain down upon him as his two servants appeared once more to collect the booty.

Standing in the center of the arena, Magnus finally lifted his arms in victory and the crowd went mad, but he wasn't looking at the crowd as a whole.

He was looking at the spot vacated by Diantha.

It occurred to him that she had just seen him kill a man, which had probably spooked her. Although he regretted that she had to see it, it was better than her seeing him laid out on the arena floor while a big Saxon smashed him to bits.

It was ridiculous for him to even care what she thought but oddly enough, he did. He'd only known the woman for a day, and already he cared what she thought. That hardworking, magnificent Spanish beauty had somehow gotten under his skin without even trying.

Infatuation? Probably.

It terrified him to consider the alternative.

⚜ ⚜ ⚜

So this is what the Ludus Caledonia is all about?

Diantha rolled those words over in her mind as she followed Isabail and Lucia into the stands overlooking the arena floor. The Fields of Mars was packed on this night, with a thousand torches lighting up the sky and the roar of the crowd electrifying the very air around them. When Isabail and Lucia had invited her to watch the evening's bouts, Diantha had no idea what to expect.

But now she knew.

This was a place of debauchery, excess, and bloodlust.

People weren't there for food and fun. They were there to watch men beat each other to a pulp, which Diantha saw during the course of the evening. There were *novicius*, or novices, as they fought their first bouts, and as the evening went on, the participants graduated to the top gladiators the Ludus Caledonia had to offer.

As Diantha sat with Isabail and Lucia, she noticed that they all observed the fighting in different ways. Isabail had come from a warring clan in the Highlands and had wielded a sword herself in her past, so she viewed the fights from a warrior's standpoint.

Lucia, on the other hand, did not come from a warring background but a much simpler one. Her father had served in a great house, so she was essentially from peasant stock. With her well-spoken manner, intelligence, and beauteous looks, she could have easily been a finely bred lady. Lucia watched the bouts with some disdain, concerned every time someone from the Ludus Caledonia was injured, seemingly watching the fights simply because her husband trained the men and she wanted to support him.

But it was clear that she didn't enjoy it.

Diantha wasn't sure what to make of it all. She did find the fighting to be exciting, but it was also quite brutal. To think that Magnus was one of the top fighters here meant that he was exciting and brutal, too. Given the way he was built—short, but extremely muscular with big arms and big thighs—she could believe it. He had obviously worked hard for his position.

She was soon to find out.

The fights went on well into the early morning hours when the next bout announced was between the Eagle and the Rutting Bull. The crowd went wild, and Diantha wasn't sure why until Isabail explained that Magnus *was* the Eagle. It was his nickname at the Ludus Caledonia, and all of the top fighters seemed to have one— names like the Beast from the East, the Sapphire Dragon, and the Hammer. All of them had nicknames in place of their real names because, as Isabail explained, that somehow made them larger than life.

And the crowds loved them for it.

If there was any confusion as to why Magnus was called the Eagle, that was quickly dispelled in the first few moments of his bout. He emerged onto the field, nearly naked but for a red cloak, a snug leather loincloth that covered his groin and buttocks, a mail apron from his waist to the top of his thighs, shoes on his feet that were secured with leather straps, and leather pads over his knees to protect them. He carried a shield with him, but no weapon.

Diantha's heart was pounding against her ribs at the sight of him. He looked like a god, strutting across the dirt of the arena, the finest form of a man that anyone had ever seen. There was nothing about him that wasn't perfect as far as she was concerned, and the pride she'd felt in knowing the man was turning into something else.

Attraction.

It wasn't that the stories of his greatness were starting to affect her judgment. Everyone thought he was great, he thought he was great, and from the reaction of the crowd, he really *was* great. It wasn't hero worship that she felt.

It ran deeper than that.

For Diantha, it was the man's kindness. He'd been very kind to her when he didn't have to be. She had been rude to him when they'd first met, but he hadn't held a grudge. When she'd come seeking his help, he'd agreed without hesitation. Even this afternoon, when they'd had some miscommunication, he'd remained kind and patient. There was something in the way he looked at her that made her heart pound. A glimmer, a certain warmth… *something*.

All she knew was that she liked it.

She knew he was special. She wondered if he thought she was special, too.

As for the Eagle, Diantha watched him fly into the air within the first few moments of the bout and kick his opponent in the head. Magnus landed on his feet, his opponent fell like a rock, and the crowd screamed for their Eagle.

It was the most astonishing thing Diantha had ever seen.

The bout had ended quickly, and Magnus disappeared into a holding area next to the arena. There were a few more fights after that, and she was fighting off boredom until the final primus bout was announced between the Eagle and the Bear.

The crowd was worked into a frenzy and the exchange of money went on at an alarming rate. As all of that was going on, Isabail and Lucia decided they'd seen enough and wanted to leave, but Diantha wanted to remain. They'd brought her to experience the Ludus Caledonia in full and she wasn't finished yet, especially with Magnus fighting the last bout. Given what had happened with the last time he fought, she was excited to see the next one.

And what a fight it was.

At least, what there was *of* it.

Magnus had delayed the start of the fight for several minutes while he removed his red cloak and adjusted the gloves on his hands. Diantha was so far up in the arena that she couldn't really see what he was doing, but his opponent was pacing around like a caged animal. There was a good deal of chest beating going on, and at one point, a big man came out to speak with Magnus. Within a short time after that, the match abruptly began.

And then it was over.

But not before Diantha saw Magnus clobber his opponent with a club. One blow to the groin, two to the head, and the man collapsed in a heap. He had to be carried away by men bearing a stretcher, and money fell onto the arena floor like snowflakes. Diantha watched, a smile on her lips, as Isabail finally tugged on her.

"Come along," she said. "We must get back tae the village before the patrons leave. It will be very crowded."

Diantha went with her, but it was reluctantly.

She rather liked watching Magnus absorb the adulation of the crowd.

By the time they cleared the arena, it was already crowded in the area where carriages and horses awaited. Men were leaving in droves, making their way to the betting cages to collect their money, and Diantha got separated from Isabail and Lucia. She was swept away with a tide of men rushing for the betting cages, which were by a viewing area that looked down over the staging area. She was about to be pushed into a fence when a hand grabbed her and she looked over to see Isabail.

"Hurry!"

Diantha summoned her strength, and her courage, and pushed through the crowd, holding tightly to Isabail. They finally made their way out of the sea of men and rushed back to the village, which was smelling heavily of cooking fires on this clear and bright night. Even though it was only a few hours until morning, many of the participants would want to eat before they retired.

Diantha slowed her pace.

"Do you think Magnus will wish to eat?" she asked. "I can procure food for him if you will just tell me where it is."

Isabail didn't say what she was thinking—that Magnus was probably already hip-deep in food with a high-paying noblewoman stroking every part of his gorgeous, naked body. That's what always happened after his victorious bouts, but she didn't want to tell Diantha that.

Somehow, she thought it might hurt her or, at the very least, set fire to that veil of innocence she had between her and the reality of what Magnus was really like. Isabail had seen that all day. The more time she spent with Diantha, the more naive she realized the woman was.

She seemed to have no idea what kind of man Magnus was.

But that would come with time.

"There is a kitchen next tae the garden," she said, pointing toward the north. "Do ye remember when I took ye there?"

Diantha nodded. "Aye," she said. "Thank you. Can I bring you something, too? For your husband, mayhap?"

Isabail smiled, touching Diantha sweetly on the cheek. "Nay, thank ye, lass," she said. "It is kind tae offer. Lor willna eat. He'll simply want tae sleep, and I'll be lucky if he makes it tae the bed before he does. If ye dunna need my help, then I'll see ye when the sun rises."

Diantha smiled in return. "You will, indeed," she said. "And… thank you for being so kind to me today. You and Lucia have been very gracious and I am appreciative."

Isabail winked at her and turned for her cottage, which wasn't too far. As she walked away, Diantha went in search of food for Magnus. She made her way through the darkened edge of the village, up a footpath, and ended up in a clearing where the garden and one of the big kitchens were located. There were just a few people in the kitchen, and she came away with her own iron pot of stew and an entire loaf of bread.

After making her way back to the cottage, she quickly went to work preparing the meal for Magnus's return. There was some excitement, welcoming home the man who had won both of his bouts for the night.

As she stoked the fire and hung the pot of stew over it to keep it warm, she prepared the small table for his meal. He had bowls and utensils in the cottage, but they looked as if they hadn't been used in months. Rinsing them out and then drying them, she put them on the table, neatly arranged.

As Diantha waited for Magnus, she tidied up the cottage. While he'd slept that afternoon, she had swept and scrubbed the larger chamber, wiping down chairs and chests, and generally cleaning. His laundry had dried and she'd brought that in, neatly hanging his tunics on the pegs outside of his bedchamber and carefully folding the bed linens.

When he awoke, he'd shuffled out of the room, yawning, and muttered something about going to the arena. He'd walked right by her, smiling sleepily, and opened the door before he realized that he should probably say something to her. Then he paused, told her again where he was going, and she simply nodded. His gaze lingered on her for a moment before he headed out into the waning day.

But there had been something in that gaze.

Diantha's heart fluttered simply to think about it. With freshly washed linens on his bed, swept dirt floors, scrubbed table, food, and clean clothing, she dared to wonder if this was what it would be like to wait for a husband's return home. She couldn't imagine doing this for Conan, but for Magnus...

It was something she could get used to.

Unfortunately, the wait for Magnus was a long one. Diantha had fashioned a pallet for herself out of rushes and blankets. It was shoved up against the wall so that her feet were near the hearth, and it was looking inviting as the minutes passed. She kept stirring the stew so it wouldn't boil down, putting water in it to thin it out as she continued to wait. She finally sat down at the table, but that was the last thing she remembered before someone was gently shaking her.

In an instant, she was halfway out of her chair.

"I'm sorry," she said before she was even fully awake. "I did not mean to sleep. I am awake."

Strong hands were steadying her, and she looked up to see Magnus grinning at her. "Easy, lass," he said quietly, pushing her back down into the chair. "It's very late. I thought for certain ye'd be in bed."

Diantha took a deep breath, rubbing her eyes. "I was waiting for you," she said. "I have food if you are hungry."

He looked at the pot on the hearth, steaming. "I suppose I could eat something if ye've gone to the trouble," he said. "I dinna expect ye tae have food waiting."

Diantha popped up again out of her chair and rushed to the hearth with a bowl in her hand.

"Please, sit," she said. "You must be famished after the evening you've had."

Magnus was swathed in a woolen cloak and his normal clothing of breeches and a tunic, so he began to remove the cloak.

"I saw ye in the lists," he said, hanging up the cloak near the door. "What did ye think?"

Diantha looked up from stirring the pot of stew. "I thought you were magnificent."

He grinned. "I am," he said. "I'm glad ye know it now."

She returned his smile, staring at the man as if transfixed until the stew bubbled and a hot drop landed on her hand. That snapped her out of her trance, and she spooned the stew into the bowl until it was full. Carefully, she brought it back over to the table and set it down in front of him.

"This came from the kitchen," she said. "I am sorry that I do not know how to cook, but I am happy to learn if it pleases you."

He sat down wearily, collecting his spoon. "If I need a cook, I'll hire one," he said. "Ye dunna need tae learn just for me. Sit down and talk tae me. Tell me what ye thought of the fights tonight."

Diantha sat down across from him, feeling giddy in his presence. He looked as if he had bathed, for his hair was still wet and there wasn't a speck of dust on him. She could smell something, too—the clean scent of pine.

He smelled as good as he looked.

"I thought it was…exciting," she said, trying to pretend she had enjoyed it. "I've never seen such fights before."

He spooned the steaming stew into his mouth. "That's because there are no fights like the ones at the Ludus Caledonia anywhere in Scotland," he said, chewing. "What did ye like best?"

"When you won."

He snorted, tearing up the bread and dipping it in the stew. "Then I pleased ye."

"I was very happy to see you win."

He took a bite of the stew-soaked bread, looking at her as he did. "So was I," he said honestly. "It seems that we have the same taste in winners."

He was jesting with her and she smiled bashfully. "I believe so," she said. "But where did you learn to fight like that? Surely it was not at Culroy. In fact, I seem to remember hearing about the lads there beating up on you regularly."

His smile faded as his attention returned to his stew. "The only thing my time at Culroy taught me was that the only person who will fight for me is, in fact, *me*," he said. "I was the beating post for those young whelps, and it continued on until the day I was released."

"Did you seek out the Ludus Caledonia to learn to fight?" she asked. "Or did they find you?"

His grin was back. "They found me," he said. "And it wasna the Ludus Caledonia. It was the Ludus Antonine in Glasgow. I'd gone there after I was released and ended up fighting in the streets for money. It was Axel who found me in the gutter after one nasty brawl, beaten and bloodied. He told me he could take me tae a place where I would be taught tae fight properly. And here I am."

"Why did you not go home after your release?" she asked.

"Because I had no home tae go tae," he said. "I know ye dunna know much about me, and ye've had the good sense not tae ask. Because ye've not asked, I'll tell ye. My father is a duke and my mother was a lady-in-waiting tae the duke's wife. I was the bastard no one wanted. When I was born, my mother and I were sent tae my mother's family at Blackwood House near Stirling. I was a tiny lad when Ambrose Stewart came looking for me and took me away tae Culroy."

Diantha was listening intently. "But how did he even know about you?"

The smile on his face was without humor. "Because the man has spies everywhere," he said. "Did ye not know that? He paid someone at my father's home tae tell him about the bastard son who lived in the Highlands. When he came for me, my mother's family had no choice but tae give me over. One doesna deny the Duke of Ayr and not suffer the consequences."

Diantha shook her head sadly. "You were so young," she said. "And you lived at Culroy most of your life?"

Magnus nodded, trying not to let those dark memories overwhelm him. "I lived there for fifteen years," he said. "I managed tae get away seven years ago and ended up in Glasgow until I was taken tae the Ludus Antonine."

Diantha was touched by his sorrowful story. "And ye've been here ever since?"

"Aye."

"But what about your father? Why did he not come for you at Culroy?"

"Because my father is the youngest brother of the king and a rebel," he said frankly. "Ambrose is a cousin tae the king and tae my father, but he sides with the king. Ambrose took me hostage against my father doing anything too stupid, but it dinna work. My father continued tae rebel against his brother until such time as an injury nearly killed him. When he stopped rebelling, I was released because of his good behavior. I was told that my father hates the very mention of me, a reminder of his own indiscretions, and his wife willna have me around."

Diantha was coming to feel a great deal of pity for him. "That is why he did not come for you?"

"Aye."

"Even after you were released?"

"He doesna know of my whereabouts and he surely doesna care."

"But what about your mother? Surely you could have gone back to Blackwood?"

Magnus shook his head. "By the time I was released, I'd not seen my mother in many a year," he said. "I was a man. Men dunna return home tae their mother's bosom tae become her burden. I had tae make my own way."

Diantha clucked softly. "I am sorry for you, my lord," she said softly. "You do not deserve such a thing."

The dark memories had Magnus in their grip. He could feel the familiar sadness and anguish creeping upon him, filling his veins like it used to. He hadn't spoken of his past in years, but suddenly in the past two days, he'd been forced to face it again. Speaking of it to Diantha had been so...easy.

She was getting under his skin more and more.

"Nay, I dunna," he said, trying to pull himself out of the familiar depression. "But it doesna matter anymore. I have made a success of myself in spite of Ambrose or my father, and I enjoy prestige and fame here at the Ludus Caledonia. I couldna want for more."

He said it firmly, as if he truly didn't care, but that wasn't the truth. Deep down, he was still that abandoned little boy with no one to care for him. That's where he first learned to build the wall around him that he kept so closely guarded.

But Diantha was succeeding in putting tiny cracks in that wall.

"You are clearly loved here," she said, reaching out and impulsively putting a hand on his arm. "I saw it tonight in the way the crowd cheered for you. You are a great warrior and that is something to be proud of."

Magnus was midchew when she put her hand on him. He stopped, looking at the hand on his arm and feeling it like a brand. He stared at it a moment, her beautiful hand over his bronzed skin. It made something in his chest churn. He suspected it was all that emotion he kept buried, struggling to get out.

Slowly, he resumed chewing.

"This is where I've found myself," he said, swallowing what was in his mouth. "I have found greatness here, but I dunna intend tae remain here forever."

To his disappointment, she removed her hand. "What do you intend to do?"

He shrugged, spooning the last of the stew into his mouth. "Travel," he said. "I want tae go tae far and mysterious places. I want tae see where the real gladiators walked. I want tae see great mountains and great rivers. I've never been out of Scotland."

She smiled faintly. "Then you must go to Navarre someday," she said. "In my town, there are ancient Roman ruins. You can see their avenues, their gutters, and the remains of their homes. When I was a child, I used to play there with other children from the village. We pretended it was our own little village. I even found a coin there once, buried in the floor of one of the houses."

Now, it was his turn to listen intently, which was something Magnus wasn't used to. He wasn't a good listener because he didn't really care about others, but with Diantha, he found himself interested in what she was saying.

"Tell me about yer town," he said.

Her smile grew as she thought on the place where she was born. "It is dry and warm most of the time," she said. "The land is arid and the village is surrounded by mountains, but a river runs near our village, lazy and green. In the summer, you can smell the rosemary on the breeze, as it grows wild on the hills. My father's castle is a great fortress, built from stone that is the color of gold. At sunset, when the light hits it just so, it looks like a golden castle."

He nodded, envisioning such a place in his mind's eye. "I canna imagine a place that is warm and dry always," he said. "Even now, during these days in August, it is warm, but that will be brief. In September, the storms will come and it will grow cold again. It would be nice tae have the warmth all year."

Diantha nodded. "I cannot wait to return to it," she said, her smile fading. "I...I am hoping that I still have a home to return to."

He could see the melancholy wash over her features. It wasn't something he understood, longing for a home that he once had, but he could feel sympathy for her nonetheless.

"How do ye plan tae get there?" he asked. "Ye speak of earning money for passage, but *how* do ye plan tae go? It willna be an easy undertaking."

She nodded, trying to shake off the melancholy. "I know," she said. "But I shall go to Edinburgh and find passage to Calais. From Calais, I can find passage to Bilbao. From there, it is only four days to Santacara on a swift horse."

It sounded simple enough, but travel was seldom so easy. "And ye plan tae travel alone?" he said. "Ye dunna plan tae hire protection?"

She shrugged. "I had not thought on it," she said. "I would have to earn more money to pay for protection."

"But it isna safe tae travel alone. Ye know that."

She nodded, putting on a brave front. "I know, but I must go home and I cannot wait for the time it would take to earn money for protection. I pray that God will protect me. That is good enough."

Magnus couldn't figure out if she was delusional or simply faithful. Either way, he thought it was a foolish stance, but he didn't say so. But he knew one thing—

She wasn't going to travel alone.

He wasn't going to let her.

He wasn't going to bring it up, not now, but he certainly intended to at some point. She may have been too honorable to take his money when he offered to pay for her passage, but he wouldn't let her refuse his money to pay for protection.

He was going to pay for it whether or not she liked it.

Or perhaps he would go with her.

That last thought crept up on him without warning, and suddenly he was reeling from the mere idea. He would *go* with her?

He'd just finished telling her he wanted to travel, so why not? Great bleeding Christ, it was a foolish thought.

He was foolish.

He was also exhausted.

Exhaustion was doing strange things to his mind.

"I must sleep," he said, rising wearily. "It has been a long night."

Diantha jumped up, rushing over to the hearth where she had a bed warmer waiting. She'd found it in the piles of clutter Magnus had in his cottage, a valuable piece of household equipment, and she immediately began to poke at the fire in the hearth for chunks of glowing peat.

"Of course," she said, using a small shovel to put the peat into the pot-like warmer. "I shall have your bed warmed in a few moments."

Magnus looked at her, crouched down on the floor. After a fight like the one tonight, he was assured of an array of women to choose from afterward. There had been more than he had ever seen waiting above the holding area, throwing money and coin purses down to him, begging to lick the sweat from his skin. He'd seen some of the women before. He'd even bedded a few of them before. Tonight, he could have had his pick.

But he couldn't seem to do it.

All he could see was Diantha.

There was a bathhouse attached to the staging area where the men would bathe after the fights, modeled after the great bathhouses of Rome. When Clegg de Lave designed the Ludus Caledonia, he'd left nothing out. Everything ancient Rome had, the Ludus Caledonia had, and the bathhouse was truly a marvel.

Built next to the Fields of Mars, it was a large stone structure on a raised floor, and servants kept the fires stoked to heat up the baths. There were both male servants and female servants to tend the bathers, whichever they preferred, and Magnus usually had his pick of the female servants.

Tonight, he'd had two males.

He couldn't even comprehend why. He'd never had that before. Usually, he'd take the female servant and expected something a little more than simple bathing assistance, but tonight, he couldn't manage to do it. When one had tried to change his mind, he closed his eyes to enjoy the experience but all he could see was Diantha. That noble, beautiful woman that had his interest.

He'd chased the servant away.

As he looked at her now, carefully putting coals into the bed warmer so she could warm his bed, he could think of a better way for her to warm it but he couldn't bring himself to say it. He couldn't even bring himself to do anything about it. She had come seeking his help, hadn't she? She was sleeping in his cottage, washing his clothes, bringing meals for him, wasn't she? Doing everything a wife would do.

A wife...

So why couldn't he do to her what he did to every single willing female he met?

He knew why. Magnus may have been an arrogant man, but he wasn't a molester. He would never lower himself. Moreover, when he was with a woman, he wanted a willing partner.

And he knew, deep down, that Diantha hadn't come to warm his bed in the way he was hoping.

But perhaps with time, she would.

Perhaps in time, he could make her want to.

Magnus continued to watch Diantha as she finished with the bed warmer and dashed into his chamber to warm his sheets, but he didn't follow. In fact, Diantha had been in his chamber for quite some time, making sure everything was nice and warm, before she realized he hadn't come into the room.

Puzzled, she went out into the larger room to see what he was doing only to find him dead asleep on the pallet she had made for herself. He was shoved up against the wall, rolled up in a blanket with his feet on the hearth, nice and warm.

He was snoring loudly enough to lift the roof.

With a grin, Diantha set the bed warmer down and went back into his chamber, returning with another blanket. Carefully, she laid it over him, making sure he was tucked in and comfortable.

That night, she slept on his bed.

CHAPTER NINE

Blackridge House
The seat of the Duke of Kintyre and Lorne

SHE WAS WAITING FOR HIM IN WHAT THEY CALLED THE Gathering Room, a vast chamber that spanned nearly one entire side of the house, facing out onto the green expanse of meadows to the south.

The woman had come in a fine carriage but without soldiers except for her coachmen, four of them, who rode fine and fat steeds, indicating wealth. In fact, everything about her carriage indicated wealth and status. He'd inspected the vehicle when he was told of her arrival, but she would not give her name, not even to his majordomo. She was secretive and quiet, demanding to see the duke with the utmost urgency.

It was pure curiosity that had brought him to the Gathering Room.

Hugh Stewart stood in the doorway of the enormous chamber, with its stone floor, paneled walls, and two magnificent hearths. It also had heavy damask curtains on the windows, and there were several because his late wife had liked the look of them. He'd never had the heart to get rid of them after she died. They'd cost a small fortune and they were all closed at the moment, giving the chamber a dim and mysterious ambiance.

Certainly, the unknown female visitor was a mystery.

"Who are ye?" he finally asked.

The woman was wrapped from head to toe in a dark-green velvet cloak with a fox lining. It looked very expensive. When she turned to him, her cloak parted near the hemline of her dress and he could see that she was wearing an equally expensive gown with jewels sewn into the hemline. But she had a hood over her head and a veil across the bottom part of her face so he couldn't make out her features.

Her eyes glittered in the dim light.

"Hugh?" she asked.

She didn't speak with a Scots brogue. To his ear, it was English. The mystery grew.

"If ye think tae pull a dirk on me, I'll not let ye get close enough," he said steadily. "State yer name or get out. I've no time for games."

"If you will close the door, I will tell you all you need to know."

Hugh took a step inside the chamber and slammed the door in the face of his majordomo, hovering out in the hall.

"There," he said. "*Who* are ye?"

Immediately, the veil came away and she pulled the hood from her head. She took a few steps toward him, but not too close. She didn't want to spook him.

"Do you know me?" she asked.

Hugh thought he might. She had a familiar look to her, a pretty woman who had aged well. "I'm not sure," he said. "I think so."

"It has been a while," she said. "At least twenty-five years, but you have changed little. You are still as handsome as I remember. I am Agnes, Duchess of Ayr."

Hugh's eyes widened at the revelation. "Of course," he hissed. "Agnes, lass, I've not seen ye in ages. What are ye doing here? Where's Ambrose?"

"He does not know I have come," she said. "I can only stay a few moments because I am expected elsewhere. I told my husband I was going to visit my sister, who lives not far from here, but my true purpose was coming to speak with you, Hugh. There is something you must know."

Hugh eyed her. "It must be important for ye tae have taken the trouble tae have come."

"It is."

He scratched his head. "Are ye tae tell me that yer husband is planning an offensive against me?" he said. "I already know, Agnes. He thinks I've allied myself with the Laird of the Isles."

"How did you know that?"

Hugh sighed faintly. He didn't want to say too much, concerned it would make it back to Ambrose. He couldn't be sure that Agnes's presence wasn't a ploy.

"'Tis the rumor," he said. "Everyone knows. Is that what ye've come tae tell me?"

She shook her head. "Nay," she said. "I've come to speak with you about your son, Magnus."

That drew a reaction. "Magnus?" he repeated. "Is he well? Has something happened?"

With those panicked questions, Hugh revealed how much he ached for his long-estranged son. It was something he kept well hidden, a suppression that had become part of his fabric. That dull ache of longing, of hopelessness, was a constant in his life, only to be revived when Magnus's name was spoken as it was now.

His son.

Seeing his reaction, Agnes put up her hand, easing him. "Nay," she said quickly. "He is well. You needn't be troubled. But I want you to know something. When Ambrose told you that Magnus wanted nothing to do with you, it was not the truth."

Hugh stared at her in confusion. "What?" he finally said. "But...that is the way of things."

"It is *not* the way of things. It is a lie."

"What are ye saying?"

Agnes took a few more steps toward him. "I am telling you that you were lied to," she said flatly. "By Ambrose. He told you that Magnus did not wish to see you, and he told Magnus the same thing—that you did not wish to see him. He purposely drove a wedge between you two."

Hugh's eyes widened with bewilderment. "But...but why?" he hissed. "Why should he do such a thing? Agnes, are ye certain?"

Agnes nodded. "I am very certain," she said. "You know that Ambrose has always been jealous of you, Hugh. You, the brother of a king, and him...a duke who inherited everything from his father. He never had to work for anything. He allies himself with your brother, the king, because he believes himself to be a great man in politics. What he did to you and your son, he did to control you. That is the truth of it. By keeping you and Magnus apart, he is controlling you both."

Hugh had to sit down. He grabbed for the nearest chair, sitting heavily in it. He had to digest what he was being told because he'd gone through most of his life believing his son didn't want to see him. But now he was being told quite the opposite.

Was it actually true?

He was having a difficult time reconciling it.

He wanted to believe, but...

"Ambrose always told me that Magnus dinna wish tae see me," he said, sounding weak and confused. "Even when Magnus was a lad, I would send him missives, but he never sent anything back tae me. Ambrose told me that Magnus burned them."

Agnes shook her head. "It is not true," she said. "He would tell Magnus you never asked for him. It was Ambrose who burned your missives."

The realization began to dawn on him. Ambrose had orchestrated the entire situation, and as that news settled, Hugh was nearly beside himself.

"My God," he muttered. "What has that man done? Magnus may be my bastard, but he is the only son I have. Ye know I've never had any children with my wife."

Agnes nodded. "I know," she said. "Hugh, there is no time to discuss this in full. I am telling you this now because Magnus is in jeopardy again. Ambrose is raising an army against you, and he wants Magnus to lead it by telling him more lies about you. He wants Magnus's sense of vengeance against you to lead his armies to victory."

Hugh looked at her, horrified. "What's this ye say?" he hissed. "He has turned my son against me?"

"Not completely," Agnes said. "I believe there may still be hope, but I do not know for certain. All I know is that you must help Magnus. You must tell him the truth, that you do not hate him, so that Ambrose cannot use him against you. Magnus is in a precarious position."

"Why do ye say that?"

Agnes was running out of time. She knew she had to get back on the road swiftly before her carriage was sighted by any number of Ambrose's allies or spies. He seemed to have them everywhere, even out here in the country, and that made her nervous.

"I saw Magnus recently," she said. "He told me that he is a warrior at the greatest fight guild in all of Scotland. I had not heard of the place, but Ambrose explained that it is the Ludus Caledonia where men are trained to be great warriors. It is also a gambling establishment where men can wager on the fights. Do you know of it?"

Hugh nodded, rising from his chair. "Of course I do," he said. "I've been there several times. Are ye telling me that my son is a warrior there?"

"That is what he told me. Were you at the Ludus Caledonia recently?"

"Last year," he said, stunned. "I must have seen him but dinna even know it. I've not seen him since he was young. I wouldna know him if I saw him as a grown man."

Agnes moved close enough to put a hand on his arm. Her gaze drifted over him. "He looks just like you," she said, a glimmer in her eyes. "He is handsome and powerful. He has your eyes, Hugh. You must go to him. *Help him.* Do not let Ambrose turn him against you once and for all."

Hugh didn't know what to say. He was overwhelmed with

everything, struggling to remain on an even keel. But he knew one thing—he was appreciative of Agnes's appearance. Her bravery had meant all the difference in his small corner of the world.

And he had no idea why she should do it.

"Why would ye risk yerself tae tell me this, Agnes?" he asked. "Ye've gone against yer husband. Why?"

She shrugged. "Because he did the same thing to me," she said. "He turned my son against me, too. He thinks I do not know, but I do. I have watched him do it to others, but for you, he seems to have a particular brand of hatred. I could not stand by and do nothing."

Hugh looked at her, long and hard. "Swear it tae me," he said softly. "Swear tae me this is all true."

"I swear to you upon my own life that it is true."

He believed her.

"Then ye canna know how grateful I am," he said. "I will find Magnus and I will tell him… I'm not sure what I'll tell him, but whatever it is, it will be the truth."

Agnes gave his arm a squeeze before releasing him. Quickly, she wrapped herself back up in the cloak, making sure to drape the veil over her face.

"I must go," she said. "You did not see me here. Tell your major-domo the same. Ambrose must not know I was here, Hugh."

Hugh opened the door for her. It was a straight path out to her waiting carriage.

"Not a word, Agnes," he promised. "I'll take it tae my grave."

Agnes wished he'd used a different choice of words. As she scurried out to her waiting escort, she found herself repeating his words in her head.

I'll take it tae my grave.

She hoped the grave it was taken to wouldn't be her own if Ambrose discovered what she'd done.

CHAPTER TEN

HE TRAVELED LIKE A ROMAN CAESAR.

Clegg de Lave, from an excellent Norman family based in Cornwall, hadn't seen Cornwall since he was a lad. He'd always had big dreams and big ambitions, ambitions that had taken him all over the known world. He'd had more experiences, adventures, and incidents than most men would have in two lifetimes, but Clegg had a bigger-than-life persona and savored everything life had to offer. He learned all he could, studied all he could, tasted all he could.

The culmination of that experience was a series of fight guilds in the south of Scotland.

The Ludus Caledonia…

The Ludus Antonine…

The Ludus Hadrian…

The Ludus Trimontium…

And the latest one, the Ludus Valentia.

Clegg had just come from overseeing the final construction of an amphitheater that was enormous and sleek, built to accommodate five hundred patrons. The Ludus Valentia was in Dumfries, in the hills to the southwest in a naturally bowled-out area that once was a lake. But Clegg drained the lake and built his complex, something he'd been working on for more than a year. Given the close proximity of the location to everything south of Glasgow and most of the Lowlands, he already had men clamoring to attend the games that would not take place for several more months.

But that was the nature of Clegg's business—supply and demand.

He fully intended to supply.

He traveled in a caravan that looked like something out of the spice trade on the rolling sands of Morocco—lavish dressings for the horses, gaily painted carriages, soldiers with lush tunics, and more. That was the nature of Clegg's flamboyance.

As his escort headed up the road toward his home of Caelian Hill, he was glad to be back at his *premier* venue. From inside his comfortable carriage, he watched the predawn landscape around him, thinking back to the days when he had come to this mountain to establish his first venue. It seemed like so long ago.

He'd built much in his lifetime.

Behind his carriage, there was a second carriage full of men. He had brought two new top warriors with him and six *novicius*, new men to try out at his largest venue. As the caravan drew closer to the top of the hill, they were greeted by men riding out from the Ludus Caledonia.

Axel was the first one to come alongside Clegg's carriage.

"My lord," he greeted Clegg. "Welcome home."

Clegg flashed his big, white teeth at his manager. "Axel," he said with satisfaction. "It is good to see you again. I have been away too long, I fear. I have missed my home."

Axel smiled in return to a man he was genuinely fond of. "Your home has missed you, but all has been well," he said. "It has been prosperous while you have been away."

That brought interest from Clegg. "Is that so?" he said. "I am pleased, then. I look forward to going over the accounting with you."

"Aye, my lord."

Clegg threw a thumb in the direction of the wagon behind him. "I have brought you more men," he said. "I journeyed to Hades to make sure all is as it should be and to collect the revenue. We must dismiss the manager, however, for I fear he is keeping some of the winnings himself."

He was speaking of the Ludus Hadrian in Carlisle, known as

"Hades," and nearly as successful as the Ludus Caledonia. Axel looked at him in surprise.

"Dismiss Gideon Lloyd?" he said. "But he has been with us a long time. His reputation is without equal."

Clegg grunted and shook his head. "That is true, but he married last year and his wife has an appetite for fine things," he said. "The woman was dripping in jewels, and I know for a fact that Gideon does not make that kind of money, so he is getting it from somewhere. I left Luther there to see if he could discover if Gideon has been cheating us. I told Luther that if he felt the man has been abusing his position, he has my permission to dismiss him."

Axel nodded. "Mayhap I will go to Hades and see for myself," he said. "Is there anything else of note?"

"Nay," Clegg grunted. "I went to Antonine, too, but everything there is as it should be. No thieving managers to report. And here? You said all has been well?"

Axel nodded. "Mostly," he said. "Nothing to report, except for last night. The Eagle had some trouble."

Clegg grew serious very quickly. "Not Magnus," he said. "Please tell me the man is not injured."

Axel shook his head quickly. "He is fine," he said. "But he was forced to kill his opponent last night, a Saxon warrior known as the Bear. The man was out to kill Magnus, and I am convinced that Magnus acted in self-defense. I am telling you because the Bear's trainer is demanding compensation for his loss, and he is demanding to see you upon your return."

Clegg didn't seem particularly concerned. "I will see him when I am rested," he said. "That could take weeks. Months, even. But send for Magnus. I want to speak with him. Did you punish him?"

Axel shook his head. "Nay, because the Bear was twice his size and out for Magnus's blood. Truly, he had no choice."

"Then there is no problem, but I would speak to Magnus anyway."

"As you wish, my lord. Is there anything else you desire?"

"Not immediately, but do not stray far. I want to hear more of what happened while I was away, but not at the moment."

They finished the rest of the journey in relative silence, with Axel escorting Clegg home as he always did. Clegg was a wealthy man, wealthier than God as the rumors went, so he expected a certain amount of respect and admiration.

When the carriage came to a halt, Axel and Wendell were there to make sure Clegg was escorted inside and his baggage collected. It was Wendell who went to the other wagon with the men inside, releasing the warriors and taking them to the warriors' village for orientation.

Somewhere in the process, word was sent to Magnus.

On two hours of sleep, Magnus answered the summons.

☩ ☩ ☩

"I hear there was a death, Magnus. Tell me about it."

Magnus was standing in Clegg's solar, which was quite possibly the most lavish chamber in all of Scotland. There were rare hides on the floor, expensive leather furniture, and tapestries on the walls from distant and exotic places. Most of all, it smelled heavily of incense that Clegg had sent all the way from Rome. He burned the stuff heavily, as he felt it kept him healthy and sane.

Magnus thought it smelled like dirty feet.

At the moment, Clegg was burning it happily, inhaling deeply of a scent he'd missed. Dressed in his usual garb of flowing robes made from expensive materials, he'd just asked a question that Magnus had been expecting, so he replied honestly.

He wasn't a man who condoned lying, in any case.

"Aye, m'laird," he said after a moment. "A man I was fighting."

"Axel said he wanted to kill you."

Magnus nodded. "He did," he said frankly. "I had beaten him in a bout before, and he would not take his money and leave. Instead, he demanded a rematch. I was told that he was known tae kill his opponents, so I knew that was his intention with me. Everyone knew it, including Axel. I had no other choice but tae kill him before he could kill me."

Clegg waved his hand in the gray ribbons of smoke rising from the incense bowl as he continued to inhale deeply. "You have every right to defend yourself, Magnus," he said. "I do not fault you for what had to be done. But we will not make a habit of this, shall we? Killing your opponents is bad for business."

"I understand, m'laird."

"Good." Clegg took one last sniff of the incense smoke and came around the table, looking at Magnus at closer range. "I was at the Ant a few weeks ago and saw many of your old comrades. They send their greetings."

Magnus grinned; he couldn't help it. Clegg was speaking of the Ludus Antonine in Glasgow where Magnus had spent several years of his life prior to coming to the Ludus Caledonia. He had enjoyed his time there immensely.

"And how is that motley group, m'laird?" he asked.

Clegg snorted. "As motley as ever," he said. "But making me money, so I do not care. I brought one of them back with me, in fact. Aurelius Finn."

Magnus's eyebrows lifted. "The Celtic Storm?" he said with surprise. "I've not seen the man in years."

Clegg could see the pleasure on Magnus's face. "You'll see him now," he said. "I knew he was your friend, so I have invited him to fight at the Cal. A happy Magnus is a victorious Magnus. Does this please you?"

"It does, m'laird, very much."

"Is there anything else I can do for you?"

Magnus's smile faded. Clegg's question had him grasping at a variety of responses. His first thought was of Diantha, something

Clegg would find out about sooner or later now that he had returned.

He wanted to be honest about it.

"Aye, m'laird," he said. "There is a...woman."

Clegg's eyebrows lifted curiously as he moved to a table containing a rock-crystal decanter of wine and matching cups. "A woman?" he said. "Someone you want?"

Magnus watched the man as he poured ruby-red liquid into a cup. "Nay," he said. "It is not one I want, at least not in the manner ye're suggesting. It is a woman I knew long ago. She has come tae me for help and I have agreed."

Clegg's curiosity grew. "What kind of help?"

"She wants tae return to Navarre," he said, which was true. So far, he'd managed to avoid lying to Clegg about the situation. "She has asked me tae help her earn money for her passage. She is very intelligent and can read and write several languages. She has offered tae help those at the Cal learn tae read and write if they wish as a way of earning money."

Clegg apparently didn't think that sounded too outlandish. There was a time when he had been adamant about not having women at the Ludus Caledonia other than comfort women for the warriors, but over the past few years, he'd greatly relaxed that stance, which was why Magnus had no fear in asking. He was certain Clegg would agree.

As it turned out, he was right.

"I have no concern with her remaining," he said. "But if she needs money, why not just give it to her?"

Magnus smiled ironically. "I have tried," he said. "She willna take it. She says she willna take money she hasna earned."

"A lady who will not take your money but would rather work for it? Astonishing."

"She is...unusual, 'tis true," Magnus said. "If ye're agreeable, I will spread the word that she's willing tae teach for a small price."

Clegg didn't hesitate. "That might be beneficial," he said. "I think some of our warriors might wish to learn. What languages does she speak?"

"She is from Navarre, so she speaks Spanish," Magnus said. "She also speaks English, French, and Catalan."

"Ah," Clegg said. "An educated woman."

"Aye, m'laird."

Clegg scratched his chin thoughtfully. "Does she know Latin?"

"I dunna know, but I shall ask."

"Do," Clegg said. "Mayhap I can give her some work. I have many volumes from Rome, written in Latin, that she may be able to translate for me. My Latin is not as good as my English."

"I shall ask, m'laird," Magnus said. "Thank ye for allowing her tae remain."

"Where is she sleeping?"

"In my cottage, m'laird."

Clegg snorted. "I might have known," he said. "Well, keep her to yourself if you wish. As I said…a happy Magnus is a victorious Magnus."

Magnus knew exactly what Clegg meant. Magnus's reputation as a womanizer wasn't something that bothered him until this very moment. He wasn't keeping Diantha in his cottage so he could ravish her nightly, but Clegg thought that was the exact reason. Magnus didn't care that Clegg thought that of him because it was a true assumption, but Diantha…

She wasn't *that* kind of woman.

He didn't like that others might assume she was.

"Ye have my thanks, m'laird," he said after a moment. "Do ye wish tae speak with me about anything else?"

Clegg shook his head. "Nay," he said, waving a hand. "You may go, Magnus."

Magnus did, heading out into the early morning, his mind lingering on the conversation with Clegg.

He purposely didn't tell the man about Diantha's association with the Duke of Ayr. Had he mentioned it, and the fact that she ran from the man, Clegg probably wouldn't have been so agreeable to her remaining. To harbor an escaped hostage was the same thing as stealing, and the fact that Diantha was at the Ludus Caledonia was putting Clegg in the path of a vengeful Duke of Ayr.

But Magnus was betting heavily on the fact that Ambrose would never find Diantha. In his mind, she was at the safest place she could be—in a warriors' village surrounded by one hundred of the most highly trained fighting men in all of Scotland. Magnus had not seen Ambrose or Conan since the day he left Culroy, and they'd never visited the Ludus Caledonia as far as he knew.

He kept telling himself that he had nothing to worry about, but deep down, he wondered if that was the truth. When he should have been heading back to his cottage to sleep, he found himself going back to the arena.

He would find solace and balance where he always found it—

In training.

CHAPTER ELEVEN

"GET OUT OF THE DIRT, YE BIG OX!"

Tay was lying on his back as Magnus yelled at him. It was late morning at the Ludus Caledonia and the advanced warriors were getting in some training before the *novicius* took over the field. Currently, it was Tay and Magnus against Galan and Bane, who were getting in some practice as well.

As Lor sat on the side of the arena with his toddler son because his wife wasn't feeling well, the four warriors went at it beneath the searing summer sun. Clouds of dust were kicking up as the men worked on a battle exercise that had them shackled to one another.

Magnus and Tay were shackled together, and Bane and Galan were shackled together. It was an exercise meant to teach them teamwork. While Magnus was light on his feet, Tay could be clumsy—his strength was, literally, his greatest asset and as Magnus had backed them away from Bane and Galan, Tay had tripped over his own feet.

Down he went.

Now, Magnus was forced to fight Bane and Galan by himself, using a wooden *gladius* that was chipping because Bane was striking at him so hard. The shield in his hand was protecting Tay as the man rolled to his knees, but Galan was too close to the scuffling and Tay was able to grab an ankle and throw the man right off his feet.

Galan went down, yanking on the chain that linked him to Bane, and Bane nearly went down as well. That was all Magnus and Tay needed to charge Bane and shove him over onto Galan.

With their opponents on the ground, Magnus and Tay stood over them and gloated.

"Tell me I'm the greatest warrior ye've ever seen," Magnus demanded, gesturing to Tay. "Dunna worry about the Ox. I'm better than he is. Tell me!"

Bane sighed heavily as he rolled onto his buttocks, fumbling with the shackle he had on his left hand.

"Ye're the most overbearing and obnoxious warrior I've ever seen," he said. "But ye have a gift, Chicken. There is no denying that."

Magnus started laughing, disengaging the pin from his shackle and letting it fall off his wrist. Lor came over from the sidelines with his towheaded son, who ran right to Bane and wanted to play with the heavy *gladius*. Bane let the boy have it and Nikki hugged it to his body, thrilled with the weapon. Lor shook his head at his son.

"What chance did the lad have?" he asked, a rhetorical question. "His mother trained as a warrior, his father is a trainer of men, and his grandfather is a clan chief. The lad was born with a sword in his hand. Soon enough, he'll be out here with us."

Nikki began to drag the sword around because it was too heavy for him to lift, but he made a valiant attempt. As Galan and Tay collected the shackles and carried them back to the servants who manned the armory, Magnus and Lor and Bane watched Nikki fight imaginary warriors.

"Is that what ye want for yer son?" Bane asked. "Do ye want the lad tae fight on the floor of the Fields of Mars?"

Lor grinned as he watched the child lug the sword around. "Why not?" he said. "What's the difference if he fights here or in the Highlands for his clan?"

Bane looked over at him. "Will ye give him a choice?"

"I will. Will ye give yer sons the same choice?"

Bane shook his head. "Nay," he said. "Ye know I canna. They'll know of their clan, but it's not a place they can ever return tae. But ye...ye can return tae the Highlands and yer wife's clan."

Lor's gaze lingered on the child a moment longer before looking at Bane and Magnus. "This *is* my clan," he said. "We're all part of the same clan. Ye're my brothers and I'd fight tae the death for ye, so that makes us family. I'm proud tae have Nikki fight for this clan. He was born here, ye know. 'Tis his home."

Magnus was listening to the conversation, a conversation he would have ignored under normal circumstances because things like clans and families and children meant nothing to him. He agreed that the Ludus Caledonia was his clan, as Lor said, because they were more of a family to him than those of his blood who had long abandoned him.

"One doesna need tae be related by blood in order tae be family," he said after a moment. "I've learned that."

Lor and Bane looked at him. "That is true," Lor said. "We all have our backgrounds, our families that we've left behind."

Magnus looked over at them. "Ye never asked me what my background was or if I have family I've left behind."

Lor and Bane continued to look at him, wondering why he should make such a statement, especially at this moment. They'd just finished training, a lighthearted but serious exercise, and were preparing to move on with their day. But this comment was unexpected, and would have been unexpected at any time because the answer to it was something that Magnus had always kept closely guarded. It seemed like an odd time to bring it up.

But Magnus evidently didn't feel that way.

Lor finally shrugged.

"Does it matter?" he said. "If ye want us tae know, ye'll tell us, but ye've made it clear that ye dunna want tae speak of yer past. We respect that."

Magnus didn't say anything for a moment. His gaze returned to the little boy playing in the dirt as his thoughts turned to the past he never spoke of. He'd done very well at forgetting it until he saw Lady Ayr in the apothecary's shop.

Now, it was heavy on his mind. Speaking of it to Diantha had done something to him. It had been a cathartic moment, more than he'd realized it would be, and she had been kind and interested in his origins. She hadn't passed judgment. Perhaps that's what he had always been afraid of—men passing judgment.

But he had come to know Lor and Bane very well over the past several months, ever since he had been brought to the Ludus Caledonia. He knew all about their backgrounds, the tragedies and triumphs, but they knew nothing about his. They were all close friends, but he knew they could never be truly close unless they knew all about him. For the first time since knowing them, he felt like lowering his guard.

Perhaps letting friends in on his past was a good thing.

"Ye've not heard about me and my background, then?" he finally asked. "If ye have, ye can say so. I willna be angry."

Lor and Bane both shook their heads. "We know ye came from Glasgow," Lor said. "That's all I've ever heard."

Magnus was still looking at the boy as he spoke. "My father is the Duke of Kintyre and Lorne," he said quietly. Then he turned to see their reactions. "My father is the youngest brother of the King of Scotland. James is my uncle."

Lor and Bane were staring at him as if waiting for him to admit he was lying. But Magnus simply nodded his head.

"It *is* true," he said. "I wouldna lie tae ye about such a thing. I know we spend a good deal of time playing tricks on one another, but this isna one of those times. I may be a prideful lad, but I dunna need tae lie tae my friends in order tae impress them. My father really *is* a duke and my uncle really *is* the king."

Lor's eyebrows lifted in astonishment. "Then what in the hell are ye doing here?" He asked the obvious. "Magnus, ye should be living in a fine house with yer own army. Ye're of royal blood, lad."

"I'm also a bastard," Magnus said quietly. "My mother was a lady-in-waiting for the duchess, and I was raised by my mother's family as an infant and then given over as a hostage tae my father's cousin. That was where I spent my entire life until seven years ago when I was released. Being directionless, with a father who wouldna accept me and a mother I dinna want tae burden, I learned tae fight at the Ludus Antonine. If ye wanted tae know the truth, now ye do. When I said one doesna need tae be related by blood tae be a family, I meant it. Ye're the only family I have."

It was a sad statement, though Magnus wasn't looking for pity. It was simply a fact, but it explained why Magnus was such a prideful man. He needed that reassurance that he was good enough, that he was accepted and loved for who he was. He would always be that discarded bastard, but at the Ludus Caledonia, none of that mattered. Lor and Bane immediately went to him and Lor reached out, putting a hand on Magnus's broad shoulder.

"'Tis their loss, lad," he said softly, warmly. "I'll take a duke's bastard as my brother and be the richer for it."

Magnus smiled weakly, perhaps a little uncomfortably. He wasn't used to such sentiment. "It seems we have something in common," he said. "Ye told me once that yer father was a Norse king who loved yer mother. It seems we're both royal bastards, from different paths in life."

"And I'm a bloody peasant," Bane snorted, breaking the spell of the warm moment as Magnus and Lor chuckled. "'Tis true! I'm no better than a weed growing out of the dirt compared tae the two of ye."

"At least ye have yer beauteous looks," Lor said. "Ye were able tae attract a wife with that face even if ye have nothing else tae offer her. Speaking of attracting a wife, what's this I hear, Magnus? Ye have a woman living with ye now?"

Magnus cleared his throat as the focus swung back on him. The subject changed and he wasn't sure he was prepared to discuss it. How could he discuss something he didn't fully understand himself?

"Aye," he said after a moment. "I told Clegg about her and he has given permission for her tae remain with me."

Lor and Bane were expecting more of an answer. "And?" Lor said. "Tell us more about her. My wife says she's Spanish."

"She is," Magnus said. He paused a moment before continuing. "I told ye that I was held a hostage for many years. She was a hostage also, but she escaped and came tae me for help. I couldna deny her."

"A hostage with the same captor?" Lor asked, puzzled.

Magnus nodded. "I dinna tell Clegg any of this, so keep it tae yerself," he said, lowering his voice. "I was the captive of Ambrose Stewart, Duke of Ayr, for many years. He kept me at Culroy Castle as insurance against my father doing anything...foolish. My father has known a contentious relationship with his brother and was constantly in a state of rebellion. Diantha was at Culroy Castle, too. Only in her case, the duke held her against her will and planned tae marry her tae his son, who is a vile excuse for a man. She escaped and has asked me tae help her earn money for passage back tae Navarre."

Now, the story was starting to make more sense. "I see," Lor said. "What is she doing tae earn money?"

Magnus shrugged. "She is educated," he said. "She wants tae teach men tae read and write for a small price."

"A teacher, is she?"

"Aye."

"Is that what ye're telling Clegg?"

"What do ye mean?"

Lor glanced at Bane. It was clear that they were both thinking the same thing.

"Magnus, we've known ye a while now," Lor said quietly. "Every woman at the Ludus Caledonia wants a piece of ye, and now ye have a woman living in yer cottage. Ye needna lie tae us about her. If she's warming yer bed, we'll not judge ye."

Magnus's brow furrowed. "I've never lied tae ye," he said. "If she was warming my bed, I'd tell ye and be proud of it, but the truth is that she's not. She's tending my cottage and doing what she can tae earn money. She's…she's not like the women I've known. She's…different."

"Different?" Bane repeated, confused. "Different how? Does she not like men?"

Magnus snorted. "I havena asked her," he said. "But I hope she does."

That piqued the curiosity of both Lor and Bane. The way Magnus said it led them to believe that there was some interest behind that statement.

"Is that so?" Lor asked, his eyes glimmering with mirth. "Do ye intend her tae warm yer bed after all?"

Magnus was feeling cornered. He almost pushed them away, but something stopped him. They knew how to woo a woman in a way that he didn't. They had wives, after all. They knew something more than he did. All he'd ever done was flex his sweaty muscles and women fainted at his feet.

He didn't want Diantha fainting at his feet.

He wanted something more.

"Not now," he said after a moment. "What I mean tae say is mayhap I do, but honorably."

"What does that mean?"

Magnus was starting to become exasperated because he was embarrassed to say what he was really thinking. It was difficult to put into words.

"It means just what I told ye," he muttered, looking at the two of them. "Since when have I ever had a woman in my bed honorably? They pay the price and I permit them the honor. I suppose that makes me nothing more than a whore. I take their money, they have their way, and I'm the richer for it. I thought that was all I wanted until…"

Lor and Bane were hanging on his every word. "Until *what*?" Bane pressed.

Magnus sighed heavily and scratched his head. "Well…how *did* ye woo yer wives?" he asked. "What did ye do that told a woman that ye thought she was special above all others?"

Bane was trying very hard not to grin, but Lor wasn't so lucky. He had a full-blown smile on his face. He patted Magnus sweetly on the side of the head.

"Marriage, my fine lad?" he said, delighted. "Do ye want tae marry this Spanish lass?"

Magnus frowned. "I dinna say marriage," he said. "All I know is that she's *different*. I've never met a lass like her. I dunna want tae do the wrong thing. I want her tae like me, too."

"Then do all of the right things," Lor said. "Say nice things. Bring her flowers. Tell her she's lovely. Women like those things, Magnus. Not just yer sweaty muscles."

That was all new territory for Magnus. Those were always things that other women did for him, not the other way around. "That's all?"

Lor nodded. "Usually," he said. "Unless ye're Isabail and ye'd rather be gifted with a new dirk instead of jewels. My wife was more of a challenge."

As he snorted, Bane spoke up. "Is it that ye want tae court her, Magnus? Or just be nice tae her?"

Magnus shrugged. "As I said, I dunna know," he said. "The lass has had a difficult life. I think she needs someone tae be kind tae her."

"And ye want tae be the one."

"I think so."

"Then ye need tae consider something else," Lor interjected. "If ye want tae be nice tae her, and ye want her tae like ye, most women dunna like competition."

Magnus looked at him curiously. "What competition?"

"The half-dozen women ye cavort with after each victorious bout," Lor said honestly. "If ye want the Spanish lass tae warm tae ye, I suspect she willna take kindly tae that. Now, the question is— can ye give up the gangs of women for just one, Magnus?"

Magnus hadn't really thought about it, mostly because the women after the games didn't mean much to him other than income. That's really all they ever were—a means to an end. But it had been their adulation and worship that he needed, too.

He wondered if one woman could supply all that he needed.

Lor and Bane were about to go in for another round of questions when Magnus discreetly waved them off because Tay and Galan were returning. Therefore, further interrogation on the subject of the mysterious Diantha would have to wait.

But come it would.

CHAPTER TWELVE

DIANTHA WASN'T SURPRISED WHEN SHE AWOKE IN THE morning to find Magnus gone.

What did surprise her was the disappointment she felt.

It was her second day at the Ludus Caledonia, and already she felt as if she'd lived there forever. She was looking forward to seeing Isabail and Lucia, to cleaning Magnus's cottage, and to finding her place among the warriors and women of the Ludus Caledonia. She knew she could fit in here if she tried, and she intended to try very hard.

The Ludus Caledonia wasn't like any other living establishment, like a castle or manse, where there was a hierarchy based on blood and tradition. It seemed to her that anyone could be anything in a place like the Ludus Caledonia, which was how Magnus had been able to make himself a top warrior in spite of his past.

He'd been able to thrive with no one holding him responsible for his past.

Rising from Magnus's bed just after sunrise, Diantha bathed quickly in cold water from the night before and with the bar of soap Lucia had given her. She dressed in the brown broadcloth that Magnus hated, but it was very serviceable for what she needed to do.

Today was going to be a great day.

Yesterday, she had cleaned as much as she could, but today she was going to do more. She was also going to ask Isabail and Lucia if they could help her find men to teach. The sooner she got to earning money, the better. The sooner she would be able to return to Navarre.

But return to *what*?

Thoughts of her father had been heavy on her mind. Last night, she'd even dreamed of the tall, golden walls of Santacara, wondering if it still belonged to her father. After all these years, she couldn't imagine why he hadn't come for her, but deep down, she suspected that she knew. Only death could keep him from her.

Still, she had to discover the truth.

She had to go home.

It was a bright morning outside, promising to be a warm day. Since she'd dirtied one of the sheets from the day before when she fell on it, she dragged it outside to wash again. Lucia was already outside with both infants, and she joined Diantha as the woman prepared to wash the sheet again. Diantha learned that Isabail wasn't feeling well, but it was still a morning of laughter and conversation, just her and Lucia. As the morning waned, the infants grew restless and Lucia took them indoors for a nap.

That left Diantha alone, but she didn't mind. She put the linen sheet up on a branch so it could dry and headed back to the cottage to see if there was anything else that needed washing. She also found herself taking a look at the cottage itself. It was made from stone with window frames of wood and a sod roof. She didn't think it needed repairs or cleaning from the outside, but she leaned in one of the window frames, peering at what she thought was a crack.

And that's when she saw it.

A big black-and-yellow bumblebee.

There were wildflowers growing around the cottage, and nearly everywhere else in the Ludus Caledonia this summer season, and she noticed a big bumblebee on the ground, lying on its back. Its legs were flailing about, showing its panic about being on its back.

Diantha was a lover of all living creatures, even those that could sting. As a child, she'd had pet lizards and tame birds, even a pet goat. Her father had called their home *la casa de fieras*, or the menagerie, because she collected so many creatures. Therefore, a bumblebee on its back warranted her sympathy.

Crouching down, she took a stick and gently flipped it over.

The little bee began to crawl around frantically, and as she studied it, she could see that it was missing a wing. It couldn't fly. She tried to get it to crawl onto the stick so she could put it back in the flowers, but it kept crawling in her direction. Timidly, she put her hand down to it and it promptly crawled upon one of her fingers.

"My poor little friend," she murmured in Spanish. "It seems that you are injured."

The bee seemed quite happy on her fingers. Diantha watched him for a few minutes, speaking softly to him as one did to tiny creatures, before putting him onto one of the wildflowers around the cottage. With her little friend safely on a yellow bloom, she headed back into the cottage to reconnoiter for more laundry.

Finding nothing left, she made her way up to the kitchen by the vegetable garden, bringing back the iron pot and having it filled with a delicious-smelling soup made from smashed peas and carrots. She collected more bread, some cheese, a jug of watered ale, and took it all back to the cottage for Magnus when he returned.

As the day peaked and the afternoon set in, Diantha did more sweeping and cleaning, including the ashes out of the hearth. When she went back outside, she noticed that her bumblebee friend had fallen from his bloom, so she brought him inside with a few flowers for nourishment and put him in a bowl on the windowsill.

With the bee tended to, she straightened out the pallet that Magnus had slept on. She felt guilty about taking his bed last night, wondering why he should choose to sleep on the floor when he had a perfectly good mattress waiting for him. Surely it had been temporary madness.

Or chivalry.

The thought made her smile. Though she didn't know what

was going on in his head, she knew what was going on in hers. That arrogant warrior with the hidden heart who charmed an arena full of people last night had her interest.

She couldn't deny it.

Emerging from the cottage to shake out the broom, she caught sight of Magnus as he headed in her direction.

⟁ ⟁ ⟁

The flowers grew everywhere.

Lor said that women liked flowers, and there were bushels of them along the edges of the Fields of Mars. White, purple, yellow—many kinds. His friends told him to be kind and sweet, and Magnus saw those flowers as his opportunity. Perhaps he would give their suggestions a try because, after all, they had wives. They knew what he didn't.

He was in uncharted territory.

Leaving Lor and Bane and the rest of them going through some exercises in the staging area, Magnus headed back to his cottage to sleep for a few hours before the bouts that night, but not before he picked a giant bouquet of wildflowers for Diantha. It was a warm day and the winds had picked up a little, coming in off the sea to the east.

Strange how he'd never really noticed things like that before— the brightness of the day, the beauty of the landscape. But he was noticing them now. The world looked beautiful in a way he'd never noticed before.

Inside, he felt…happy.

He was going to see Diantha again.

With thoughts of her on his mind, he was halfway through the warriors' village when he realized that people were giving him strange looks. It occurred to him that he was parading through the village with a giant bouquet of flowers and looking like a fool. He didn't look like the fearsome warrior with the fearsome reputation.

Everyone he passed looked at him oddly to the point where he was so embarrassed that he tossed the flowers aside.

But that didn't solve the problem.

With the wind whipping up, one of the flowers blew up behind him and stuck in his hair, so as he was closing the distance toward his cottage, he had a yellow daisy sticking up out of the back of his head. Now, people were looking at him and laughing, and he had no idea why. It got to the point where he was starting to scowl at people, who quickly averted their gazes, but somehow, he could feel them laughing behind his back.

Lor and his stupid suggestion of flowers!

Magnus's cottage was ahead on the rise. He could see Diantha outside, smacking a broom against the side of the cottage. Puffs of dirt flew into the air, disappearing in the breeze. She turned around and caught sight of him, and he would never forget the expression on her face. Something between surprise and delight.

Was it possible she was actually *glad* to see him?

He was sorry that he'd tossed away the flowers.

"*Buenos días,*" she said. "That means 'good day.'"

He couldn't help the smile on his lips as he closed the distance between them. "Good day," he said. "Busy, I see."

She nodded eagerly. "More cleaning, more washing," she said, but her gaze was inevitably drawn to his head. "And may I say that you are looking quite lovely today."

He frowned. "What do ye mean?"

Reaching up, she plucked the flower from his dark hair, her eyes twinkling at she showed it to him. Magnus took one look at it and rolled his eyes.

"So *that's* why everyone was looking at me strangely," he said. "I had a weed in my hair."

She laughed softly. "I think it looked rather pretty."

He ran his hand up the back of his head just to make sure there were no more green stragglers.

"Then put it in yer hair," he said. "It'll look better."

She did, tucking it behind one ear, and Magnus thought it was about the sweetest thing he'd ever seen. "Like that?" she asked.

A smile played on his lips as he looked at her. "Like that."

He wanted to say more to her, but he wasn't sure what, exactly, to say. Lor had told him to tell her she was lovely, and he thought he had. Sort of. He told her the flower would look better on her, hadn't he? But he wasn't sure what more he needed to say and it made him nervous. In a desperate bid to change the subject, he pointed to the broom.

"I thought ye did the cleaning yesterday," he said.

Diantha was still smiling as she looked at the broom in her hand. "Oh, I know," she said. "I did quite a bit of it, but there is always something more to sweep or clean. Truthfully, I am enjoying it immensely."

"Are ye?"

She nodded, tendrils of dark hair in her eyes. "At Culroy, all we did was sit around and watch each other sing or paint or dance," she said. "Did you know that about Lady Ayr? She never believed in labor for noblewomen. We could only have refined interests, which is why I can read and write so well. When I wasn't reading, I was writing."

"Oh?" he said, warming to the conversation quickly. "What did ye write?"

She shrugged bashfully. "Poems, mostly," she said. "Sometimes memories of my life at Santacara. I even wrote a story once."

"What about?"

"A little Roman boy from the Roman ruins at Santacara," she said. "He lost his dog and set out with his friends to find it."

"Did he?"

She grinned. "He did," she said. "A terrible woman had stolen the dog and refused to give him back, so the little boy and his friends outsmarted her. Confidentially, the woman in my story was a duchess with a mean husband."

She meant like Lady Ayr and he chuckled. "Good on ye," he said. "She deserved it."

Diantha laughed, a tinkling sound that set Magnus's heart to racing. "She did, indeed," she said. "She deserved that and much more. But Lady Ayr aside, are you hungry? I have food inside if you are."

He was but mostly he was just glad to see her again. Each day found her more charming than the last.

"I can eat," he said. "Will ye eat with me?"

Diantha nodded. "I will," she said, gathering the broom and heading for the door. "I thought that I might ask the cooks here to teach me how to cook. Do you think that is a good idea?"

She pushed open the door, entering, and he followed close behind. "If ye wish it," he said, shutting the cottage door. "But I told ye that I dunna expect ye tae cook for me."

"I know," she said, setting the broom aside. "But I would like to learn. One should never stop learning, you know. There is always something new to know."

He sat down at the table as she went over to the hearth, stirring something in the pot over the low flame.

"I suppose that is true," he said. "That is why I train every day. It keeps my skills sharp, but sometimes I learn something new. But dunna tell the others. I dunna want them tae think they can teach me anything."

She snorted. "Is that where you went this morning? To train?"

He nodded, realizing there was a pitcher of watered ale on the table, and he poured himself a cup. "Aye," he said, smacking his lips after taking a drink. "That is what every warrior at the Cal does, every morning. We train."

Diantha began spooning the thick pottage into bowls. "Is it permissible to watch you train?"

"If ye wish."

She nodded. "I would like to," she said. "I find it fascinating to watch you fight. And as I watched you last night, I realized something."

"That I am the greatest fighter ye've ever seen?"

She grinned. "That is true," she said. "But I realized something else."

"What?"

"That there is great strategy involved."

He leaned back in the chair, a lazy smile on his face. "Lass, that's most of the battle," he said. "I can be the strongest man in the world, but that's not going tae win over brains."

She approached the table, setting the soup bowls down—one in front of him, one in front of her. "I saw that last night," she said. "That man you were fighting in your last bout was twice your size. He was big and mean and angry. But you used your head and not your brawn when you defeated him."

Magnus dug into the pottage with gusto. "I had no choice," he said, mouth full. "The man was going tae kill me, so I had tae be smarter—and faster—than him."

She looked up from her soup, watching him as he shoveled food into his mouth. "You knew he was going to kill you?"

"Aye."

He didn't seem concerned about it and she couldn't understand why. "Didn't your commanders know?" she asked. "And they still let him fight you?"

Magnus shrugged. "Of course they did."

"But why?"

"Because they knew I could defeat him."

Diantha thought about that, but she realized that she didn't like any of it. Magnus was allowed to fight against a man who wanted to kill him? What if he had succeeded?

What if she had witnessed it?

The thought made her shudder. She had been excited to watch the games again tonight, but now she wasn't so sure.

"Will he be back tonight?" she asked. "To fight you again, I mean."

He glanced at her as he tore up a loaf of bread. "Nay," he said after a moment, handing her the soft, white middle. "He willna be back."

"You're sure?"

"I'm sure."

"That is good," she said, visibly relieved. "But there are more fights tonight, correct?"

He nodded. "Four nights a week," he said. "After tonight, there will be two days of rest before the next fight night."

Since Magnus wasn't fighting that beast of a man tonight, Diantha felt a little better about it. She settled down to her meal.

"What do you do on the days you are not fighting?" she asked.

"Train."

"Do you always train?"

He nodded. "I do," he said. "Tae be the best, you must work at it."

"There is nothing else you do?"

"Nothing else."

She took a sip of her soup before replying. "You said you wanted to travel," she said. "Do you not want to go places and see things when you have time away from fighting?"

"There is not enough time to do that in just a few short days."

"But you think about it?"

He was halfway finished with his soup, now dipping bread into it and taking big bites. "Mayhap a wee bit," he said. "But the time for travel is not now. The time now is for work. It sounds strange, but when I was first released from Culroy, I felt...lost. Lost until the Ludus Antonine gave me a sense of belonging. It gives me a sense of security, of purpose. This is my home. My friends and I were speaking about it today—we *are* a clan. We are brothers, if not in blood, in spirit. It is the time now tae be with them."

She understood what he was saying, in theory. "I envy you,"

she said. "I do not belong to anyone or anything, which is why I immediately started working here. I need that sense of purpose, too. I want to feel as if I belong, at least for the time I am here. That reminds me... Have you asked around to see if anyone wants to learn to read and write?"

He sopped up the last of his soup with the bread. "Not yet," he said. "But I will."

"Thank you," she said, smiling. He was almost done with his food so she jumped up, taking his bowl away. "Let me bring you more."

He waved her off. "Not now," he said. "I am going tae sleep a few hours before the bouts tonight. I'll eat a little when I awaken."

She nodded, setting the bowl aside so she could rinse it out. Magnus was finishing off the last of his watered ale when he noticed the bowl with flowers in it. Then he noticed the crippled bumblebee. Setting his cup down, he peered into the bowl.

"What's this?" he asked.

Diantha went over to him, standing next to him as he took the bowl from the ledge. "That is my new friend," she said proudly. "He is missing a wing and cannot fly. I put him in the bowl so he would not be eaten by birds."

As Magnus watched, she put her hand into the bowl and the bumblebee climbed into her palm, scooting around. Magnus leaned over, watching the bee as he moved around.

"And he doesna sting ye?" he asked, incredulous.

She grinned. "Nay," she said. "I think he likes being in my hand. It is warm and comforting. I think he likes me."

Magnus watched as she crouched down next to the table, holding the little bee in her hand and speaking softly to it. In truth, his gaze was on her and not the bee. He'd never seen anything so sweet and lovely and nurturing, pure in every sense of the word. He'd never known a woman like Diantha, and more and more he was becoming enchanted by everything about her.

The rescue of a bee seemed like something small and insignificant, but in truth it was not insignificant at all. It reflected a compassionate nature that he had never seen before, someone with so great a heart and soul that even a little bee meant something to her.

For a moment, he just sat there and stared at her. He couldn't seem to do anything else. Then he gently grasped her chin, leaned over, and kissed her tenderly on the cheek.

It was a thanks for showing him something he'd never seen before.

Beauty in its finest form.

"I think he does, too," he whispered.

Without another word, he headed into the smaller chamber to sleep, shutting the door behind him.

It took Diantha a solid hour to catch her breath.

Chapter Thirteen

The fights that night had been full of dust and sweat and blood.

In the fading heat of the August night, the torches of the Fields of Mars were ablaze and the arena seats packed with patrons. It was so crowded that people were sitting in the aisles. The purses were big this night because it was Theme Night, meaning the warriors had selected a favored country or favored legendary hero, and they were fighting on behalf of that country or hero.

Clegg de Lave had returned to his *primus* venue, and he walked the arena floor before the fights began like a conquering caesar. He was swathed in white robes and had a turban on his head in the style that Diantha had seen in her youth when caravans would cross from the Mediterranean coast on their way to Portugal. Clegg lifted his hands benevolently, and the crowd cheered wildly for the man who made this entire way of life possible.

Diantha didn't see much of Clegg because he quickly retreated into his private box above the staging area where he could watch the fights unimpeded. The bouts soon began, and she discovered that there were a good deal of Englishmen in the lists this night. When a young warrior by the name of Warenne de Soulant, fighting for English honor, won his first bout against a *novicius* Scotsman, the English patrons erupted in victory, which turned into a brawl with the Scots patrons.

That happened three times.

Seated over on the left-hand side of the arena with the rest of the warriors' women, Isabail and Lucia and Diantha laughed at the fighting going on. It was sheer ridiculousness. Isabail was feeling much better after having rested all day, and at one point, she ran over to the fighting and clobbered some hapless Englishman on the head. It was all great fun to her, this former warrior woman, and she returned to her friends quite happy and satisfied at having gotten in a lick in a fight.

But her joy was short-lived.

Lor had been in the lists, breaking up the fights with some of the other *doctores* and sentries who kept order at the Ludus Caledonia, and he saw his wife get in a good belt. When the crowd had settled down, he came over to her, giving her a look that suggested she was in a good deal of trouble, and pulled her out of her seat.

At the top of the lists, he scolded her, shook a finger at her, and she took it until she finally threw her arms around his neck and kissed him passionately. Lucia and Diantha were watching all of it, giggling when Isabail kissed him. It had the desired effect because Lor cooled down, returning to the arena floor as his wife returned triumphantly to her seat.

She'd won the battle.

The later bouts were between the more advanced warriors, including two new ones that had been brought in by Clegg. One man was big and pale, with flaming-red hair, and went by the name of the Celtic Storm. He fought a man who was about half his size, and it was an excellent fight, but in the end the Celtic Storm triumphed.

The second new warrior was a little more interesting. He was tall and sinewy, with well-defined muscles and dark skin that was glorious and glistening. He went by the name the North Star and he battled against a seasoned warrior known as the Beast from the East.

It was the most exciting match yet.

It went on for a very long time, until both men were so exhausted they could barely fight any longer. The crowd, who had been screaming for the duration of the match, became abruptly silent when the North Star and the Beast from the East got into a wrestling match that saw the Beast from the East get the upper hand by flipping his opponent onto his face. The North Star was slowly suffocating in the dirt until the field marshals broke up the fight and declared the Beast from the East the victor.

But barely.

In all, it had been an exciting night of excellent matches. Lucia had paid for warmed wine when the vendor came around, and the women drank their spicy wine, discussing the matches with glee. The wine made them giggly and they were genuinely enjoying themselves.

Especially Diantha.

Three days ago, if someone had told her that her life would change so much in just a matter of days, she would never have believed them. She was truly happy for the first time in her life, with women who had already become her friends, and she was fast becoming enamored with a man who, until two days ago, had been just a faded speck in her memory.

Now, she could think of nothing else.

It was the kiss that had done it.

She could still feel it on her cheek, sweet and delicious. He had been so gentle about it that she found it difficult to believe that the same man who could fight so viciously was capable of such tenderness.

He had kissed her and then he'd gone to sleep. But when he awoke, she was still in the cottage, sitting by the hearth mending one of his torn tunics with some thread Lucia had given her. He'd smiled at her, she'd smiled in return, and he'd quit the cottage without speaking a word.

But he didn't need to.

There was something in the air.

Therefore, Diantha was quite excited to see him fight on this night, and she was learning quickly that Magnus only fought the later, more important rounds. As the wind that had been blowing through the complex all day picked up and clouds began to blow in from the east, covering the moon, Magnus's bout was announced.

It would be the Eagle against the Celtic Storm.

The crowd went mad.

The Celtic Storm was the first one out onto the arena floor, lifting his arms and bellowing at the crowd, who managed to cheer for him in a mediocre manner. But the moment Magnus came out, the crowd was on its feet, screaming as if Jesus Christ had just made an appearance. There was hooting and yelling going on, but down in the first row of the lists, there was something else happening.

A solid row of exquisitely dressed women, waving perfumed kerchiefs.

Diantha hadn't noticed them last night, but from her vantage point tonight in a different seat, she could see them clearly. Already, the women were throwing things onto the arena floor where two young men rushed out to collect everything. Seated next to Isabail, she craned her neck to see all of those lovely, well-dressed women.

"Who are they?" she asked, pointing. "Wives?"

Isabail wasn't sure who she meant. "Who?"

"Those women," Diantha said. "They are throwing things onto the field. Are they wives of patrons?"

Isabail realized who she was indicating. But she found herself reluctant to tell Diantha that they were the brigade of women who had come to seek Magnus's favor.

"Those are wealthy women who like tae come and watch the bouts," she said carefully. "They are throwing money onto the field tae indicate their esteem for the fighters. Like a reward."

Or an enticement. But she didn't say so. She watched Diantha accept the explanation with no trouble.

"Oh," Diantha said, not sensing anything out of the ordinary. "Do the women come often?"

"Every night there is fighting."

"Are their husbands here?"

"Probably not."

That was as far as Diantha's questions went and Isabail was grateful. She'd spent enough time around the woman to realize she was fond of Magnus, and she didn't want to tell her the truth—that all of those women were there *because* of Magnus. They were hoping to spend time with him after his bout, licking the sweat from his body or doing any number of things to him.

That's what Magnus was known for.

Isabail caught a look from Lucia, who shook her head faintly as if thankful Diantha wasn't pushing the point. Sometimes, Magnus actually went to those in the front row and kissed a hand or two, or turned around so they could see his impossibly muscular buttocks, which he would happily flex for them.

On a night like this, he was virtually nude but for the chainmail briefs around his pelvis. The rest of him—that magnificent chest and those powerful arms—were glistening with sweat in the warmth of the evening.

And every woman in the front row was filled with lust.

Thankfully, Diantha was oblivious. Her gaze was on Magnus as he remained on the opposite side of the arena floor, away from the women who were trying so desperately to get his attention. He was fussing with his gloves again, but once those were finally secure, he lifted a hand to the crowd and their screams resumed in earnest.

But he was looking in Diantha's direction.

At least, she thought he was. She stood up on her seat and waved an arm at him, and far down below, he waved back. It was brief, but that was enough. He acknowledged her and Diantha was fairly aglow.

Then the match started.

The crowd had decided that it was much better to stand while

Magnus was fighting, so everyone was on their feet. Diantha couldn't really see anything unless she stood on her seat, so she stood on the stone bench and watched Magnus stalk a man who was taller and broader than he was.

It was like watching a cat toy with a mouse.

The Celtic Storm didn't stop smiling through the entire match. He watched Magnus as the man stalked him, and soon enough, he was yelling at him, daring him to charge him. Magnus grinned and waved at him. For a while, it almost seemed like two friends toying with each other. They were laughing at one another, challenging one another, until the Celtic Storm got tired of waiting and rushed Magnus, swinging his *gladius* in a fairly precise manner.

But Magnus was fast. He darted out of the way at the last moment, causing the Celtic Storm to lose his balance with his momentum. Magnus came up behind him with the intention of using a finishing move, but the Celtic Storm whirled on him. Magnus was forced to bring up his shield, the only weapon he used in most of his bouts, to block a strike from the Celtic Storm.

But he had some of his own momentum going and he managed to spin out of the way of another strike, coming up behind the Celtic Storm once again. His strategy was clear—to get in behind the man so he couldn't take a full swing at him—but the Celtic Storm seemed to know that. He managed to reach around and grab hold of Magnus's shield, yanking on it, and Magnus was abruptly in front of him.

But that would do the Celtic Storm no good. Magnus still had hold of his shield and used it like a battering ram, throwing his weight into it and knocking the Celtic Storm backwards and onto the ground. Or at least down to one knee. As the Celtic Storm tried to rise, Magnus went airborne and kicked him in the side of the head.

He went out as quickly as if someone had blown out a candle. And with that, the match was over.

The crowd went mad, screaming Magnus's name. Money rained down and servants dashed out onto the field again, collecting every little coin as Magnus lifted his hands to the crowd.

The roar was deafening.

"Come on!" Lucia said. "It is finished for tonight. Let us leave before this crowd disbands."

She and Isabail were already on their feet, running up the steps that led to the exits, but Diantha was slower. She was moving, but her gaze was on Magnus down on the arena floor.

She couldn't seem to move away from the sight.

After he acknowledged the crowd and even looked in her direction, or so she thought, he bent over the Celtic Storm, who was starting to stir. A couple of trainers had come out onto the arena floor and were helping the big redhead come around as Magnus put his hand on the man's head, seemingly trying to bring him around as well.

Lucia and Isabail were up at the top of the steps, beckoning Diantha to hurry, and she began to move faster when she saw Magnus help his dazed opponent to his feet.

She thought that was a sweet gesture.

The crowds were moving swiftly to cash in on their bets and Diantha was caught up in the flow, but she found Lucia and Isabail at the top of the arena.

"Where do the men go when they come off the arena floor?" she asked.

Lucia pointed toward the north. "There is an area next tae the arena," she said. "They call it the staging area."

"Can you see the men?"

"Aye," Lucia said. "There is a fence. It is where people will go tae inspect the combatants for the night before making their wagers. Or you can see them when they are finished for the night."

"Will they be gathered there now? The fighters, I mean."

Lucia nodded. "Probably," she said. "Why?"

Diantha grinned. "Because I want to see Magnus," she said. "The only time I ever see him is when he is fighting, but I would like to see him after his fight. He was magnificent, don't you think?"

Isabail had been listening. Given that all of the women who had come to the Ludus Caledonia to see Magnus would also be over at the staging area, she didn't think it was a good idea for Diantha to go over there.

"It will be very crowded," she said. "Ye probably willna be able tae see him. Let's go back tae the cottages and wait for the men there."

But Diantha was caught up in the thrill of victory. "I just want to see," she said. "If it is too crowded, I'll go back to the cottage. But I would like to see where the men go after a fight. It all seems so exciting."

Isabail was shaking her head but she didn't want to say anything more, concerned that Diantha would get suspicious and she would end up explaining something she didn't think it was her place to explain. What Magnus did with women was his own business, but Diantha...she had such a pure view of the man.

She thought he was a hero.

Isabail was afraid that view was about to be tarnished.

"It will be very crowded," she said again, weakly, as they were jostled by the crowd around them. "I think it would be better if..."

Diantha flashed her a grin. "I will not be long, I promise," she said. "I just want to see, just this once."

Before they could stop her, she was off. Isabail and Lucia watched her go.

"What do we do?" Lucia hissed.

Isabail grunted unhappily. "We'd better follow her," she said. "At the very least, we can divert her attention from the women who have come tae shower Magnus with money and gifts."

Lucia rolled her eyes and dashed off, pursuing Diantha as the woman headed toward the staging area. Isabail quickly followed.

Oblivious to her friends' concern, Diantha was nearing an area at the end of the arena where there was a big iron fence. She could see people milling around it but as she drew closer, she began to see all of those well-dressed women who had been in the front row of the lists. She could already smell the perfume.

Curious, she pushed her way through the crowd until she came to the iron fence, which was poised on an overlook with the staging area down below. Looking down, she could see several men milling about, some having fought that night. She didn't see Magnus, but her vantage point wasn't very good.

She could, however, see an iron staircase leading from the staging area up to a gate next to the iron fence that was guarded by a pair of sentries. As she watched, one of the gladiators came up the steps and through the gates, and the women surged in his direction. They were pawing at him, slipping him coins, and he seemed more than willing to go along with them.

That's when Diantha realized who the women were.

What they were.

And that's when she started paying attention to the chatter.

"Where is the Eagle?" one woman cried. "We want the Eagle!"

Other women chimed in, demanding the Eagle. Diantha knew that meant Magnus, and she was baffled about these women demanding Magnus. Certainly, he was gorgeous to look at, but it never occurred to her that they might be here for him. Magnus wasn't that kind of man…

Was he?

As Diantha stood there, increasingly confused at what she was hearing, a woman a few feet away was speaking loudly to her friends.

"They say he never takes the same woman twice," she said. "I was fortunate enough tae have the Eagle last month and the man turned my legs tae water. I couldna walk for hours afterward."

She and her friends tittered lewdly. "I've not had him yet!" one whined. "I've heard he has a manhood as big as a rutting stallion. I've heard he can go all night and all day and never rest!"

Her friend, who was seemingly a Magnus expert, nodded emphatically. "I just bent over, spread my legs, and let him do the rest." She giggled. "It was like mating with a bull."

"I wish he would choose me tonight!"

"Nay, *me*!"

They were arguing about it now as Diantha stood there, stunned with what she was hearing. She looked around, listening to other conversations, and realizing that every woman here was speaking of the Eagle. They had their money out, in some instances their coin purses held high, badgering the sentries at the gate and demanding the Eagle.

Her Eagle...

Diantha was starting to feel sick.

"What are they speaking of?" she asked, turning to Lucia and Isabail. "Are they... Does he actually take money from them?"

Isabail and Lucia were looking at her in various stages of grief. Neither wanted to answer, yet she was asking a direct question. It was Isabail who finally spoke.

"Magnus is very popular," she said. "He has no woman, no wife. He is very handsome. Surely such a man is not expected to remain...celibate."

Her words were like a blow to Diantha's gut. She couldn't breathe. But nothing Isabail had said was shocking or untrue.

Surely such a man is not expected to remain celibate.

It occurred to her why, exactly, these women were here.

"Then he takes money from these women in exchange for... companionship," she said quietly.

Isabail looked at Lucia, who gazed back at her fearfully. "Diantha, it isna as simple as that," Isabail said, wondering how on earth she was going to explain this. "The Ludus Caledonia is modeled after the gladiator schools of Rome, and in ancient times, wealthy women paid well tae have the company of the finest gladiators. Many of the other warriors here do it, too, but they all have free will. They are not forced intae anything. Sometimes they do it for no money at all, but sometimes...they do."

"And Magnus does."

"Ye'll have tae ask him, sweetheart. If it matters tae ye, ask him."

Diantha was looking at her as if Isabail had just ripped all of her guts out and left them on the ground. There was anguish in her expression that was difficult to describe. Nay, she didn't have to ask Magnus anything.

She already knew.

Before she could reply, a great cry abruptly went up from the crowd and they turned to see Magnus coming up the iron steps toward the gate. Women began screaming, throwing money and articles of clothing at him, calling his name.

Eagle!

Eagle!

Diantha was rooted to the spot, unable to move as he came to the gate and the sentries opened it. Suddenly, he was being rushed by women who were throwing their arms around his neck, pressing their lips against him, and he was slammed back against the gate as the females attacked.

Diantha's last vision of him was with a redhead's mouth affixed to his.

That's all she needed to see.

Blinded by tears, she turned away and was immediately swallowed up by the crowd.

"Diantha!" Isabail cried. "Diantha, *wait!*"

She started to run after her, but there were too many people blocking her path. Being pregnant gave her pause when she thought about pushing through the crowd. She didn't want to injure herself or her baby. Beside her, Lucia grasped at her.

"Nay, Issie," she said. "Tell Magnus. If he wants tae go after her, let him. I fear we may only do more damage."

Isabail was miserable. "I couldna lie tae her," she said. "She asked me a question and I had tae answer."

Lucia nodded. "I know," she said. "'Tis not yer fault. But Magnus…damnation, this is *his* fault."

Over by the gate, Magnus had managed to disengage the women who were grabbing at him, including the one who had laid a big fat kiss right on his lips. He pushed through them, but it was difficult. Everyone was grabbing at him, trying to hand him money. One woman even ripped her bodice, exposing her breasts to him. But he didn't look; the only thing he saw was Isabail, waving her long arms at him.

"Where is Diantha?" he asked, prying some woman's hand out of his hair. "I saw her heading in this direction. Where is she?"

He was trying to get away from a mob of women who just wouldn't let him go, and Isabail and Lucia ran to his aid. They began slapping hands away and shoving women aside, pulling Magnus free of his adoring throng. Wisely, they pulled him into the crowd of men who were waiting for their payoffs, blocking the women who were following.

"She knows, Magnus," Isabail said as she dragged Magnus through the crowd. "She wanted tae see ye as ye came out of the staging area, but she saw all of those women waiting for ye and she heard some speaking about sharing yer bed."

They were nearly through the crowd at that point, but Magnus came to a halt. He had an expression on his face that Isabail had never seen before, something between horror and dismay. The supremely confident and arrogant warrior wasn't at all himself.

The arrogance was gone.

"She…" he began, stopped, and started again. "She heard them speaking of me?"

Both Isabail and Lucia nodded. "It wasna very nice what they said," Isabail said. "They said ye were a rutting bull in bed, hung like a stallion. She heard it all."

Magnus stared at her, the impact of those words hitting hard. At any other time, he would have been proud to know how women spoke of him, but now...

Now, he wasn't so proud.

It certainly wasn't anything he wanted Diantha to hear.

He started to look around frantically. "Where did she go?"

"She ran off," Lucia said. She put her hand on him, forcing him to look at her. "Magnus, I've spent the past two days with Diantha, and I believe the lass feels something for ye. She looks at ye as some kind of hero, a savior, and it never occurred tae her that ye have all the failings of a mortal man. I'm not judging ye for what ye do with yer life because it's *yer* life, but Diantha dinna know ye had that side tae ye. I believe she thought ye tae be perfect and chaste, and when she heard those women, she was hurt. She ran off in tears."

"Christ," he hissed, closing his eyes briefly. "I must find her. I must explain."

"Explain *what*?" Isabail wanted to know. "Magnus, dunna just explain tae her. Be *honest* with her. If ye want tae keep on with the parades of women in yer bed, then ye need tae tell her so she doesna build a world around the fantasy of ye being a pure and perfect man. At least let the lass know about ye. At least then ye'll have been honest with her so there are no misunderstandings."

She was right.

Magnus knew that Isabail was absolutely right. Perhaps he should have done it from the start, but it had never occurred to him. He'd never thought a simple act of helping a frightened woman would turn into something else, a feeling that was more than he could comprehend. It wasn't Diantha's business what he did with his life. But coming to understand her as he had in just the short time they'd known each other, he didn't want her to think poorly of him.

Something else Lucia had said had his attention.

The lass feels something for ye.

Those were the most important words he'd ever heard.

"Do ye really think so?" he asked Lucia. "About her feeling something for me. Do ye really think so?"

Lucia nodded. "I do," she said. "She's such a sweet lass, Magnus. Realizing that part of ye tonight… It broke her heart. She thought ye were someone that ye weren't."

He groaned, feeling sick. "I never thought that…" He stopped when he saw the expressions on Lucia and Isabail's faces, and he knew this wasn't the time for excuses or regrets. It was a time for action. "It doesna matter what I thought. I must find her. I'll deal with the rest later."

He was off, leaving them behind as he bolted through the warriors' village and back to his cottage, praying that Diantha was there. He didn't know what he was going to say to her, but he knew one thing—he had to be completely honest with her. Somehow, someway, her kindness and compassion had done something to him. There was a transition going on inside of him, something that was shifting from selfishness to selflessness.

For once, he was thinking about someone else.

For once, he was caring about someone else.

He had to tell her so.

His cottage was ahead and he bashed into the door, slamming it open, only to find it empty. He ran back into the smaller chamber, so neatly made up by Diantha, and that was empty, too.

She wasn't in the cottage.

Trying not to feel panic, Magnus looked around, noting that Lady Ayr's fanciful dress was still there, hung up on a peg by the door. The hearth was gently snapping and the cottage was neat and orderly. Untouched. Even the bumblebee in his bowl was sleeping on his flower petals, undisturbed.

She hadn't come here when she'd run off.

But she was out there, somewhere.

And he was going to find her.

He started to run out but realized he was still dressed in his mail loincloth and shoes. The wind was picking up outside and the clouds were starting to gather, sure signs of a summer storm, and among his other fears, he was concerned that Diantha would get caught in it.

Quickly, he stripped out of his clothing and donned leather breeches and a tunic, the first clothing he could find. Yanking on his boots, he rushed out into the predawn morning.

As it turned out, Lucia and Isabail had alerted their husbands, and Magnus found himself with several of his friends willing to help him search. As the patrons still filtered out of the Ludus Caledonia, the warriors who had fought all night went on the hunt for a lovely Spanish lass who mattered to Magnus very much.

By the time the sun rose, a storm had rolled in and the rain was pounding.

But Diantha was still missing.

CHAPTER FOURTEEN

THE RAIN WAS POUNDING.

In the brown broadcloth dress that Lucia had loaned her, Diantha was soaking wet as she headed into Edinburgh along the same road she had traveled to reach the Ludus Caledonia.

She was in mud up to her ankles and cold, but none of that mattered.

Nothing mattered any longer.

Her goal was simple—she was going to make her way to the docks north of Edinburgh and see if she could get work on a ship heading for France or Navarre. There were docks in Leith, she remembered Lady Ayr mentioning, so that was her destination. She was going to go home, back where she belonged, and forget about brutal Scottish dukes and beautiful gladiators who let every woman in Scotland sample that beauty.

She was going to forget about Magnus.

If she could.

It was just after dawn. Diantha had been walking perhaps two or three hours at the most since leaving with the droves of carriages and horses departing the Ludus Caledonia after the games were over.

It had been easy to lose herself in the crowd, filtering out into the night, before finally leaping onto the back of a carriage as it puttered down the road. She been able to ride a little way until the coachman caught her and made her get off, and she had been forced to resume her walk.

The rain had come heavily just before sunrise and she'd ducked into St. Eustace's Church for a few minutes, just to get out of the rain, before heading back out into the weather. She probably could have remained longer at the church, but she wanted to put as much distance as possible between her and the Ludus Caledonia.

She wanted to forget she'd ever known the place.

The road into Edinburgh was the same one she'd traveled before, so she ended up walking off the road, near the trees, so she could hide if needed. The trees also provided a little protection from the rain, and at one point, she found a branch on the ground that was thick with needles. Picking it up, she used it to shield herself from the weather.

But she was still very cold and very wet.

As the sun began to rise, Diantha started to sneeze, knowing she'd caught a chill but trying to ignore it. Her throat was starting to feel scratchy, but she ignored that, too, unwilling to surrender to any illness. She had to make it into town and find shelter, perhaps in another church. Surely a church would let her dry out and wait for the storm to pass. Her stomach was also rumbling a bit, but she couldn't address that at the moment.

One problem at a time.

The mud was thicker as she walked nearer to the trees because of the drainage, so she was forced back onto the road. The rain was starting to lighten up and the clouds were parting in spots, emitting bright sunlight onto the wet, green earth.

She dared to turn around once and saw the green hills behind her, the hills that concealed the Ludus Caledonia. But seeing those hills brought tears at what she'd left behind, a life she'd been so happy with. She was already grieving the loss.

But there was no use in looking back.

She passed another church, a small one, and decided to stop because her body was crying out for rest. Her scratchy throat was growing worse, as was her sneezing, so she thought it might be best to stop for a while. Perhaps she could regain her strength a little if she were only to rest. Given that she hadn't slept all night, her exhaustion was compounded.

The church was small and dark, but the door was open and she entered timidly, looking for a quiet corner. It was dank and cold inside, but it was better than nothing at all. She went straight to a corner near the door and sat down, leaning against the cold stone, just to close her eyes briefly.

Sleep claimed her before she realized it.

⟁ ⟁ ⟁

She wasn't at the Ludus Caledonia.

After two hours of searching, Magnus had come to that conclusion. There had been a lot of people at the Ludus Caledonia last night when Diantha had run off, so he could only imagine she had either lost herself in the crowd or found someone who could offer her a ride. If she had walked out, there was still a chance of locating her, but if she'd gotten into a carriage with someone, there was no telling where she'd gone.

Magnus was trying very hard not to panic.

Lor, Bane, Galan, Tay, and even Aurelius Finn, the big Irishman that Magnus had beaten in his bout last night, were helping him search. Clegg was aware of the situation and had given permission for Axel and Wendell and Milo to help in the search as well. They were all looking for the woman in whom Magnus placed a good deal of stock, asking no questions but simply offering their help because it meant so much to him.

But two hours later, Diantha de Mora hadn't turned up.

The search area would have to expand.

There were training sessions to take place that morning, so Axel and Wendell went to work with those men while the rest of the *doctores* helped Magnus. By sunrise, they were all on horseback, horses from Clegg's collection of fine animals, and they set off to hunt for the lady in the surrounding area.

Before they split up, however, each man had a direction and a goal. Magnus and Lor were heading directly into Edinburgh along the main road while Bane took the eastern road. Tay and Galan headed west, toward Dalkeith, while Milo and Aurelius would search the hills surrounding the Ludus Caledonia. There were a lot of trees a lady could lose herself in.

Unfortunately, Lor was delayed in departing because Isabail wanted to go with him. She felt responsible for Diantha's departure and very much wanted to help, but in her condition, stress and possibly long hours on a horse wouldn't be good for her, so Magnus took off while Lor tried to convince his wife to rest and wait. No one, not even Magnus, could seem to convince Isabail that the situation wasn't her fault.

The last Magnus saw of Isabail, she was weeping in Lor's arms.

Magnus was riding a magnificent dappled stallion named Tempest, who had been a gift to Clegg from a Portuguese duke who had spent three solid months attending games at the Ludus Caledonia. Tempest was young and excitable, but massive and sturdy, endless in his energy. Magnus took the horse down the road from the Ludus Caledonia, through the trees, and onto the main road that ran along the base of the hills.

His only plan at that point was to retrace Diantha's original path to the Ludus Caledonia from Edinburgh, ending at the apothecary shop where they'd first met. He was hoping that she had gone back to that shop because she was familiar with it, so that was his destination.

It was his one and only hope.

But first, he intended to check every church, tavern, and inn along the way, hoping she might have gone inside one of them for shelter from the rain. The weather had been warm and dry until last night when the summer storm rolled through, and it had turned the dusty roads into a soupy mess in places. Magnus could see carriage tracks and footprints along the road, but there was no way of knowing if any of those footprints belonged to Diantha.

The first church he came to was St. Eustace at the crossroads in Morningside. The church was dotted with worshippers at lauds, or the morning prayers, and he walked through to see if any of the faithful were Diantha. He didn't see her, and the priests, in the middle of the mass, refused to answer his questions.

Frustrated, he continued northward. The storm had mostly blown away at this point, although there were pockets of rain now and again. A short time later, he could see another church, small and nearly hidden in some trees. He pulled the horse to a halt just outside the door, leaving the beast to chew on the wet green grass as he made his way inside.

It was dark and smelled of rot. The floor leaned and the pillars that held up the roof looked as if they were barely strong enough. There were a few people up near the altar and he made his way up there to speak with them, but they seemed to be fearful of his presence. He managed to corner an acolyte, who denied seeing anyone who looked like Diantha. The priests tried to chase Magnus away until he told them that he was looking for a woman.

Then they pointed to the door. He thought they were pointing *at* the door, demanding he leave, until he saw what they were indicating.

A figure slumped into a corner.

Magnus's heart leapt into his throat as he rushed over to see that it was, in fact, Diantha. She was damp and dirty, slumped against the stone wall and sleeping like the dead. As he watched, she coughed and sputtered, but she didn't wake up.

Magnus had never been so glad to see anyone in his entire life. In fact, he could feel the unfamiliar tug of tears, something completely foreign to him but indicative of the emotion he felt.

For her.

Kneeling down, he reached out and gently shook her.

"Diantha?" he whispered. "Diantha, wake up."

She grunted and her eyes lolled open, but she shut them again.

As she was drifting back off to sleep, he shook her once more and her eyes rolled open again, but she was staring at the wall. Magnus's hand was on her knee and he patted it gently.

"Diantha? Look at me, sweetheart."

She blinked. Then, slowly, her eyes moved in his direction until she was focused on him. For a moment, she simply stared at him.

"Magnus?" she asked weakly.

He smiled. "Aye. 'Tis me."

She didn't say anything for a moment. "Am I dreaming?"

"Nay. 'Tis me."

By her expression, she was becoming a little more lucid when she realized that he wasn't a dream. Sitting up, she jerked her leg back, away from his touch.

"Go away," she hissed. "*Regresa a tus putas. No quiero verte de nuevo.*"

She was quickly growing furious and cagey, but he remained calm. "I dunna know what ye just said, but I can guess," he said. "Diantha, ye must let me explain."

He tried to touch her knee again, but she batted his hand away. "I told you to go back to your women because I do not want to see you again," she said. She sounded raspy and weak. "I want you to leave me alone. I was stupid to have gone to the Ludus Caledonia for your help."

"Why?"

"Because you are not who I thought you were. You...you are not an honorable man!"

He could see her lower lip trembling as she spoke, and he remembered what Lucia had said to him.

The lass feels something for ye.

Truth be told, he felt something for her, too.

He wasn't going anywhere.

Shifting, he sank onto his buttocks, watching her recoil from him. He could see the anguish in her eyes, anguish he had put there when she discovered the unsavory truth about some of his activities. Magnus knew he would only have one chance to change her mind about him.

He never wanted anything more in his life.

"Will ye at least give me a moment of yer time tae explain?" he asked. "All I ask is one moment. If ye still want me tae go after that, I'll go. Please?"

She turned away from him, looking back to the wall. She sniffled, then she coughed, and the tears began to come.

"You need not explain," she said hoarsely. "You do not owe me anything, Magnus. I am only a woman who came to you for help. How you have lived your life is none of my affair, so you owe me nothing. But I cannot be a party to what you do. I will find my own way home to Navarre, without your help, so you can return to the Cal and resume your life. I am sorry to have troubled you."

He watched her closely as she spoke. "Ye dinna trouble me," he said. "It was no trouble at all. But I made a promise tae ye and I intend tae keep it."

"What promise?"

"Tae help ye earn money."

She closed her eyes, covering her mouth when she coughed. "You need not concern yourself," she said. "I will make it on my own."

She was being stubborn. He understood stubborn people because he was one of them. Under normal circumstances and with anyone else, he would have walked away. In fact, he wouldn't have even made the effort to go after her. But this was the woman who had forced him away from his selfishness. In just a few days, she had done more for him, and showed him more, than anyone else had in his lifetime. He wasn't so arrogant and stuck in his ways that he didn't see that.

She was the key to a door on the future he could never have imagined.

He couldn't walk away.

"I know ye can make it on yer own," he said quietly. "There is no doubt in my mind that ye can do anything ye set out tae do. I've never met anyone like ye, Diantha. Ye have a strength in ye that is beyond anything I've ever seen in a woman. I knew the moment ye came tae me that I was unworthy of ye."

She kept her face turned to the wall, but he could see a single tear trickling down her cheek. It tugged at his heart, strangling him, because he wanted very much to comfort her. But he couldn't.

They had to get a few things straight first.

"I'm sorry I'm not who ye thought I was," he said. "But I've lived my life with no regrets. I've worked hard tae achieve a great deal in the face of adversity. Ye must remember that I'm a man who belonged tae no one, a duke's bastard who was used as a pawn and then tossed aside when I no longer served a purpose. I have no one to answer tae other than myself. Do ye understand that?"

Another tear trickled from her eye but she didn't reply. He continued.

"The Ludus Caledonia saved my life," he said. "I willna apologize for the life I've lived there, but I will explain it tae ye so ye understand. Every coin I earn is in defiance of a father who never gave me anything. Every cheer from the crowd is praise telling me that I mean something tae someone, and every woman I take tae my bed has been the assurance I've needed tae believe that I'm worthy. Mayhap that is wrong of me, or dishonorable, but it's the truth. I've done what I needed tae do for myself. I'm the most selfish bastard ye'll ever meet, and I'm not ashamed of it."

By this time, Diantha's eyes were open and she was looking at him. "I suppose if you are going to be something, then you might as well be proud of whatever it is you are," she said. "As I said, you needn't explain anything to me. I simply do not want to be a part of it."

He shook his head, his eyes glimmering at her in the weak light.

"Not ye," he said. "Ye're too good for the likes of me and every-thing about me. Do ye not understand? Ye're an earl's daughter, an honorable and beautiful woman the likes of which I never thought would even speak tae me. I'm so unworthy of ye, Diantha, but since I met ye, I've come tae see a kind, compassionate, and sweet woman I'd give the world tae be with. I've never felt that way before about anyone. I always thought I knew what I wanted and it dinna include a woman in my life. But ye...ye've made me reconsider that."

Diantha stared at him a moment before looking away. The tremble in her lower lip was growing worse.

"You're a beautiful, intelligent, and vibrant man, Magnus," she said hoarsely. "You're the most beautiful man I've ever seen. I will admit that I thought you could do no wrong. You were kind and generous with me, and I put you on an altar like something to be worshipped because you were my savior. You saved me from a horrible life at Culroy. I wanted you to be perfect, but it was my mistake for expecting you to be flawless."

"It's hard when those ye think well of fall from their perch," he murmured. "I dinna mean tae fall, Diantha, but I canna change what I've done in the past. Men have pasts and women do, too. I'm not as perfect as I want people tae believe. I know I have my faults. But I suppose that is difficult for ye tae understand because ye have no faults at all. Ye *are* perfect."

Diantha looked at him a moment, eons of untold longing in her eyes. There was much she wanted to say and couldn't. After a moment, she simply looked away.

"Please go," she whispered, closing her eyes. "There is nothing more to say, Magnus."

He wasn't moving. "If ye wish it, I will, but I must ask ye a ques-tion first," he said. "Will ye answer truthfully?"

She stiffened. "I will not lie if that is what you are suggesting."

He shook his head. "That's not what I'm suggesting," he said. "I simply want a truthful answer."

"Then ask."

"Do ye feel something for me?"

Her eyes opened but she didn't look at him. For the longest time, she simply stared at the wall, unblinking.

"Why do you ask?" she finally said.

He could hear the pain in her voice. "Because if ye dinna, ye wouldna be so upset about this. About me. Please, Diantha…tell me what ye feel."

She turned to him once more, her face a mask of confusion, of defiance, and of surrender. She sighed heavily but ended up coughing, covering her mouth with her hand.

"I was proud to be your friend," she said. "I was proud to tend your home. I was proud of *you*."

"Proud enough tae love me?"

She blinked and her eyes filled with a lake of tears. She looked away once more. "I will not love a man who has let every woman in Edinburgh taste him."

"Could ye love a man who swears ye'll be the only woman for him from this moment on, for as long as he lives?"

Her head jerked to him, her eyes wide. She was looking for any hint of jest in his expression, any suggestion that he was simply telling her what she wanted to hear so he could have his way in all things. But she didn't see that at all. Magnus's expression was open, honest…

Vulnerable.

"You asked me how I feel," she whispered. "Don't you even know?"

His hand, which he'd kept away from her since she recoiled, lifted. He held it out to her. "Nay," he said. "I can only guess. Will ye please tell me the truth?"

Diantha looked at his hand, tears filling her eyes and rolling down her cheeks. He wanted to feel her flesh in his, but she wasn't going to give in.

Not yet.

"I…I adore you," she whispered. "But I adore someone who does not exist."

"How do ye know unless ye let me try?"

She sniffled, wiping at her cheeks. "I do not expect you to change for me, Magnus. I do not want us both to be disappointed."

He was still holding his hand out, still begging her to take it. "Ye must let me try," he murmured. "Diantha, ye make me want tae be a better man. Will ye not even let me try?"

She was still wiping her cheeks. "You haven't yet told me how you feel."

"Isna my presence here proof of that?"

He had a point, but she wasn't going to accept it. She wanted to hear it from his own lips. "You made me tell you how I feel," she said. "Tell me or I will not go with you."

Magnus kept his hand up, outstretched to her, but he was struggling with his reply. He finally grinned, embarrassed.

"I've never had tae tell anyone what I feel," he said. "No one ever cared enough tae ask."

"I'm asking."

He pondered his answer for a moment. "I told ye that ye make me want tae be a better man," he said. "Ye're kind and compassionate and genuine. Ye willna take what ye havena earned. Ye're as beautiful as a new sunrise. Ye're a woman of unusual strength and I told ye that I'm unworthy of ye, but I want tae be. I've never had a woman whose respect I so badly wanted. What do I feel? I dunna know yet, but I know I dunna want tae be without ye. Whatever I'm feeling, I want it tae grow. I want tae be the man ye thought I was because I want tae make ye happy. Does that tell ye enough or must I go on?"

He had explained himself well enough without really giving her a direct answer. But for Diantha, it was enough to ease her wounded heart. She wanted so badly to believe him because he seemed truly repentant. But she knew it would probably be diffi-cult for him to change his ways.

From what she'd heard, she wasn't entirely sure he could commit to one woman.

Still...she couldn't refuse him because whatever she was feel-ing for him seemed to demand forgiveness. The feelings were pre-cious and fragile, but oh so glorious.

She couldn't cast them off so easily.

"I hope I am not making a mistake," she said after a moment.

A hopeful smile came to his lips. "I swear I'll try my hardest so ye never regret it."

Diantha thought about that. Then she sighed faintly and lifted her hand, putting it into his palm. He lifted it to his lips, kissing it sweetly. It was a kiss of hope, of implied promises for the future.

Never had a kiss meant more.

"Let me take ye home," he whispered.

Stiff, sore, sick, and achy, Diantha shifted from her seated posi-tion as he held her hand and helped her rise. Once she was on her feet, she put both hands on his face, forcing him to look at her.

For a moment, they simply stared at each other. Magnus didn't try to touch her or hold her because this was her moment. She was drinking him in, deciding if he was worth the risk. After a moment, her dark eyes glimmered, just a little.

"You are still the most beautiful man I have ever seen," she murmured.

He smiled faintly. "I'll make ye a promise, Diantha," he said. "I canna erase the past, but I can make a promise for the future. From this day forward, ye'll be the only woman for me, Diantha Marabella Silva y de Mora. I swear that tae ye on my honor as a warrior of the Ludus Caledonia."

A weary smile spread over her lips. "Hearing you say my name like a Highlander makes me think that you mean it."

"Did I say it right?"

She laughed softly. "Beautifully," she said. Then she was forced to quickly lower her head and sneeze. "I fear I have caused you much trouble, Magnus. I hope you think I am worth it."

It was his turn to put his hands on her face, forcing her to look at him. He studied her big soulful eyes, her red nose, her lush and dreamy lips. His gaze drifted over everything about her, the fine lines, the contours.

"Strange," he said. "I can honestly say that I've seen many women, but I never really *looked* at them. What I mean is that I've never looked into their eyes. I've never stopped long enough to care about anything other than myself, but now...I *see* ye, Diantha. Ye're the only woman I've ever really looked at."

Diantha was quickly forgetting her hurt, even though she was trying to keep some measure of self-protection up. But with Magnus, it was so easy to let it all go because she believed him.

She *wanted* to believe him.

"What do you see when you look at me?" she whispered.

A light came to his eyes. "Everything I want tae be."

With that, his mouth slanted over hers. She tried to pull away, given that she was sniffling and ill, but his big arms went around her and she was lost. Magnus kissed her fully, deeply, tasting everything about her in a way he'd never tasted anyone before. It was an awakening for him, acquainting himself with a woman who, in two days, had taught him everything he wasn't and everything he wanted to be.

He wanted to discover more about her.

He wanted to discover everything about himself *through* her.

They had the rest of their lives to do that.

"Come along," he murmured against her lips, finally releasing her. "Let me take ye home."

Diantha was so overwhelmed by his kiss that she stumbled as he tried to lead her away. Magnus quickly realized that she was cold and stiff, and he let her go long enough to remove the cloaks he was wearing, both of them, and put them around her, fastening them tightly.

It was his first lesson in thinking of someone other than himself.

He'd learned it by nearly losing something more precious than he could possibly comprehend.

PART THREE

Et a Tribus Militibus

(A Clan of Warriors)

Chapter Fifteen

THE DAY WAS BRIGHT, BUT NOT FOR LONG. THE STORMS OF autumn were beginning to show themselves, and the Cal had experienced two major rainstorms in as many weeks. The shutters to the cottage were open but Diantha kept a close watch on the sky, prepared to close the shutters against the rain at any moment.

Magnus was at the Fields of Mars, training with his fellow fighters, while Diantha was making curtains for the windows with oiled canvas she'd obtained from a woman who came to the Ludus Caledonia now and again, selling her wares.

Diantha had paid for it with her own money. She'd earned quite a bit of it teaching reading and writing to a few of the more advanced and worldly warriors. Her two prize pupils were Tay and Aurelius, although Aurelius had been somewhat of a challenge. He was very bright but very stubborn, and when he didn't understand a lesson, he would often throw something or kick something purely out of rage.

The first time Aurelius threw a tantrum, Diantha had been shocked. The second time, she had ordered him away and not to come back until he could behave himself. Somehow, Magnus had caught wind of the tantrum and he nearly came to blows with Aurelius, his old friend, until Diantha stopped it and scolded them both.

Aurelius never had a tantrum again after that.

But it didn't stop him from kicking the table leg now and then.

In fact, she was expecting Aurelius when the training at the arena was over, so she was hurrying to finish at least one of the curtains she intended to hang. With the weather expected to grow worse, she wanted the curtains up to help keep the drafts and weather out of the small cottage.

The little cottage itself had transformed under her careful hand, with hides on the floor, two very comfortable chairs in front of the hearth, and a second, smaller bed where her pallet used to be, surrounded by a canvas curtain that hung from the ceiling.

She may share Magnus's cottage, but she still didn't share his bed.

In fact, he hadn't even tried to coerce her into it. He'd been a perfect gentleman since she'd tried to run away, seemingly content to go at whatever pace she was comfortable with when it came to their budding relationship. He did kiss her, though, and kiss her often, and there were times when she could feel his stiff manhood through his breeches, but he never said a word about tending to it.

After his bouts, he still received all of the hero worship he always had, with the exception of selecting a woman to spend time with. He collected all the money thrown at him and flexed his sweaty muscles for screaming admirers, but he ducked out of the arena on the south side where no one was waiting for him.

Except Diantha.

She was always waiting for him.

And she tended to him sweetly and gently, something he'd never had in his entire life. As Diantha sat next to the open window with her sewing in her hands, she smiled as she thought of their latest escapade, the Battle of the Beds. Magnus would take the smaller bed if he had the opportunity to, forcing her to take the larger one, and vice versa. He was trying to be chivalrous, but she wasn't the one fighting nightly, so she wanted him to have the more comfortable bed.

They argued about it constantly.

It was all part of coming to know each other better, of learning to work together, and of understanding the attraction that grew stronger by the day. Magnus had lost none of his arrogance, but somewhere in the midst of it all, he had softened his edges. His arrogance didn't carry over too much with Diantha, whom he'd grown a heart for. Everyone could see it, especially Diantha. He was everything she knew he could be.

He'd told her once that she made him want to be a better man. Now, he was proving it.

Over in a big bowl, her little bumblebee was starting to stir. He was still alive, her wingless friend, and he had an elaborate living space for a bee with fresh flowers and honey water to drink. He still crawled on her hand and sometimes slept on her, and there was no one more fascinated with the bee than young Nikki. In fact, he called Diantha "Bee," something that stuck to the point that everyone, including Magnus, called her Bee.

Sweet Bee, as Magnus would say.

More clouds began to roll in from the east, distracting Diantha from her bee because she very much wanted to get the oiled canvas finished, so she picked up her sewing pace. She was nearing the end of the last seam when there was a knock on her door. Before she could answer, Isabail came in with Nikki in tow.

"Here," she said, laying out a set of curtains identical to the ones that Diantha had been working on. "I finished these and none too soon. Looks as if the rains are on their way."

Diantha nodded, glancing at Isabail's handiwork as Nikki went straight for the bee bowl.

"Bee!" he cried happily.

Diantha smiled at the little boy, who was extremely careful with the bee, even at his young age. With the child occupied, Diantha stood up to show Isabail her curtains.

"These should do nicely," she said. "Thank you for your help with them. I couldn't have finished them all on my own."

Isabail wasn't the greatest seamstress, but she got the job done. "We'll loop hemp rope through the seams at the top and the bottom so ye can open and close them," she said. "Can ye mind Nikki? I'll go hunt for the rope."

Diantha was happy to watch the boy. "Of course," she said. "He can help me watch the bee."

With her son occupied, Isabail slipped out. No sooner did she leave, however, than there was a knock at the door. Diantha opened it to Aurelius. Enormous and muscular, he had skin as white as cream, pale-blue eyes, and big, straight teeth. He smiled timidly.

"*Buenos días, Señorita Abeja,*" he said. *Good day, Lady Bee.*

Diantha was teaching him Spanish. Spoken in his heavy Celtic accent, it sounded funny to the ear, but he was trying very hard to learn. She smiled politely at him.

"*Buenos días,*" she said. "*Cómo estás hoy?*"

His smile vanished and he stared at her, trying hard to think of the answer. Then his eyes widened and his grin returned.

"*Bueno,*" he said.

Diantha laughed softly. "Excellent, Aurelius," she said. "Come in. Nikki is visiting today."

Aurelius came into the cottage, filling it up with his bulk. He sat down on one of the chairs at the table, next to where Nikki was standing. The little boy pointed out the bee and flowers to Aurelius, who pretended to be interested. As that was going on, Diantha stood over by the hearth.

"Let us see how much you remember from last week's lesson, Aurelius," she said. "Did you write the words like I showed you?"

Aurelius nodded. "Aye, Lady Bee," he said. "I wrote them twenty times in the dirt."

"Good," she said. "Now, what's this?"

She was pointing to the fire in the hearth. Aurelius's brow furrowed as he thought on the question. "*Fuego,*" he said.

"Very good. And this?"

She was pointing to the stone wall. He continued to look thoughtful. "*La pared,*" he said.

Diantha praised him. She went through about ten more everyday household items, and he remembered all of them. Pleased, she moved back over to the table where she had some sentences written down on vellum, but his last word question was for the bee in the bowl.

"*La abeja*," he said.

"Abeja!" Nikki echoed.

Diantha laughed at the toddler, who was just learning to speak English. "Excellent, Nikki," she said. "Now I have two students."

Aurelius was perfectly happy sharing his lesson with Nikki, who was surprisingly attentive for a toddler. He ended up sitting on Aurelius's lap, listening to Diantha's lesson as she taught Aurelius small sentences related to household or everyday phrases, his favorite being *Me gustaría agua.*

I would like water.

The lesson went on for about a half hour before Magnus returned, and Nikki jumped off Aurelius's lap to run to Magnus, who greeted the child fondly. He didn't pick him up or hug him, but simply put a big hand on the boy's head and asked him about his visit with the bee. Magnus wasn't hugely fond of children, mostly because he'd never been around them, but he was learning, little by little. Nikki seemed to have a great affection for him, and Magnus genuinely liked the child.

Magnus's return, however, signaled the end of the lesson, and Aurelius paid Diantha two silver coins in exchange for his homework, which was writing phrases in the dirt that she had written down on a piece of vellum. No kicking or anger this time, which was progress where he was concerned. When he was gone and Nikki ran back over to the bee in the bowl, Magnus took Diantha in his arms.

Freely and fully, he did that these days. He embraced her long and sweetly whenever he saw her, holding her against him and savoring the feel of her soft body against his. Sometimes, he just stood there and held her, inhaling her scent, feeling her heartbeat through her clothing. Her heart thumped so hard sometimes that he could feel it mingling with his own.

"Did that big Irishman throw anything today?" he asked.

He felt her giggle. "Not today," she said. "He was well-behaved."

"Good," he said, releasing her so he could look her in the face. "And ye? What have ye done since I left ye this morning?"

She pointed to the table with its curtains and little boy. "Sewing," she said. "And Nikki and I have been watching the bee."

He wasn't much interested in the sewing or the bee. He was looking at her face. "Can I kiss ye in front of the lad?"

"You know what happened when you did that the last time."

"He cried."

"Do not feel too bad. Isabail says he cries when Lor kisses her, too."

Thwarted by a temperamental child, Magnus let her go and went to sit at the table as Diantha went to the hearth to prepare his meal. She always had it waiting for him. Whenever he came back from training, he would eat, nap, and then go to the Fields of Mars for the evening's fights. On the evenings when he wasn't fighting, they would sit before the fire and talk of any number of things.

Over the past two weeks, their lives had changed so much.

But it was a wonderful change for them both. Diantha put a bowl of boiled beef in front of him with a second bowl that contained honeyed carrots. Half a loaf of bread ended up next to him, and Nikki became interested in the food.

Diantha gave the child his own little bowl and Magnus put carrots and soft pieces of bread in it, which Nikki happily devoured. He was just making his move for Magnus's beef when there was another knock on the door and Isabail entered without being invited. When she saw Magnus, she gasped.

"I am sorry, Magnus," she said. "I dinna know ye were in here."

Magnus grunted. "Take yer glutton of a child out of here," he said. "He wants all of my food."

Fighting off a grin, Isabail went to collect her child, who wasn't too happy at being taken away from Magnus and the beef. He whimpered as she took him out, and they could hear his crying as it faded away.

"Poor Nikki," Diantha said, bringing her own bowl of beef over to the table. "He only wanted to eat with you."

Magnus scowled. "He wants everything I have."

She laughed softly. "You are doing very well at sharing with him."

"If I dunna, he'll scream and ye'll probably berate me, so I have no choice."

He made a good stab at being disgruntled, but he didn't really mean it. Diantha continued to smile as she dug into her meal. "How was training today?" she asked.

He shrugged. "The same," he said. "Clegg has a special visitor from Provence, a warlord who is said to be the richest in all the land. He wanted tae watch us train, but I have a feeling he is here tae make an offer for one of us."

She slowed her chewing. "He wants to buy one of you?"

Magnus nodded. "He will buy out the remainder of our contract with Clegg," he said. "Ye know that when a man comes tae fight for the Cal, he promises tae give it seven years of his life. In two years, my contract will be finished, and I'll be free tae do as I wish."

Diantha stopped chewing entirely. "And if this warlord offers to buy out those last two years, does that mean you will go to Provence?"

Magnus shook his head. "I'll not go," he said. "We have the choice of accepting an offer or not, and I'll decline. I've declined eleven offers since I've been at the Cal. I like it better here than in some warlord's army."

Diantha had to admit that she breathed a little sigh of relief. "I am sure they offer a lot of money for you. You are worth every pence."

He shoveled beef into his mouth. "Of course they do," he said. "They always do. More money than most people see in a lifetime, but I still willna accept it. I think Clegg would rather have me here, so he doesna push me. Too many people come tae see me fight and he doesna want tae lose that income."

Diantha resumed her meal with gusto, confident that Magnus wasn't about to end up somewhere in Provence.

"Do you see yourself remaining here for the foreseeable future, then?" she asked.

He sopped up beef juice with his bread. "For a while, anyway," he said. "The Cal has made me very wealthy from the purses I've won and the women who've paid tae—"

He suddenly froze, remembering who he was talking to. He looked at her, his expression full of remorse.

"I'm sorry," he said. "I dinna meant tae—"

She cut him off, though not harshly. "Do not worry so," she said. "You told me that part of your life is over and I believe you. But I acknowledge that it *was* part of your life. It cannot be undone."

It was his turn to heave a sigh of relief as he reached out and grasped her hand, squeezing it. "I will be honest," he said. "The money is the only thing I miss. The rest of it…it had become habit. Sometimes, it's difficult tae break a habit. But it is surprising how much I canna stand tae look at another woman when I know ye're waiting for me. Ye're the only woman I want tae see."

She smiled, watching him kiss her hand over the tabletop. "I see them at the gates near the staging area, still waiting for you," she said. "I've also seen you flex your muscles for your adoring throng so they'll throw more money at you."

He bit his lip to keep from smiling guiltily. "Does it distress ye? If it does, I willna do it anymore."

She laughed, mostly because he looked so guilty. "As long as you do not touch them and they do not touch you, I am unconcerned," she said. "Besides…they have good taste. They may want you, but I *have* you."

He snorted. "A very wise attitude," he said. "The money is for us, after all."

She cocked her head. "Us?"

He nodded, returning to the last of his food. "Money tae pay for passage back tae Navarre," he said. "Money tae travel the world. Money for a home for ye. For us."

The smile was back on her lips. "A home for *us*?" she repeated. "Magnus, are you proposing marriage to me?"

"I dinna say marriage, ye greedy woman. I said a home."

She was trying hard not to laugh. "So you intend to buy a home for us but not marry me? I am not entirely sure I like that."

He wouldn't look at her. "Ye live with me here and we're not married."

"Do you ever want me to share your bed?"

He shrugged. "Mayhap. I havena decided."

He was teasing her. She ripped her hand from his grip. "Is that so?" she gasped, though she was mostly jesting. "You conceited whelp! I'll go find another man to tend house for if this is your attitude."

He started laughing. "I'll kill any man ye try tae charm," he said. "Ye'd better stay with me. Only I know how tae handle ye."

"You think so, do you?"

He finally looked up from his food, a grin tugging at his lips. "Of course I'll marry ye if ye're going tae cry about it," he said. "Is that what ye want tae hear?"

She shook her head slowly. "Magnus, you are as romantic as a bellyache," she said with disapproval. "Ask me nicely and I may agree."

"Ye'll agree any way I ask ye."

"*Eso crees, querido?*"

The only word he recognized was *querido*, a sweet term she'd been calling him for the past few days. It meant "darling" or "sweetheart" in Spanish. But he didn't recognize anything else, and his lips pressed into a flat line.

"If we're going tae argue, have the decency tae do it in English."

She began to laugh. "You are far too confident. A man with humility is appealing."

"A man with humility doesna get the prettiest lass in all the world," he said. "I've got ye and I intend tae keep ye, Bee."

Diantha didn't have the energy or the desire to keep up her act of indignation. When he started flattering her, she caved easily.

"Very well," she said. "If it will make you happy, I will marry you."

"If it'll make *ye* happy, I'll marry ye."

"When?"

He set his spoon down. Standing up, he went to her and pulled her up from her seat. Wrapping his big arms around her, he kissed her deeply, his tongue licking her lips and tasting the watered ale on them. His hands moved down her body until they came to her buttocks, which he clutched through her garment. She gasped when he pulled her pelvis against his and she could feel a hint of arousal.

"The sooner the better," he murmured. "I dunna know how much longer I can hold out. 'Tis torture sleeping in a bed, knowing ye're in the next room and I canna lie down beside ye. Not for the act of it...but because I just want tae hold ye and never let ye go."

Diantha wrapped her arms around his neck, squeezing tightly, her supple body pressed against his.

"I never imagined I would want that, too, but I do," she murmured. "I love you, Magnus. I cannot remember when I have not loved you."

He stopped fondling her. After a moment, he pulled back to look at her, his eyes glimmering with bewilderment and joy.

"Why?" he finally managed to say. "I feel as if I've done nothing tae earn it."

She reached up, gently cupping his face. "But you have," she said. "You *are* who I thought you were, or at least you are trying very hard to be. I never have seen anyone work harder, but at the same time, you have been effortless. It has not seemed like work at all. I have always known the sensitive, compassionate man that is inside you. He exists, no matter how hard you pretend otherwise."

Magnus grinned, embarrassed. "He's only there for ye."

"I know."

"Do ye want tae know something?"

"What is it?"

"I love ye, too."

She giggled. He laughed. It was the first time he'd said it outright to her. Suddenly, she was in his arms and he was spinning her around until they were both dizzy and giggly. It was delirium, it was joy. It was everything they hoped it would be and more.

It was everything.

Eventually, he settled down, long enough for her to direct him back into the bigger bed so that he could sleep for a couple of hours before he had to go to the arena. She pushed him down onto the bed, but he grabbed her and she ended up falling atop him.

As Diantha struggled to push him away and get up, Magnus's mouth found the flesh of her neck and shoulder, suckling her skin, tasting her.

"Nay, *querido*," Diantha said, weakly trying to get away from him. "You must sleep."

He had her in his arms, in bed, and he wasn't going to let her go. "I will," he murmured against her flesh. "In a moment."

Diantha knew this wasn't a good idea. The more they discovered each other, the more they kissed, the more they wanted in a physical sense. Diantha was a maiden, but even she felt fire stirring in her loins when he gently kissed her neck and shoulder. Everything about the man set her on fire in ways she didn't fully understand, but she knew she would, one day.

She had to admit that she was looking forward to it.

As he peeled back her dress, exposing her right shoulder and much of her right breast, she tried to give him one last shove, but she ended up losing her balance and falling off to the side. Magnus was on her in a flash, his mouth on her. One arm was pulling her closer while the other edged the top of her dress down lower.

"Magnus, please," Diantha whispered. "If you do not let me go, you will never get to sleep."

Her words said one thing, but her body said another. Her hands were on him, clutching him, and she wasn't resisting him in the least. He lifted his head to look at her.

"Do ye want me tae let ye go?" he purred.

"Well…"

"'Tis not a difficult question. Ye do or ye dunna."

Before she could answer, he slanted his lips over hers, kissing her lustily. His arms went around her, pulling her tightly against him, drowning her in a passion she'd never before known. It was on the tip of her tongue to be firm and demand he release her. But gazing up into that beautiful masculine face, she couldn't bring herself to do it.

She lusted after him as badly as he lusted after her.

Magnus knew he was lost the moment she latched on to him with her soft mouth. He lost himself in her honeyed lips, his hands entangled in her hair. He was more forceful in his kisses than ever before because, for the first time, he felt as if she had no restraint. *He* had no restraint. She was giving him permission to touch her, and touch her he would.

The broadcloth dress she was wearing came off as his eager hands stripped her. Somehow, his lips never left her mouth, and before Diantha realized it, her dress was off and so was her shift. They lay in a pile next to the bed. Magnus lavished kisses upon her mouth, her face, as he removed his own clothing.

Suddenly, they were both naked.

Magnus's big body came down on Diantha's soft, slender one, enveloping her in power and heat. His mouth left her lips, feasting on her neck as he moved down her body. He tasted every inch of skin on her shoulders and arms before depositing lusty kisses on the swell of her bosom. A big hand kneaded her breasts as his lips finally found her nipples, moving from one to the other hungrily.

Beneath him, Diantha squirmed and gasped.

His weight on her was significant and she instinctively parted her thighs. His lower body slipped through, finding rest upon the mattress as his upper body covered her torso. She was delicious and nubile in every way, and as one hand slipped beneath her to grasp her tender buttocks, the other slipped down her flat belly as his mouth began to move along her abdomen.

Magnus knew what he was doing and Diantha let him.

In truth, she was in a haze of delight. She was only thinking of how deeply she loved him. They were to be married, were they not? Already, she belonged to him, body and soul. All she could feel was her love for him and a primal need she was trying to understand. It was flesh against flesh, and Magnus wasn't shy about sharing his experience with her, but he also had some restraint.

Not much, but enough.

But surely it was going to kill him.

He was engorged and instinct demanded he plunge his body into Diantha's virginal one, but he resisted. He'd never had anything pure in his entire life until he met her and somehow it just didn't seem right to take that innocence now. He wanted their first time together to be as man and wife, not because he was so lustfully hot for her that he couldn't control himself.

Even so…he wanted her to enjoy every minute of what he was doing.

He wanted her to long for what was to come.

They were both nude, and although he'd made no attempt to touch her below the waist, his hand began to move, lower and lower, until he was at the fluff of dark curls between her legs. He touched her ever so gently, feeling her jump at the unfamiliar newness of his touch but very much wanting her to become accustomed to it.

To crave it.

He began to stroke her, just a little, just enough to acquaint her with his touch, but she was so new to this and so highly aroused that within just a few strokes, she was convulsing beneath him with her first climax. Of course, that fed the fever in his blood and it took the greatest of effort not to satisfy himself, too. He was in a painful situation, but he simply didn't want this to be about him. It had always been about him and he always had plenty of women to do anything he wanted them to do to satisfy him, but not now.

Not with Diantha.

At this moment, he just wanted to touch her.

As Diantha's tremors of passion died away, he gathered her up in his arms and tried not to think about the massive erection between them. He tried to think about that old woman his friends tried to trick him with in Clegg's chambers those weeks ago, anything to drive down his heated blood, but he found that he couldn't. He didn't want anything to take away from this moment with Diantha.

"I love ye, Bee," he whispered. "Until the end of all things, I'll love ye."

Dazed from her first sexual experience, Diantha felt his words as they reached into her, grasping her heart and holding fast. For a woman who had never really known the warmth of a human touch, or the love of anyone other than her long-ago father, she felt as if she were living in a dream, something surreal and glorious. She found herself praying she would never awaken from a dream where only Magnus existed.

"And I love you," she whispered, kissing his chin. "Sleep now. I will be here when you awaken."

With a delighted grin, Magnus pulled her closer, her naked

body up against his, and closed his eyes. He was snoring softly before Diantha could draw another breath.

As a storm rolled in from the east and a gentle rain began to fall, they stayed as they were—warm and safe and cherished—all afternoon.

CHAPTER SIXTEEN

"WHEN WERE YE LAST HERE, DA?"

The question came from Conan as he and Ambrose rode in the duke's fine carriage into the heavily guarded Ludus Caledonia. Rain was falling gently, and in the distance, lightning was carving through the sky. But the weather hadn't kept away those who lived for and loved these games.

The Ludus Caledonia was packed, as usual.

"It has been years," Ambrose said, keeping a sharp eye out for anyone he recognized, Magnus especially. "I came here with yer uncle. The man likes tae gamble."

Conan was keeping an eye out, too. The complex of the Ludus Caledonia was truly something to behold in scope and architecture. The massive walls of Caelian Hill were off to his right as the crowd was funneled down into an area that was between a vast village of cottages and the arena known as the Fields of Mars. As the rain fell gently, the Ludus Caledonia was just getting started.

"I canna remember seeing so many people outside of a village," Conan said. "With this place hidden in the hills, it's an astonishing sight."

Ambrose nodded, but he wasn't interested in idle chatter. Thunder rolled overhead as his carriage came to a halt. He'd brought six men-at-arms with him, men who were assigned with guarding his carriage and possessions, and he left those men settling the horses and taking the carriage off of the main road while he and Conan disembarked.

Ambrose had a destination in mind.

"I must find someone who serves here and knows the games," he said. "I have…questions."

Conan nodded. He was of the same mindset. The two of them set off, walking up to an area that contained food vendors and wager tables meant for the exchange of money. It was already busy and heavy with soldiers protecting the money flow. There was a man standing in front of the wager tables, directing traffic, and Ambrose walked up to him.

"Do ye serve here?" he asked.

The worker, dressed in a tunic the same scarlet color of the banners that flew over Caelian Hill, nodded. "Aye, m'laird."

"I have a question about who will be fighting tonight."

The man pointed to another table that had a canvas wall behind it. It was canvas stretched over a frame of wood, and the bouts for the night were written upon it. Ambrose and Conan rushed over to the schedule, which looked like a family tree. The fights were listed by number to make it easier to place a bet. They both peered up at it, but what they saw made no sense.

"The Beast from the East and the Celtic Storm?" Ambrose said, puzzled. "The Flaming Sword against the Glasgow Bull? Where are the *names*?"

"Those are the names, m'laird," a man standing near the table answered. He was also dressed in the scarlet tunic of the Ludus Caledonia. "Were ye looking for someone in particular tae wager on?"

Ambrose scratched his head. "I havena been here in many years, so I've forgotten how things are done," he said. "Do we not know the names of the fighters?"

The man nodded. "They are not secret if that is what ye mean," he said. "But our patrons would rather bet on the Glasgow Bull than a man simply named John. It's better if they have a more exciting name."

Ambrose looked up at the schedule again. "Who is the fighter named Magnus Stewart?"

"Ah," the man said, pointing to the bottom of the schedule. "He is a *tertiarius*, our top fighter. They call him the Eagle."

"*Magnus?*" Conan blurted out. He couldn't help it. "*He* is yer top fighter?"

The man smiled confidently. "When ye see him fight, ye will understand," he said. "He is a guaranteed victory if ye want tae bet on a sure thing."

Conan's mouth was hanging open. He looked at his father, who seemed just as surprised. That sullen, short, and petulant young lad they'd tormented all those years had evidently made something of himself. Conan was perhaps the least bit intimidated at that point but unwilling to admit it. He'd always been able to lick Magnus, but current evidence was pointing to a change in that usual outcome.

He was beginning to wonder what they would find at the end of this trail.

Ambrose, too, was increasingly curious. The Ludus Caledonia was well known to have the best fighters in the world, so the fact that Magnus had made it to the top was quite astonishing. Like Conan, he was the least bit wary of what they would find when they finally came face-to-face with Magnus.

He clearly wasn't the youth who had left them seven years ago.

"Is there somewhere we can see the warriors before they fight?" he turned to ask the man in the scarlet tunic.

The man pointed over to the east, where the arena was. "Do ye see the fence next tae the arena?" he asked. "The big iron fence that runs between the top of the arena and the building next tae it. See it?"

Ambrose was straining to see, but he did indeed see a big iron fence with pikes at the top of it. "Aye, I see it."

"Ye can view them from there," the man said. "The fence overlooks a staging area used by the warriors before they go out onto the arena floor. But ye mightna see Magnus there. He's usually inside before his bouts. He'll go there afterward, though."

That was the information Ambrose was seeking. But there was one thing more.

"The man who owns the Ludus Caledonia," he said. "I've forgotten his name."

"Sir Clegg de Lave."

"Of course," Ambrose said, pretending to be forgetful. "How foolish of me. I'd like tae speak with the man. Can ye direct me tae him?"

The man continued to point over toward the fence. "His private viewing chambers are over by the fence," he said. "Tell the guards. They can tell ye if he's receiving audiences tonight."

Ambrose shook his head. "Ye dunna understand," he said. "My name is Ambrose Stewart. I am the Duke of Ayr and Magnus is my cousin. I wish tae see Sir Clegg. Find someone who will take me tae him."

The last few words were icy, a demand couched by a polite request. The man in the scarlet tunic realized the seriousness of the situation and the request. Very quickly, he was moving.

"Come with me, m'laird," he said. "I'll take ye tae him. Come!"

Ambrose looked at his son, giving him a knowing expression before following the man in the scarlet tunic. Conan followed close behind, still marveling at the crowds, at the bustling complex that was the Ludus Caledonia. It was difficult to believe that Magnus had thrived at this place.

Soon enough, they were going to find out just how much he had thrived.

And what his price was.

With any luck, Magnus would once again belong to the House of Ayr.

☘ ☘ ☘

In the staging area below, there was a chamber carved into the hillside where warriors could gather outside of the range of the curious crowd. It was a cold and dank chamber, not particularly comfortable because Clegg never liked his warriors to be too relaxed before a fight.

He always wanted them edgy and ready to move.

Magnus was sitting on a stone bench, fixing one of the leather straps on his gloves. He was sitting with Tay and the African fighter known as the North Star. Samuel Gondar was his real name, a tall, lanky, and silent man who mostly kept to himself, but he seemed to like Magnus. At least, as far as Magnus could tell. He'd never really spoken to him, but he seemed to gravitate in his direction.

Galan was also there, as he was going to fight a bout on this night. As far as *doctores* went, Galan was relatively new, having been a seasoned warrior until his promotion to trainer. From time to time, he was given permission to fight. Tonight, he'd be fighting against a new warrior who had arrived with his liege only today, a man all the way from Athens who went by the name of Poseidon's Wrath.

"I hear you are battling the winner of my bout tonight," Galan said as he sat down next to Magnus to retie his shoes. "Careful, Chicken. We might be scratching each other's eyes out at the end of the night."

Magnus grinned. "The Eagle will always win over the Sapphire Dragon," he said, referring to the persona Galan went by when he was fighting. "I'll be there tae wipe yer tears when it is all over, so dunna let Whale Dung get too close tae ye."

Galan burst out laughing. "Whale Dung?" he repeated. "I think the man's name is Poseidon's Wrath."

Magnus turned his nose up at that. "Like I said…Whale Dung," he said. He eyed Galan. "I saw the man earlier today as he trained. He's got a mighty right fist and he uses it frequently, so watch yerself."

"'Tis true." Aurelius came over to stand with them, fussing with a piece of forearm protection. "I saw him train, too. He's big and nasty and old. How did the man get tae be so old living this kind of life?"

"Mayhap he's immortal," Magnus said. He stopped fussing with his glove and looked at Aurelius. "But I'll tell ye now that I intend tae live tae a very old age, but I dunna intend tae be a warrior my whole life."

Galan frowned. "You?" he said, standing up. "You are the best there is, Magnus. For you to be anything less would be a waste of material."

Magnus eyed Galan as the man headed over to the rack containing helms. Galan usually wore one, and a particular one at that, and Magnus watched him as he plucked his favorite helm.

"We canna be warriors all our lives," he said. "Is that all ye wish for yerself, Galan? Tae fight yerself right intae the grave?"

Galan plopped the helm on his head, moving it around to adjust it. It was the type of helm that went down over both cheeks and the bridge of his nose, leaving his eyes and mouth clear.

"Nay," he said. "I'll return home at some point to the Welsh Marches and serve my eldest brother when he inherits my father's lands, but I will return a rich man. As the third son, I have had to earn my own money. I shall be richer than my brothers, both of them."

Magnus knew something about making his own way. But since it was his style not to open up about his personal life or past, he didn't commiserate with Galan. He simply returned his focus to his glove, or at least he pretended to, but he kept an eye on Galan as the man fussed with his helm.

"Return while ye're still young," Magnus said. "Find a good woman and have many good English sons."

Something wasn't right with Galan's helm and he pulled it off to inspect it. When he pulled it off, however, it was clear that someone had sabotaged it. Wherever the helm had touched him, his cheeks, forehead, and the bridge of his nose, it was black. His dark hair was also plastered in black, but not realizing this, he rubbed at his chin and ended up smearing it everywhere.

Magnus started to laugh. Tay and Aurelius caught sight of Galan and they, too, started to laugh. Over in the corner of the chamber where Lor and Bane were reviewing last-minute strategies with a few *novicius* who would fight this night, they heard the laughing and turned to see Galan covered in soot.

The trickster had struck again.

Galan had no idea why everyone was looking at him and laughing until he looked at his hands. They were covered in ash. He growled angrily.

"Chicken," he boomed. "This is *your* doing!"

He had rubbed the soot over his face so much that his brightest features were his eyes, blazing among the ashes. Axel picked that moment to enter the chamber, having come from Clegg's private viewing box above, and he shook his head reproachfully when he saw Galan smeared with soot. The tricksters were at it again. But Galan was so angry that it was hilarious, so he fought off a smile.

"Clean yourself up, de Lara," he said. As Galan rolled his eyes at the obvious, Axel sought out Magnus. "Eagle, Clegg wishes to see you."

Magnus was still laughing at Galan, still fussing with his glove, but he stood up and headed in Axel's direction.

"What's afoot?" he asked him.

Axel simply threw a thumb in the direction of the staircase that led up to Clegg's chambers.

Magnus made his way up the stone steps, still chuckling at Galan, still lighthearted from the day in general. It had been a day of days and his mood was better than it had been in a very long time. In fact, he couldn't remember ever being so happy. Diantha had agreed to marry him, he'd managed to put one over on Galan, and for the first time in his life, he was looking forward to the future.

There was everything to be happy about.

Little did he know that all of that was about to change drastically.

CHAPTER SEVENTEEN

"Come in, Magnus."

Clegg was standing on the balcony that overlooked both the staging area and the arena floor beyond. He had a straight line-of-sight view to everything, even now as the rain fell and those working in the arena struggled to keep the hundreds of torches lit for the coming events.

Magnus had come up the stairs that dumped into the rear of the room, a private staircase meant only for the warriors when Clegg summoned them. They were never allowed to come through the front entrance, or at least rarely. Magnus had often been an exception to that rule.

Clegg turned to the warrior as he entered.

"Magnus," he greeted.

"M'laird," Magnus returned. "It is going tae be a sloppy night if this rain keeps up."

Clegg nodded, glancing to the gently falling rain once more. "We've had nights like this before, haven't we?" he said. "I can remember seeing you covered from head to toe in brown muck many a time. All of this slippery mud makes for interesting bouts."

Magnus grinned. "Messy ones, anyway," he said. "Axel said ye wanted tae speak with me?"

Clegg nodded. "I do, indeed," he said. "Sit down a moment. I just had an interesting conversation about you."

Magnus sat down. "About me?" he said. "Who with?"

"The Duke of Ayr."

All of the joy and happiness Magnus had been feeling died at that very moment. In fact, he could feel himself stiffening, from the bottom of his feet all the way up to the top of his head. He bolted to his feet and didn't even realize he'd done it.

"Ayr?" he hissed. "*Here?*"

Clegg nodded. In fact, he was watching Magnus's reaction very closely. "I take it from the tone of your voice that this does not please you."

Magnus was ready to explode right through the roof. "Not in any way," he said, struggling to control his shock and his temper. "He is here? Tonight?"

Clegg nodded again, more slowly this time. "Magnus," he said after a moment, "I know little of your background before you came to the Ludus Antonine. I know that Axel found you fighting in the streets of Glasgow but little else. A man's background doesn't matter to me, but the duke tells me you are the son of the king's youngest brother, Hugh."

Magnus was starting to tremble. "I am his bastard."

"I see," Clegg said. "You are a man of royal blood. I should have known."

Magnus was beginning to twitch. "It hasna been a blessing if that's what ye mean."

Clegg wasn't sure what he meant, but Magnus's reaction was interesting. The duke had also made it seem that Magnus was his beloved, long-lost nephew, and clearly Magnus didn't feel that way. The man looked like he did when he was in a fight for his life in the arena—edgy, coiled, ready to strike. But there was something more, something Clegg had never seen from him before.

There was hatred there.

Clegg lifted a hand to him.

"Magnus, please sit," he said quietly. "Tell me about yourself and of your relation to Ambrose Stewart. His son is here, also, by the way."

Magnus stopped twitching and his eyes widened. "Conan?"

"Aye."

That had Magnus bolting for the door. Clegg called out to him, but Magnus was running, running from the front door and through the arriving crowds. A cry went up when some people realized the Eagle was in their midst, but he was running so fast that he was through the crowds before they could work up a good cheer.

He was heading for the warriors' village.

His legs were pumping, and his chest felt as if it were ready to explode as he ran at top speed. He sailed through the warriors' village and to his cottage on the rise. He crashed into the door, slamming it back on its hinges.

"Bee!" he bellowed. "Diantha!"

The cottage was empty.

Panic consumed him. Magnus spilled out of his cottage, preparing to run back to the lists and find Diantha sitting there among the crowd, but voices coming from Lor's cottage caught his attention. He rushed over to the cottage, pounding on the door. Quickly, it was yanked open and Isabail was standing there.

"Magnus!" she gasped. "What in the world is—?"

Magnus caught sight of Diantha standing behind Isabail, and he nearly bowled the woman over in his haste to get to Diantha.

"Shut the door," he hissed at Isabail.

The door slammed and Magnus threw his arms around Diantha, never more relieved in his entire life. In fact, realizing she was safe and sound brought tears to his eyes. He actually thought he was going to start weeping. He stood there for a moment, holding her, reassuring himself that she was well.

In his embrace, Diantha could feel him trembling.

"Magnus?" she said, deeply concerned. "What is the matter? What has happened?"

He wasn't ready to let her go yet so he stood there a moment longer, squeezing the breath from her, before answering.

"Thank God," he said, sounding exhausted and strained. "Bee, ye must promise not tae panic. Please. I need yer calm head. Can ye do this?"

Diantha finally pulled away from him, greatly puzzled. "Do *what*?" she said. "Magnus, what *is* the matter?"

Magnus sighed heavily, trying to regain his composure. "Ambrose is here," he said. "So is Conan. They have been tae see Clegg. They know I am here."

As he watched, Diantha's eyes widened so much that they were surely about to pop from her skull. "The duke?" she gasped "And...and Conan?"

He nodded. "I dunna know what they want yet, but I will find out," he said. "I wanted tae make sure ye were safe first and tell ye not tae go tae the arena tonight. Stay in the cottage, lock the shutters, and bolt the door. Dunna open it for anyone but me. Do ye understand?"

Diantha nodded. She didn't panic and she didn't cry out, but her hands were at her mouth in shock and as Magnus watched, tears filled her eyes and spilled over. She collapsed against him, weeping fearfully, and he hugged her tightly.

"I know," he whispered to her. "I know ye're frightened. So am I. I'm sure they dunna know ye're here, so that is why ye must stay in the cottage and not come out. They'll leave and all will be well again, do ye hear? We just have tae get through tonight."

Diantha nodded, wiping her eyes and struggling to compose herself. "As you say," she said. "I'll be all right. But, Magnus... they're *here*? How would they have known to come here?"

Magnus shrugged. "I told Lady Ayr this was where I was," he said. "Clearly, she told her husband and he's come tae see for himself. I'm sure that's all it is."

"You're positive?"

"Aye," he said confidently, though he wasn't sure he felt all that confident. "I just dunna want him tae see ye, so ye must stay out of sight."

"I'll keep her with me, Magnus," Isabail said. "Ye needna worry. I can handle a sword. If he wants her, he'll have tae go through me tae get her."

Magnus looked at Isabail. *Pregnant* Isabail, still willing to fight for her friend. Reaching out, he touched her sweetly on the cheek.

"Ye're a bold and foolish wench," he said softly. "But ye're the best kind of woman. Ye dunna even know why we're so frightened, but instead of asking questions, ye're making offers. If ye'd keep her here, out of sight, I'd be grateful."

Isabail nodded, fighting off a grin because he was. Magnus had never been the kind or sweet type, but the introduction of Diantha had seen that aspect of his personality change considerably. He was still arrogant, still a peacock, but now he was more...human. Warm, humorous, delightful at times.

Isabail liked the new Magnus.

As she went to check on Nikki to make sure he hadn't awakened with all of the commotion, Magnus returned his attention to Diantha, who was wiping away the last of her tears. Their eyes met and she forced a smile, assuring him that she was composed.

"I will wait here for you," she said softly. "Fight well, *querido*. Do not let the presence of Ambrose and Conan distract you. They are not worthy of your attention. They have come to gawk, so let them. But ignore them."

He smiled, appreciating her words of encouragement and support. He had to admit that he was concerned about being distracted. And in his business, distraction equaled failure.

He didn't want to fail.

"I willna be distracted so long as ye remain here and safe," he said. "But please...dunna come tae the arena for any reason."

"I will not. I promise."

He took a deep breath. "Good," he said. "Now, I must return tae Clegg. I ran out of his private chambers so quickly that I'm sure he thinks I've lost my mind, but I—"

There was a knock on the door, cutting him off. Immediately, he went into defensive mode.

"Get intae the back chamber with Nikki," he told her. "Get there and stay there until I tell ye tae come out."

As Diantha dashed into the rear chamber, Isabail emerged. She shut the door behind Diantha and calmly walked to the front door.

"Who comes?" she asked evenly.

There was a pause. "Issie, have ye seen Magnus?"

It was Lor. Isabail looked at Magnus, who nodded his head, and she opened the door to find her husband, Bane, Axel, and Clegg standing outside. Before Isabail could answer, Magnus showed himself.

"I'm here," he said, looking to Clegg. "Forgive me for running out on ye, m'laird. I...I had tae tend tae something."

Clegg held up a hand. "Magnus," he said quietly, "we are all your friends and we love you. Clearly, this duke has something over you, from your reaction to the news that he has come to the Cal. I have told you that I do not care about a man's past so long as he performs, but in this case, I must ask. Will you tell me what your dispute is with the Duke of Ayr?"

Magnus looked to Lor and Bane. They already knew of his royal connections. But until tonight, Clegg and Axel had not. Clearing his throat softly, he prepared to tell them. It was less difficult this time around because he had already told Diantha, and he had told Lor and Bane. No one judged him, no one ridiculed him. It made it easier to reveal himself to those who loved him.

It was only fair that Clegg knew, considering it was now on his doorstep.

"My father is the Duke of Kintyre and Lorne," he said. "I am his bastard. He is the youngest brother of the king and Ambrose Stewart is a distant cousin. His great-grandsire and my father's great-grandsire were brothers, so it is a hundred years ago with bloodlines that have been watered down through the generations. But Ambrose wants everyone tae believe we are closer than that and that he is more important than he is."

He paused to let the information sink in, but Clegg nodded his encouragement. "Go on."

Magnus did. "When I was a small child, Ambrose took me away from my mother's family and held me hostage against my father," he said. "My father isna allied with his brother, the king. He has sided against him, but seven years ago, the situation was such that I was no longer needed as a hostage, so I was released. Knowing my father wanted nothing tae do with me, I went tae Glasgow tae seek my fortune. Axel, that's why ye found me fighting in the streets. I was angry and I was directionless."

Axel, as well as Clegg, was listening intently. He nodded his head faintly as if coming to understand the motivation behind an angry and violent young man who had weaponized that rage.

"Then Ayr was your captor," Clegg said.

Magnus nodded. "Aye," he said. "And a cruel one at that. His son, who is the same age as me, was my tormentor. A rotten, vile excuse for a man if there ever was one, and his father never stopped him. It was a terrible way tae grow up, beaten by a bully time and time again, unable tae fight back because when I did, I was punished for it."

So much of Magnus's manner and behavior was coming clear in that brief statement. "But what of your mother?" Clegg wanted to know. "Was there no one to help you?"

Magnus shook his head. "There was nothing she could do," he said. "My mother was a lady-in-waiting tae the Duchess of Kintyre and Lorne, and we were sent away as soon as I was born. I've not seen her since I was very young. I dunna blame her for not helping me. In fact, I'm glad she dinna because it probably would have made things worse. I had tae learn tae stand up for myself. It has made me who I am."

"But if your father disowned you, why did Ayr hold you hostage?" Axel asked. "Your father surely would not care what happened to you."

Magnus shrugged. "'Tis a true fact," he said. "I would agree with ye, but mayhap there is a small part of him that does. Mayhap he doesna hate me as much as I've been told. But the truth is that Ayr *did* hold me hostage, for fifteen years. Fifteen hellish years. I've not seen the man since I was released and the news that he is here is...troubling. I dunna know why he would come tae see me, not after all this time."

"I can answer that," Clegg said. "You ran out before I had the opportunity to tell you. He came to buy your services, Magnus. He has made an incredibly generous offer to buy out your contract so that you may serve him."

Magnus's eyes widened. "But...but he's not even seen me fight," he said. "The man hasna seen me in seven years. Why would he make such an offer?"

Clegg shook his head. "I do not know," he said. "But I can tell you this, Magnus. I am an excellent judge of men. My business depends on it. I could tell from the moment the duke started speaking that something with him was not as he wanted it to seem. It is my sense that his offer for your services is not because he wants you. It is because he either wants something *for* you or *from* you. I do not know which. But even before I knew anything about him, there was something in his eyes that suggested something... dark. I did not like the feel of him."

Magnus nodded faintly. "Yer instincts are correct," he said. "He is a conniving, petty man. I dunna know why he should want tae buy my contract, but no good can come from it. If I served the man, he would make my life hell for the rest of my life. I must absolutely refuse."

Clegg smiled faintly. "I already did," he said. "I told him that your contract would remain with me indefinitely. He was not pleased in the least and offered me twice the money. I still refused and he left in anger. I do not know where he went, but my sentries are looking for him. He may have gone to the arena or he may have left. In any case, you should be on your guard, Magnus. He may try to find you. He wants you very badly."

"He'll not get near ye," Lor growled. "If ye see him, point him out tae me, Magnus. I'll not let the bastard near ye."

"And me," Bane said. "What's the son's name? Conan? I'll beat the bully right out of the whelp. Give me the privilege, Magnus. Let me hurt him."

Magnus looked at his friends, more touched by their protectiveness than he could possibly express. He wasn't an emotional man because he'd long learned to suppress any feelings he might have, and what he had shown had never been much more than conceit or humor. At the moment, however, he was feeling so much more.

It was enough to bring a lump to his throat.

"What did ye call us once, Lor?" he said quietly. "A clan of warriors? It is true. We *are* family. I'd kill for ye a thousand times over, but when it comes tae ye offering tae defend me, it feels...strange. I know ye dunna mean that I canna defend myself, though. I know ye mean it because we are brothers and ye'd defend me tae the death."

"We *are* brothers," Lor insisted. "We'll get through the night and make it known that Ayr isna welcome. We dunna want him and his bastard of a son here."

Magnus looked to Clegg; it was his establishment, after all. Only he could say who was allowed to remain and who was not. But Clegg agreed with Lor.

"When he is found, I will have him and his son removed," he said. Then he smiled weakly. "A happy Magnus is a victorious Magnus, is he not? I must keep you happy and you must make me money."

Magnus couldn't help but chuckle. "That is true," he said, his smile fading. "But I dinna tell ye all of it, m'laird. I came back here tae make sure Diantha was all right."

"Why should she matter in all of this?" Clegg asked.

Magnus sighed heavily. "Because she, too, was a hostage of Ayr," he said. "Ambrose took her as collateral against her father, a Navarre warlord, who wanted support from Ayr. Ambrose took her but never provided her father with the support he promised, and he's been holding her hostage ever since. She's an heiress tae her father's titles and lands, and it is Ambrose's intention tae marry her tae his son. She escaped and came tae me for help. I know I should have told ye all of it, m'laird, but I truly never thought Ambrose and Conan would come tae the Cal. But if they happen to see her now…"

The implication wasn't lost on anyone, least of all Clegg. But he didn't seem to take it too seriously, as evidenced by his expression. He cocked his head as if thinking about the ramifications of a duke finding his son's runaway bride at his establishment, but just as quickly pushed the concern aside.

"You ran back here to tell her to remain out of sight for tonight?" he asked.

Magnus nodded. "I did."

"Understandable and wise."

Magnus was surprised he'd gotten off so easily. He'd expected a rebuke at best, but Clegg seemed to understand his reasons. "I will tell ye now that if they discover her and try tae drag her back tae Culroy, I will kill them both before I allow that tae happen," he said. "Just so ye're clear on my reaction. I wouldna let her go with them. I'd kill them or die trying."

Clegg simply nodded. "I know," he said. "Diantha is important to you and because you are important to me, she is as well. Tell her to remain out of sight until we are sure the duke and his son have been located. They do not know she is here, but we would not want them to see her accidentally."

"Agreed, m'laird."

It seemed that everything that needed to be said was now out in the open. The situation was identified, and there was nothing to do now but wait until Ambrose and Conan could be located and removed from the Ludus Caledonia. Everyone was willing to protect Magnus, and Diantha, from men evidently determined to do them harm.

Perhaps they had done harm in the past, but for the future... Magnus and Diantha would be free of them if Clegg and the others from the Ludus Caledonia had anything to say about it.

"The games are beginning," Axel finally said. "We must return."

Clegg nodded, turning for the Fields of Mars in the distance. "Let us see that tonight's games are the best we have ever had," he said. "Magnus, your last bout is to be against Poseidon's Wrath. You will shine, lad."

Magnus was following with Lor and Bane. "But Galan has a bout with him," he said. "What happened?"

Clegg grunted. "Someone put soot in his helm and it got into his eyes," he said. "The man's eyes are so red that he tells me he can hardly see, so he has been forced to forfeit his bout. That means you will face the beast from Athens at the end of the night. Mind that you do not let Whale Dung shite upon you. And that is a direct quote from Galan."

Magnus started to laugh, looking at Lor and Bane and seeing that they were laughing, too. In the long line of jokes and tricks they had all played on one another, Galan was having the last laugh with this one. He would forfeit his fight so that Magnus would have to face a fully rested warrior. Clearly, Axel and Clegg were in on it, too, because soon they were all roaring with laughter as they headed over to the Fields of Mars.

But it would be the last moment of levity for some time to come.

Hell was coming.

☙ ☙ ☙

It had been a long night of blood and brutality against a soft mist that fell steadily, coating everything and everyone with a layer of wet. As the night deepened, the field became muddier no matter what the field marshals did to it. They spread buckets of sand to absorb the water. But toward the end of the night, it was a slippery mess.

The spectators in the lists were wet and cold, but the abundance of hot buttered ale made them quite drunk, so they didn't care. They had been screaming all night, throwing coins to their champions but heartily condemning those they didn't like with catcalls and hisses. It had been a wild and unpredictable evening.

The spectators' excitement was something that hadn't gone unnoticed by Ambrose and Conan. They sat in the middle of the lists, down toward the field so they could get a good look at Magnus when it was finally his bout. After they'd left Clegg in a rage, they'd gone to the lists to wait for the games to begin and they had been sitting in the same spot for hours.

It had been a long and uncomfortable wait.

"I dunna care if I ever see this place again," Conan muttered. "I dunna want tae come back here, but what are we doing tae do about Magnus? We canna buy him."

Ambrose had been brooding about that all night. It was rare when he was denied anything so he hadn't learned to gracefully accept a refusal of any kind. He'd been mulling over the problem all night.

"If I could only see him," he said. "If I can talk tae the man, I know I can convince him tae come with us."

"How can ye talk tae him if ye canna get near him?"

The crowd around them was becoming restless because the field marshals were trying to prepare the field for the next bout. Ambrose yanked his son closer to him so he could be heard over the buzz of the crowd without shouting.

"The servant that took us tae Clegg told us that the warriors can be seen in the staging area after the bouts. He said we would likely see Magnus there."

"He did."

Ambrose looked at him. "Magnus willna be there all night," he said. "He's got tae leave sometime and find his bed."

"Where's his bed?"

Ambrose threw a thumb over his shoulder. "Ye saw all of those cottages tae the west," he said. "My guess is that is where the men who fight here live and sleep. If we can wait for him over there…"

Conan's face lit up. "Of course," he hissed. "We'll wait for him tae make his way home."

Ambrose nodded, but then he turned around and noted a few soldiers in the scarlet of the Ludus Caledonia who had been standing in the same place all night, watching him. He grunted as he returned his focus to the field.

"I suspect Clegg is having his men watch us," he said. "Soldiers from the Cal have been watching us since we arrived in the lists. We'll have tae lose them in the crowd."

Conan very much wanted to turn around and look, but he resisted. He didn't want to tip the soldiers off.

"Do ye think we can?" he asked.

"I think there are a great many men here and it would be a simple thing tae lose two men in a crowd of hundreds."

"I'm ready when ye are."

Ambrose shushed his son when he saw the big Saxon emerge onto the field. He was the man who announced the coming fights. Ambrose and Conan waited with great anticipation for the next announcement.

The Eagle and Poseidon's Wrath.

The crowd went mad.

"It's him," Conan muttered, poking his father. "Finally! This is Magnus's fight!"

Ambrose shushed his son loudly as the crowd around them began to cheer to earsplitting proportions. Everyone was on their feet, so Ambrose and Conan rose, too.

The bout they had been waiting for was about to begin.

The first one onto the field was a large, muscular man with flowing silver hair. He came out onto the field with a big iron trident and a blue cape, shouting at the crowd, who loudly condemned him because he was to fight their champion. He would bellow angrily at the crowd and they would bellow angrily back. Some even began to throw rocks at him but were quickly quelled by the arena guards. As Poseidon's Wrath settled into one corner of the field, Magnus made his appearance.

A scream arose that could be heard all the way to Edinburgh and beyond. Magnus walked out on the wet field in his customary fighting garb, complete with his flashy red cloak. He lifted a fist to the crowd in acknowledgment, and the money began to rain down on the field. A well-dressed woman in the front row actually climbed over the wall and ran out onto the arena floor, but she was quickly corralled by the field marshals. She screamed for Magnus and fainted, then was promptly carried off.

Magnus was in his corner of the field, removing his cloak before adjusting his gloves as he always did. Whether or not they needed it wasn't the point. It was simply something for him to do while stalling the start of the event, time enough for his opponent to be thoroughly demoralized to hear how much the crowd loved him. It was a ploy and always had been, but Magnus was brilliant that way. He'd learned to use the energy of the audience to his advantage.

Magnus had his head down, looking at his gloves, but in his periphery, he could see his opponent. He'd seen the man in practice, so he had an idea of what he would be facing. The man was big and powerful, but clumsy. He'd seen that right away. He would be no match for Magnus's speed, and Magnus wanted to end this as quickly as possible. He wanted to get back to Diantha and wait out the night until Ambrose and Conan's departures were confirmed.

Although he couldn't see them, he knew they were in the audience, watching him. Of that, he had no doubt. The rain began to fall heavier and lightning began to light up the sky overhead, peppered with big cracks of thunder. A storm had rolled in, in earnest, and that electricity was feeding the crowd. They were screaming Magnus's name, now pounding on the floor of the lists in rhythm. The sound was deafening. Magnus stopped fooling with his gloves and went to the iron frame on the sidelines that held an assortment of clubs.

Although he rarely used a weapon, tonight he was going to make an exception because Poseidon's Wrath was big enough that he just might not go down with one swift kick to the head. If one didn't do it, Magnus was fairly certain he wouldn't have a second opportunity. Therefore, he selected a solid club and signaled to the field marshals that he was ready.

He would delay no longer.

Poseidon's Wrath had a club and a shield, and he charged Magnus across the muddy arena. Magnus approached him steadily, waiting until the last moment to dart out of the way just as his opponent brought his club around in a blow that would have surely taken his head off.

As Magnus moved aside, the momentum of the swing threw Poseidon's Wrath off-balance. The man tried to turn around because Magnus was now behind him, but he ended up falling over into the mud. Magnus charged, using his club to deliver a series of heavy blows around the man's head so he had to lift his shield to protect himself. That left his tender belly exposed and Magnus's last blow was right to the man's abdomen.

It was a brutal hit.

Poseidon's Wrath was in pain. He lay there a moment before slowly rolling to his knees. Magnus didn't give him a chance to rise. He jumped on the man's back, threw the club across his neck, and began to pull. His opponent was in a bad way as he was slowly strangled and he tried desperately to dislodge Magnus, who held fast. It was like riding a wild horse as the man bucked about, but slowly Poseidon's Wrath began to fade. Little by little, his actions lessened until he collapsed onto the ground.

The crowd went wild.

Magnus removed his club and pushed himself off the man as the field marshals ran forward to make sure his opponent wasn't dying. Just as Magnus turned for the crowd to decry his victory, Poseidon's Wrath suddenly came alive and tossed the field marshals aside. Magnus was just turning around to see what the commotion was about when a giant fist came flying at him.

Caught in the jaw and neck, Magnus went flying.

The crowd screamed with horror as their champion went skidding through the mud, crashing into the wall of the arena. Poseidon's Wrath roared as he charged Magnus, who was dazed from the blow, but not so dazed that he didn't see the man bearing down on him. As Poseidon's Wrath bent over to grab him by the throat, Magnus rolled out of the way and Poseidon's Wrath went crashing, headfirst, into the wall.

With the world rocking unsteadily, Magnus leapt to his feet, grabbed Poseidon's Wrath by his long silver hair, and smashed his head twice into the wall, so hard that he split his opponent's forehead. But he did it once more because he was terrified the giant would try to rise up again and kill him this time, so he wanted to make sure he was incapacitated.

Poseidon's Wrath fell into the mud, this time for good.

Rubbing his throat, Magnus backed away from the man as the crowd stood in stunned silence. He continued to back far away as the field marshals once again approached Poseidon's Wrath, only timidly this time in case his opponent was playing dead. Magnus's hand still on his throat, he finally raised a fist to the crowd in a show of victory. When they saw this, they began to chant his name, over and over again.

Eagle!

Eagle!

Magnus acknowledged them as Axel came out onto the field. He went to Magnus first.

"Are you injured?" he asked.

Magnus shook his head, coughing. "I dunna think so," he said. Then he rubbed his jaw. "I may have a loose tooth, but nothing that willna heal."

Axel nodded, looking him over. "I can send a physic to you should you want," he said. Then his gaze drifted over to the crumpled opponent. "I must speak to Clegg about these foreign warriors. They seem to think that this is a killing field and we cannot allow that, not for any of our warriors."

Magnus looked over at Poseidon's Wrath, now on his back. His entire face was bloody from the split scalp. "It isna the first time this has happened and it willna be the last," he said. "Dunna worry about me, Axel. There's no man alive who can kill me in combat."

There was the peacock again, arrogant and confident. Axel flashed a grin at him before making his way over to his opponent to make sure the man wasn't dead. As the crowd screamed and money continued to rain down, Magnus quit the field. As he came to the edge of the arena, Lor and Bane and Galan were waiting for him.

"You survived Whale Dung, did you?" Galan said, a twinkle in his eyes. "I will admit I had a brief moment of doubt when he hit you with his big fist."

Magnus was unstrapping his gloves. "If he'd hit ye with that blow, we'd be picking ye up in pieces, little lass," he said, glancing at him. "Yer eyes look well enough now."

Galan grinned. "They were well enough to see you fly across the arena when Whale Dung hit you."

"It'll be yer last look," Magnus said. "Drink it in, sweetheart. It'll never happen again."

As Galan laughed softly, Lor put a hand on Magnus's dirty shoulder. "That was quite a blow," he said. "Are ye sure ye're all right?"

Magnus nodded, moving his jaw around. "Truth be told, it was surprising," he said. "I will admit that I saw a few stars."

"Just a few?"

Magnus laughed. It had been more than that, but he wasn't going to admit *that* part of it. The group chuckled, mostly with relief because the ending could have been much worse for Magnus had he not been so swift or alert.

"It's over now," Bane said. "We'll retreat tae Lor's cottage and make the women serve us food and drink. Let's make a night of it and wait out the departure of Ayr and his son."

Magnus had nearly forgotten about the pair because he'd been so caught up in his fight. He was grateful for the reminder, but he was also grateful that Bane wanted to stay with him until the threat had passed.

It was a true mark of friendship.

He smiled weakly.

"Let me get the grime off me," he said, referring to the obvious—his entire backside was covered in mud. "I doubt Bee would appreciate me if I showed up like this, so I need tae clean up. Quickly, though. I want tae return tae her as soon as I can."

The group seemed to be in agreement. "If ye want, I can go tae her now as a measure of protection while ye bathe," Lor said. "There's no need for me tae go tae the bathhouse with ye."

They had walked into the staging area by now, full of workers and competitors after the night's events. People lined the fence overlooking it, screaming Magnus's name as he entered the area. But Magnus was focused on his friends.

"I'd be grateful," he said to Lor. "I'd feel better if a man were there. Isabail is a fearsome warrior, but she's with child, Lor. I dunna want her tae risk herself or her babe."

Lor was in full agreement. He was about to turn for the stairs leading up to the exit when Magnus suddenly threw out a hand, stopping him. When Lor looked at him curiously, he could see that Magnus's gaze was on the fence above.

"Great bleeding Christ," Magnus muttered. "There they are."

Everyone strained to catch a glimpse of what he was referring to. "Who?" Bane demanded. "Where, Magnus?"

Magnus didn't gesture, but his unblinking gaze was fixed on something along the fence.

"On the left side near the end," he said, his voice full of danger. "The man with the gray hair to his shoulders and a beard is Ayr. The man standing next tae him, taller and blond, is his son."

The group spied them, like hunters sighting prey. Bane started to move, but Magnus stopped him.

"Nay," he said. "Tell Clegg. He said he would remove them, so let him do it. Leave it at that for now."

Bane wasn't in agreement. He began pounding a fist into his hand. "They'll return unless we deter them," he said through clenched teeth. "Let me deter them, Magnus."

Magnus tore his gaze off of the pair long enough to look at Bane, a smile on his lips. "Ye're a bloody brute and I love ye for it, but let Clegg handle the situation for now," he said. "Ambrose is a duke, after all, so Clegg should be the only one tae throw him out. But if he returns…"

"If he returns, I'll make him wish he hadna," Bane said.

Magnus nodded slowly. "Exactly."

That seemed to satisfy Bane's bloodlust. Meanwhile, Galan was still standing with them, wondering what was going on. Tay and Aurelius had joined them also, all of them looking up into the crowd, evidently sighting something that had Magnus greatly upset, but the newcomers had no idea why.

"What's happening?" Galan finally said. "What's the problem, Magnus?"

Magnus didn't mind if Galan knew, but he didn't want to have to explain the whole sordid story again. He'd done enough of that lately. He tore his gaze from the view above and turned to Galan, Tay, and Aurelius behind him.

"Men from my past who want tae do me and Diantha great harm," he said simply. "I'm hoping they'll leave without trouble, but if they dunna…I'll give them more trouble than they can possibly imagine."

It was a simple enough explanation that had Galan, Tay, and Aurelius posturing angrily as Lor gave them a description of the offenders and discreetly pointed them out. At that point, Magnus just wanted the evening to be over. Truth be told, his head and jaw were hurting from the blow, and he was focused on getting over to the bathhouse and cleaning up.

And then he wanted to get home to Diantha.

Bypassing his usual routine of posing for the screaming women, he simply headed for the bathhouse with Tay, Aurelius, and Galan in tow. Lor and Bane remained behind, watching Ayr and his son up above and their reaction to Magnus's departure. As soon as Magnus left, they left.

But neither Lor nor Bane had a good feeling about that.

"Get word tae Clegg that Ayr is still here," Lor said. "I dunna understand why the sentries havena located the man and his son and escorted them out. They were here, in plain sight, and I'm sure they were in the lists, too. Why not toss them out?"

Bane wasn't quite sure, but he had a suspicion. "More than likely because it would bring many unanswered questions tae see a pair of spectators bodily removed from the lists," he said. "Mayhap Clegg is simply waiting for the moment when there willna be a thousand witnesses around. He doesna want tae upset his guests, guests he depends on for his income."

That made sense to Lor, but he still didn't like it. "Possibly," he said. "Find Clegg and tell him where we saw the pair. I'll see ye back in the village."

With that, the men parted, but there was a sense of trepidation in the air. Without knowing for certain that Ayr and his son had been seen leaving the Ludus Caledonia, or had been physically removed by Clegg's sentries, there was always that fear of the unknown.

If they couldn't see them...*where* were they?

CHAPTER EIGHTEEN

THE RAIN WAS POUNDING BY THE TIME THE LAST OF THE patrons were leaving the Ludus Caledonia, traveling down the hill on the water-slicked road. The storm was churning overhead, lighting up the night sky, which made those who worked at the Ludus Caledonia extra vigilant in making sure everyone got out safely.

The exit, and there was only one way in and out, was heavily manned, as was Caelian Hill and some of the areas where stores or things of value were kept, like the stables. With all of the sentries focused on these areas, it was easy for Ambrose and Conan to slip over to the edge of the warriors' village and hide in a copse of trees.

And there they waited.

It had been an hour, at least, if not more. They sat amid the wet branches and foliage, waiting for that one brief and shining moment when Magnus would come into their view.

Provided he didn't enter the encampment another way.

That was always a possibility.

"Do ye think they're still looking for us?" Conan asked quietly as the rain gently pelted him. "The guards, I mean. Do ye think they're still looking?"

Ambrose was hunkered down, wet and miserable, but he ignored it. He had a greater purpose in mind that superseded his personal comfort.

"Aye," he answered. "Soon, our carriage will be the only one left, so they'll assume we're still here."

"They'll be looking for us in earnest then."

Ambrose knew that. "I'm not leaving before I have a chance tae speak with Magnus," he said. "I know I can convince him tae come with us."

Conan wasn't so sure. Now that he'd seen Magnus fight, he

wasn't sure about anything any longer. He looked at his father, seeing how determined the man was. When his father took on this mood, nothing could convince him otherwise.

"I'm still not sure how," he said after a moment. "If we're honest with ourselves, it wasna as if Magnus had a good life at Culroy. He was a prisoner and treated like one. Those times werena kind tae him. He'll look at us and be reminded of those years, Da. The man dinna like us."

Ambrose's hawklike gaze was focused on the encampment of small stone cottages. "He'll forget about his dislike when we offer tae help him," he said. "I told ye that, lad. We can convince him that we will help him take revenge on his father."

Conan snorted. "Da," he said slowly, "I dunna know if ye really saw the man fight tonight, but I'll tell ye now that he doesna need us. Somewhere in the past seven years, Magnus became a world-class warrior."

"I saw."

"Did ye *truly* see? Did ye see the way he destroyed a man twice his size?"

Ambrose looked at him. "I saw everything," he said. "He's the best warrior I've ever seen, but if he has any chance at revenge against Hugh, then he'll need an army behind him. *My* army."

"That's what ye're offering him?"

"That's what I'm offering him."

Conan was eager to wreak havoc on Hugh Stewart at any given chance, but he was starting to think that his father might be delusional. The Magnus they saw tonight wasn't that same frightened boy his father seemed to think he was. He seemed to think he could still manipulate Magnus into doing his bidding.

But Conan wasn't so sure. Still, he shut his mouth because at some point his father would start calling him a coward, or worse, and Conan didn't want to get into it with him. Not now. He'd sit tight and let his father do what he needed to do.

It was better than arguing with him.

The encampment was coming more alive now that those who worked over at the Fields of Mars were retiring for the night. The smell of cooking fires filled the air, and they could see men and women moving around below and hear an occasional dog bark. It was probably an hour or two before dawn, and the clouds above were still riddled with thunder and lightning, though not as bad as before.

Perhaps it would clear before morning.

Conan was starting to doze off, feeling cold and drowsy, wishing he was in his bed. He was coming to think that Magnus had already made it into one of those cottages and they simply didn't see him. He was about to say something to his father when one of the cottages on the rise to the west caught his attention.

They'd seen a couple of men go into one of those cottages earlier. There were women waiting for them because they had seen them. The cottages were far enough away that Conan and Ambrose couldn't see things in clear detail, but close enough that they could see something of the people. When the doors to the cottages opened up, light streamed out and they could see them fairly clearly.

But those cottages had remained quiet since the men returned about a half hour ago. It was assumed everyone had gone to sleep until a door of one of the cottages opened and a small child darted out into the rain. A woman bolted out after him, calling out to him. They could hear her calling the child's name—

Nikki!

The door to one of the other cottages opened and a man spilled out, rushing after the woman, who had just captured the child. The little boy was whining and crying as the woman carried him back, escorted by the man. They could hear voices as the woman and child were swiftly escorted back into the cottage and the door slammed.

But by this time, Conan was on his feet, stunned by what he had just seen.

"Da!" he hissed. "Do ye know who that woman was?"

Ambrose was still watching the encampment. He hadn't paid much attention to the escaped child, the woman, or the man.

"What are ye talking about?" he snapped. "Sit down before someone sees ye!"

Conan didn't sit down. His shock was turning to outrage. "Da, that was Diantha!"

Ambrose forgot all about the encampment. He bolted to his feet, his attention in the direction Conan was indicating.

"*Diantha?*" he repeated. "Are ye certain?"

Conan nodded quickly. "I *saw* her," he insisted. "Did ye not hear her voice? With the Spanish cast? It *was* her!"

Ambrose hadn't seen her, nor had he been paying attention, so he was genuinely perplexed. "How can ye know that for certain?" he said. "'Tis dark out, so how could ye see her?"

Conan was absolutely convinced. "Because I heard her voice," he said. "I saw her when the light from the cottage shone upon her. Da, I swear, it *was* her!"

Ambrose's thoughts were quickly shifting from the return of Magnus to the sighting of Diantha de Mora, here at the Ludus Caledonia of all places. Diantha, the woman he intended for his son to marry, had disappeared over two weeks ago and no amount of searching had been able to turn up her trail. Several days ago, they'd finally given up because they'd run out of ideas as to where the woman could have gone.

Some said the docks to find a ship to sail home. Some said the seedy west end of Edinburgh where the cutthroats and outlaws lived. Agnes had even suggested that she had been abducted.

Perhaps she had been…but here she was at the Ludus Caledonia.

Ambrose hadn't seen her, but if Conan was convinced, so was he.

"Damnation," Ambrose finally blurted out. "What in the bloody hell is she doing here?"

Conan shook his head. "I dunna know," he said. "But she's mine. I want her back!"

He started to charge through the foliage on his way to the cottage where he'd last seen her, determined to pound the door down and retrieve what belonged to him, but Ambrose grabbed his arm.

"Nay, lad," he said. "Dunna go rushing in. This encampment is full of men who fight for a living, and ye dunna want tae risk ending up in a battle. If she's here, it's possible that she's become the woman of a fighter. Mayhap she was stolen by one of them."

Conan was furious. "But she's *mine.*"

Ambrose yanked on him, pulling him out of the trees. "And I'm going tae get tae the bottom of this," he said. "But we go tae Sir Clegg. He mayna even know she's here, but whatever the situation, the man canna refuse tae return her tae her betrothed. If he resists me, I'll not only bring the law on him, but the church as well. He'd be in for a world of trouble."

Conan was rushing along beside his father's purposeful marching. "Do ye think this has anything tae do with Magnus?" he asked. "She's here...and he's here. And she disappeared the same day Agnes saw Magnus. He must be part of it!"

Ambrose shook his head. "Dunna get yerself in a snit," he said. "They may know each other, but I canna say. Ye know we dunna let the men mix with the women, unless yer mother is careless and allows such a thing. Who's tae say? But we've found Diantha and I want her back. Ye'll marry her immediately and we'll be done with it."

Conan was in full agreement. He was still astonished by what he'd seen, but he'd swear on his life that he had, in fact, seen Diantha. He'd known the woman for years, an heiress who would give him a sizable chunk of Navarre.

That was all she was worth to him.

And he wanted her back…no matter what.

☙ ☙ ☙

"My lord?" It was Axel. "Are you awake?"

Clegg had just lain down on his massive, elaborate bed that was made to look like a Roman barge. It was an enormous piece of furniture that had to be assembled inside the chamber because it was so big and elaborate. Curtains of pale gossamer fabric hung from the ceiling, surrounding the bed and making it look like something surreal from another time. It could have easily accommodated five men had Clegg not kept it so piled up with pillows, because with all of those lumps of fabric, it could only accommodate one man.

And that was all Clegg had ever intended.

Hearing Axel's voice, he opened his eyes and grunted.

"What is it?"

Axel came into the chamber, going for the table where the candles were located that Clegg had so recently blown out. Using a flint, he relit them.

"We have a problem," he said quietly. "The Duke of Ayr is in your solar, demanding to speak with you."

That wasn't something Clegg wanted to hear, not at this hour. Not at *any* hour. He sat up, running his fingers through his long silver hair.

"Great gods," he muttered. "What now? I thought I gave orders to escort him and his son from the Cal."

"He and his son have seen Diantha."

Suddenly, Clegg wasn't so sleepy. He pushed the curtains back, looking at Axel with some trepidation in his expression.

"*What?*" he hissed. "How did this happen?"

"I do not know."

"Does Magnus know?"

Axel shook his head. "I do not believe so," he said. "But I do not know for certain. The duke is demanding to speak to you about Diantha. He says that she is his son's betrothed and must therefore be returned immediately. I fear he can make trouble for you, my lord."

Clegg was clad in a sleeping tunic, a heavy thing made from the finest lamb's wool. He went to his wardrobe and grabbed the first robe he came to, a massive creation made from silk and fur that cost more than some men made in a lifetime of work.

"He cannot truly make trouble for me, but he can cause a stir," Clegg said as he pulled the robe on and secured it. "The man is a bully and a buffoon, a nasty combination. I saw that earlier today. You shall be with me when I speak to him, but summon my Praetorian first. I intend to order Ayr and his son away from the Cal and I suspect they will not go willingly. What I want to know is how they even saw her. Magnus assured us that she was remaining out of sight."

Axel shook his head. "I do not know, my lord," he said. "They did not say how they saw her, only that they did. I will summon your guard immediately."

Clegg simply nodded, running his fingers through his hair again to slick it off his face as he descended to the floor below where his elaborate solar was located. As Axel disappeared into the shadows to summon Clegg's private soldiers, men he called his Praetorian Guard whose sole responsibility was protecting him and his keep, Clegg entered his solar.

The duke was standing at Clegg's table, rifling through the pile of vellum on it, while his son was drinking Clegg's very expensive Italian wine.

That behavior set the tone for Clegg's mood.

It wasn't good.

Incensed, he walked up to his table and yanked all of the vellum that Ambrose was inspecting onto the floor. When Ambrose looked up at him, startled, Clegg's silver eyes were blazing.

"Unless you want me to enter your private room and look through all of your papers, I suggest you immediately step away from my table and find a chair to sit upon," he said. Then he looked over at Conan, with the chalice halfway to his lips. "Put that down, boy. You were not invited to partake of my refreshments."

Clegg's tone was nothing to be trifled with. Conan immediately set the wine down, but Ambrose, who had moved away from the table but had not found a chair, spoke up.

"Ye have a woman here that belongs tae us," he said angrily. "Diantha de Mora. I saw her in the encampment of cottages and I want her returned immediately."

Clegg was not impressed nor moved by the request. "The warriors' encampment is forbidden to guests," he said. "You were where you should not have been."

"That woman belongs tae me!"

"You have violated my good graces for the last time, Ayr. You do not make demands of me in my own establishment."

Ambrose was starting to turn red in the face. He wasn't used to being denied, now twice in one night.

"If ye dunna return that woman tae me, I will go tae the magistrate in Edinburgh and tell him that ye have stolen her," he hissed. "Then I will go tae the church and tell them that ye refuse tae return my son's betrothed. Ye canna fight both the church *and* the law, de Lave. I suggest ye rethink yer stance. This can all go away quietly if ye simply return her tae me."

Though the Duke of Ayr was quite angry as he spoke, Clegg found that he was actually amused by it. He'd called Ambrose a bully and a buffoon, and he was right on both accounts. But he needed to stall for time until Axel and his guard arrived, even though he very much wanted to kick both Ambrose and his son right in their arses and chase them from his solar. It was clear that they were a pair of jackals.

He was coming to pity Magnus and Diantha a great deal.

"In the first place, there are many women here at the Ludus Caledonia," he said, forcing himself to stay calm. "What makes you think this particular woman is here? And why would she even be here? I do not know anyone named Diantha de Mora."

"I saw her," Conan blurted out. "She was chasing a child and I saw her go intae one of the cottages."

"And you know this for certain?"

"We can go tae the cottage tae confirm it."

Clegg shook his head. "I will not go into the warriors' village and wake up one of my warriors just because you are chasing ghosts," he said. "As I said, we have many women at the Ludus Caledonia. Mayhap this woman merely looked like the one you are looking for."

Conan was losing his temper. "It was *her*," he insisted. "She ran away more than two weeks ago, and we have been searching for her ever since. Now I suspect that she has been here all along. She is my betrothed and I want her back, do ye hear?"

Clegg remained calm in the face of a very angry young man. But what he said next was going to make him even angrier.

"Prove it."

Confusion washed over Conan's features. "Prove what?"

"That she is your betrothed."

Conan's mouth opened in outrage as Ambrose intervened. "Of course we can prove it," he said. "Bring her tae me. I will tell ye that the woman is Diantha de Mora."

Clegg looked at the man. "You could say that about any woman I brought to you," he said. "I will not take your word for it."

Ambrose was aghast. "Ye would doubt the word of a duke?"

"I would doubt the word of a man who has clearly come to the Ludus Caledonia for something other than entertainment."

When Ambrose geared up for a nasty retort, Clegg pounded a big fist on his desk, shaking the table.

"Shut your lips and listen well," he snarled in an uncharacteristic show of nastiness. "When you first came here, it was to purchase the Eagle's contract and I denied you. Now, you have allegedly found a woman who you say has run away from you, a woman you tell me is your son's betrothed. You've done nothing but make demands of me and change your story since your arrival, so I would not believe anything out of your mouth. Bring the woman's father to tell me that she is, indeed, his daughter and that she is betrothed to your son and I shall believe him. But you, my lord, I do not believe at all. You have all the credibility of a viper in the Garden of Eden, and I want you out of the Ludus Caledonia before I do something you will regret. Is this in any way unclear?"

Both Ambrose and Conan were looking at Clegg as if the man had committed an unforgivable offense. In their minds, he had. He had denied their wants. They looked at each other, sputtering in outrage, wanting to shout at Clegg until their demands were met but they could both see that it wasn't going to happen.

Clegg had taken a stand.

It had not gone in their favor.

Conan started to speak, but Ambrose stopped him.

"Very well," Ambrose said, quivering with anger. "We shall leave. But this isna over, de Lave. I shall return, and when I do, ye will be very sorry ye dinna cooperate. This I vow."

They were moving for the chamber door, Ambrose dragging Conan, who very much wanted to continue the argument. Just as they reached the door, Axel appeared with several guards. Since Axel was a very large and very intimidating man, Ambrose passed him a long look as he slid past him, pulling Conan along.

Clegg moved away from his table, going to the chamber door and watching his Praetorian escort Ambrose and Conan out of Caelian Hill and to the area where their carriage was stationed in the darkness. Even when they disappeared into the night, he did not breathe a sigh of relief.

He knew this wasn't over.

"Go after my guard and tell them not to leave that contingent until their carriage is clear of the Cal," he said to Axel. "Make sure they leave."

Axel nodded, following the guard out into the misting night. Even though Clegg knew his orders would be carried out, he knew without a doubt that he hadn't seen the last of Ambrose, Duke of Ayr, and his son, Conan.

Nay…he hadn't seen the last of them at all.

Slipping out of the keep, Clegg headed for the warriors' village.

CHAPTER NINETEEN

"Why were ye chasing after Nikki?" Magnus asked, trying not to become irate. "I told ye tae stay out of sight, yet ye ran after the boy? *Outside?*"

Diantha's head was lowered as Magnus scolded her, and rightfully so. They were back in their cottage after he'd come to retrieve her, but he was stewing about the fact that she'd gone outside of the cottage after he'd told her not to. Lor had let it slip that he'd had to chase both her and his son down.

Now Diantha was facing Magnus's wrath.

She braced herself.

"I could not let him run away," she said, trying to explain. "I was sleeping with him while Isabail was helping Lucia with the twins. They're both sick, you know. They have runny noses and with Bane at the arena, Isabail went to help Lucia."

Magnus was standing by the door, his big arms folded angrily across his chest. "So she left ye with Nikki."

"She did."

"And he climbed out of bed and escaped."

Diantha nodded. "One moment we were asleep, and the next he's climbing out of the bed and running away. I had to go after him."

Magnus grunted and rolled his eyes, seeing that she hadn't been willful about disobeying him, but the result was still the same. She had exposed herself to a world that had Ambrose and Conan hiding somewhere in it.

Magnus gestured in the direction of Lor and Isabail's cottage next door.

"Lor and Bane had returned from the arena before this happened," he said. "Why dinna ye let Lor run after his own son?"

"Because he was in Bane and Lucia's cottage at the time. I was the only one with Nikki."

"But I told ye tae stay out of sight for yer own good. Do ye understand that?"

"I do. But I could not let Nikki run away, *querido*. Surely *you* understand that."

Magnus did, but he was shaken. Angry and shaken. Still, there was no use berating her more than he already had because he knew very well she couldn't have let the boy simply run off. Therefore, he let it drop.

But he was still on edge.

As he stood there and wearily rubbed his face, Diantha dared to lift her head and look at him. He seemed particularly brittle, but that was understandable given the day's events. She also noticed a big bruise on the left side of his jaw.

"How was your bout?" she asked. "I am sorry I missed it."

He grunted, turning for the table and planting himself in a chair. "Dunna be," he said. "A giant hit me so hard he loosened one of my teeth."

Her eyes widened. "You were actually struck? How did it happen?"

"Trickery and stupidity," he said, but he didn't want to speak further on it. He looked up at her, reconciling himself to the fact that she was safe. That was all that mattered in the end. Reaching out, he grasped her hand. "Is there something for me tae eat, love? I could use something."

She nodded quickly. "Bread and cheese," she said. "There is a little leftover meat from earlier today."

"I'll eat it."

Diantha rushed around pulling together a meal for him. Normally, she would have had it ready, but her inability to go to the kitchen had hindered that. Soon enough, Magnus had bread and cheese and warmed-over beef in front of him, which he chewed gingerly because of his loose tooth.

Diantha poured him the remainder of the watered ale she had, putting it in front of him as he silently ate. He was pouting and she let him, sitting down across from him but not making any attempt to change the focus off of her. She'd let him get it out of his system and then they would move on. As she'd come to discover, his fits of anger didn't last long. He was quick to temper, but quick to forget.

She'd simply let him forget.

As Magnus finished his meal in silence, Diantha tended to her bee by moving him over near the hearth so he would have some warmth. The little bee was slowing down, nearing the end of his life cycle, and it saddened her to know he'd soon be gone. She planned to bury him beside the cottage, among the flowers that he had loved. As she stood by the hearth, she put her hand into the bowl and the little bee slowly climbed into her palm where it was warm.

"My little friend will soon be gone," she said, peering at the wee beastie. "He is the first thing that ever really belonged to me, the first thing that ever needed me. Mayhap that seems strange to say that about a bee, but I will always remember him with fondness. He was the first thing that ever made me feel needed."

Magnus looked over at her. "I need ye."

"You were the second thing."

She looked up from the bee and grinned at him, a jest to lighten his mood. Magnus fought off a smile as he finished the rest of his ale.

"I was the first and *only*," he said. Then he softened a little. "Ye know I'm not angry with ye, sweetheart. But knowing ye left the cottage... That frightens me."

Diantha put the bee gently into the bowl. "I know," she said. "Believe me when I say I would not have done it had there been any other way. But I could not let the baby run off."

He held up a hand to stop her from explaining again. "I know," he said. "Ye're compassionate and responsible. I see that every time ye take care of the bee, or teach Aurelius how tae write in Spanish, or chase after Nikki because Isabail is too tired tae do it. But if I lost ye…I wouldna know how tae go on."

She set the bowl down near the warm stones of the hearth and went to him, wrapping her arms around his head, avoiding his tender jaw.

"You'll not lose me," she whispered. "I'll be with you forever, *querido*. You and I are meant to be together, for always."

He put his arms around her torso, his head against her chest, hearing her heartbeat steadily in his ear.

"Ye'll sleep with me tonight," he said. "I promise I willna try tae seduce ye, but I want ye in the same room with me. I dunna want ye out of my sight."

Diantha understood. In fact, she was grateful for his sense of caution. "Of course, Magnus," she said. "I would not feel safe away from you tonight."

He looked up at her, kissing her torso when she smiled down at him. Then he stood up, taking her by the hand and leading her toward the back chamber where the comfortable bed awaited.

A knock on the cottage door stopped him in his tracks.

"Quickly," he muttered. "Intae the chamber."

As Diantha dashed inside, Magnus shut the door behind her. Over near the hearth was a heavy iron fire poker and he silently picked it up, wielding it in one hand as he made his way over to the door.

"Who comes?" he demanded.

"It is Clegg, Magnus."

Magnus threw the bolt and opened the door to reveal Clegg standing there in a glorious robe. The rain had mostly stopped and Magnus invited the man in, out of the damp and the cold.

"What's amiss, m'laird?" Magnus asked with some apprehension.

Clegg turned to him, his robes swishing. "I have just ordered

Ayr and his son away from the Ludus Caledonia," he said. "But I fear they will not stay away. Magnus, they saw Diantha. They want her returned to them."

As Magnus's eyes widened, the door to the smaller chamber flew open and Diantha appeared. Her face was taut with shock.

"It was an accident," she said, already in tears. "I was tending Isabail's little boy and he ran away from me. I had to chase him, but I was not out of the cottage more than a minute, I swear it."

She started weeping and Magnus put his arms around her, comforting her. "Dunna worry," he said, kissing her forehead, but the truth was that he was very worried. He looked at Clegg. "She was only ever next tae the cottage. If they saw her, it meant they were in the warriors' village where they shouldna have been."

Clegg was looking between Magnus and Diantha. "I know," he said. "I would not be surprised to know that they had been prowling this entire encampment, but they seemed quite outraged that Diantha was here. They have threatened to bring the church to force me to return Conan's betrothed, and if that happens, I cannot protect her, Magnus. She will have to go back."

Magnus knew that. He looked at Diantha, who was terribly upset. The worst had happened, what they had all feared, and she was to blame. But then again, no one was. It was an accident. Gently, Magnus touched her face before returning his attention to Clegg.

"Not if I marry her first," he said. "She has agreed tae marry me. We'll simply do it as soon as possible."

"You'll do it now," Clegg said firmly. "Although Ayr and his son have been escorted away from the Cal, I suspect that knowing she is here, they will not go far. They will return. My sentries are vigilant, but they cannot be everywhere. It is possible they will return in stealth and try to take her."

Magnus's jaw flexed, indicative of his emotions. "Even when I marry her, they may try tae take her from me," he said, trying not to feel defeated. "M'laird, I know I told ye that I had no desire tae fight anywhere other than the Cal, but as long as that pair is on Diantha's scent, she'll not be safe here. Is it possible tae go tae the Ludus Hadrian in Carlisle or the Ludus Trimontium in Berwick? I must put distance between Diantha and Ambrose."

Clegg nodded. "Of course, Magnus," he said. "I will send you wherever you wish to go with a full escort. But right now...now, you must marry Diantha and consummate the marriage. Once you are free of the Cal, wherever you end up, you will marry her again in the presence of a priest so that the union may be recorded properly."

Magnus looked at Diantha, whose tears had faded by this point. She was gazing up at him with utter trust in her eyes, knowing he would do the right and good thing to keep her safe. He smiled faintly.

"I've never been married before," he said. "Everyone I know has been married by a priest."

Clegg shook his head. "You can do it now, in this very cottage," he said. "You do not need a priest to officiate or a mass. Simply tell Diantha that you take her as your wife, and the deed will be done. Do it now, Magnus. Hurry."

His smile grew as he gazed into her eyes. "Diantha Marabella Silva y de Mora, I take ye as my wife," he murmured.

As she realized that they were about to become husband and wife, Diantha lit up with joy. She put her hands on his face, gently touching him, hardly believing that the moment had finally come.

"Magnus Stewart, I take you as my husband," she whispered.

Magnus leaned down, kissing her sweetly, feeling his love and adoration for her burst forth from every pore of his body. Never had a moment in his life meant so much. Never had he felt such contentment.

Whatever came, he knew he could face it so long as he had her.

"Ye have been mine since the beginning of time, and ye'll be mine until the end of all things," he murmured against her lips. "I wish I had a ring tae give ye, something tae express what it is I feel. I promise I'll get ye one as soon as I can."

Clegg, who had been watching the exchange of vows with a mixture of emotion, spoke softly.

"I think I can help," he said softly.

As they turned to him, Clegg reached into the neckline of his robe, pulling forth a golden chain with something on the end of it. He pulled the chain over his head, unfastening the clasp and pulling off the charm. He held it up into the light.

It wasn't a charm, but a small golden ring with an elaborate flower design on it. Something like that was meant for a woman, not a warrior of Clegg's status. When Magnus and Diantha looked at him questioningly, he smiled weakly.

"This belonged to a woman I loved long ago," he said. "Her name was Benedetta and we were married for a very short time before she died of a fever. I could never bring myself to marry again, and I have carried the ring I gave Benedetta for all of these years as a reminder of what I loved and lost. But now…now, I would be honored for Diantha to wear it. I can see the love between the two of you, something I once shared with Bennie, so I would like to give you this ring to carry on that love. Please… wear it for her."

Diantha was tearing up again, deeply touched by Clegg's gesture. He was an intensely private man, and not even Magnus had heard of Clegg's long-lost wife. But Clegg was holding the ring out to Diantha and she put her hand out so he could drop it into her palm. It was truly an exquisite piece of art with the flowers and filigree on it. Diantha and Magnus inspected it closely, seeing that there was an inscription written inside of it.

"I see words," Magnus said. "What does it say?"

Clegg smiled weakly, his gaze on the beautiful little ring he'd worn on a chain for forty years.

"I gave it to her before we were married, as a token of my intentions," he said quietly. "It says Tempus Veniam Nostrum."

"'Our time will come.'" Diantha translated the Latin words, looking at Clegg with great sympathy and tremendous gratitude. "Oh…my lord, it is so beautiful. Surely it means a great deal to you. Are you certain you wish to part with it?"

Clegg wasn't certain, but it was time he did. He wanted to see the ring which was given for love continue in that vein. With him, it was simply an object of memories. But with Magnus and Diantha, it was the symbol of what it had always been meant to be…

Love.

"I am not parting with it," he said. "I am simply giving it to Magnus to give to you for safekeeping. But I will ask one thing."

"Of course, my lord."

"When I die, I wish for the ring to be buried with me. Will you make sure of it?"

Diantha smiled, reaching out to gently touch his arm. "It will be returned to you, I promise. I will take good care of it until that time comes."

Clegg could feel himself getting pulled down into a bog of emotion by something he'd not thought of in many years. Rather than allowing himself to become swept up in those bittersweet memories of a woman he'd loved long ago, he forced himself to return to the matter at hand. It was the very reason why he'd come. Lifting Diantha's hand, he kissed it. Then he headed to the door.

"Your time is now, both of you," he said. "Do what needs to be done and I shall arrange transport south."

Magnus stopped him before he could get through the door entirely. "Ye have my everlasting gratitude, m'laird," he said. "Ye canna know what this means tae me. Tae us. We'll never forget it."

Clegg's yellowed eyes glimmered in the weak light. "A happy Magnus is a victorious Magnus," he said. He winked at the pair. "Here is to our victory this night."

With that, he was through the door, out into the coming dawn. Magnus shut the door behind him, throwing the bolt before turning to Diantha. He was trying to think of something meaningful to say to her at such an important moment, but she held out the ring to him.

"Put this on me," she said.

He took the little ring from her, slipping it onto her right hand, which was customary in Christian marriages. He looked at the ring for a moment before kissing it and her finger.

"I had no idea Clegg was married once," he said. "I feel as if he has given us something of great importance tae him and I'm hesitant tae accept it, tae be truthful."

Diantha looked at the ring, which was a little large, but not terribly so. "I know," she said. "I feel the same way, but he seemed to very much want us to have it. It was very kind of him to do so."

Magnus nodded, still looking at the ring, before his gaze trailed up to her face. He looked at her a moment, hardly believing he'd just married the woman.

But nothing had ever felt so right in his entire life.

"Lady Stewart?" he said softly.

She looked up at him, grinning at the use of her new name. "Aye?"

Magnus tilted his head in the direction of the rear chamber where the big, comfortable bed was. "Shall we make this official?"

Diantha nodded with great anticipation. "We shall."

With a sly grin, Magnus took her by the hand and led her back into the smaller chamber.

It was dark and cold in the room. There was a small brazier in the corner used to heat the chamber, but it sat empty. Magnus didn't bother with such things as heat and light. At the moment, he had one thing on his mind and it had nothing to with lighting fires in a brazier.

He intended to light one elsewhere.

Without a word, he sat Diantha down on the bed and completely disrobed before her. That gorgeous, muscular, nude form was now on full display, and although Diantha had seen him without his clothing before, this was the first time she'd really gotten a good look at him unimpeded. As she studied him, the words from that woman long ago came to mind.

I've heard he has a manhood as big as a rutting stallion.

Diantha had seen stallions before. She was fairly certain the woman had been right.

But her view of his enormous and erect manhood was cut short when he sat down beside her on the bed, his eyes drifting over the clothing she was wearing. It was another old dress, this time from Isabail, and full, white cleavage daringly peeked out from the neckline. Magnus's gaze was lustily drawn to it. One arm went around her shoulders as the other went to her torso, and he pulled her close again, his mouth on her cheek as the hand on her torso began to gently stroke her belly.

"Ye're so incredibly beautiful," he murmured, kissing her neck. "I dunna know what I have done in life tae warrant such a prize as ye, but know that I will always treat ye with the greatest respect. I'll love ye 'til the end of time, Bee, I swear it."

Diantha's eyes were closed as he nuzzled her neck, the hand on her belly moving gently to her rib cage. She was so overcome by his hot breath on her skin that she threw her arms around his neck, falling back onto the bed and pulling him with her. Magnus gladly lay down, his nude body half covering her own.

His seeking lips slanted over her mouth and he kissed her deeply. The hand on her belly moved to the underswell of her right breast, and she gasped softly as she felt his hand against her bosom. Already, her heart was racing at his touch and Magnus lowered his head to gently kiss her shoulder. As he nuzzled her soft, warm skin, his hand moved up and enclosed her right breast. He fondled her gently and Diantha groaned when she realized how good it felt.

She wanted more.

Magnus heard her groan and his kisses resumed with force. His hand on her breast grew bolder. Fingers slipped along the neckline, trying to pull it away somehow, but the bodice fit snugly against her body. He was forced to take a moment to disrobe her and Diantha helped him. In fact, she was working faster than he was. Lifting her arms for him, he removed both her dress and her shift in one swift motion.

Magnus was on her again in a flash; his mouth was on her soft cleavage and his palm against her naked breast. A taut nipple rubbed against his hand and his hot mouth descended upon it, suckling furiously.

Diantha gasped as his hot, wet mouth pulled her nipple into a hard little pellet. He had already managed to wedge himself in between her legs, his big body covering her, and Diantha welcomed it. She lusted after the man as badly as he lusted after her, and everything he was doing to her was new and wonderful and wicked.

She demanded more.

Magnus could feel Diantha writhing beneath him, her nubile body reacting to his touch. Her flesh was delicious and he nursed hungrily at her breasts, but there was such a magic to the moment that he paused in his onslaught, admiring her naked body, the voluptuous lines of her breasts and hips. He'd never been so aroused in his entire life. There was only one thing he wanted now and that was her body, impaled by his, claiming her as his own, as it was always meant to be.

But he was also aware that a man of his considerable size could quite possibly cause her some pain in their first experience together. He'd bedded virgins before, and he suddenly had visions of Diantha crying in pain as he eased into her. That wasn't something he was willing to chance, for he wanted her to crave his body as much as he craved hers.

He had to show her how marvelous this could be.

It started when his hand moved to the dark curls between her legs. She was quivering, her body instinctively hot for him. Magnus gently insert a finger into her virginal passage and Diantha was so wet that there was no pain or tightness at all. In fact, she groaned softly and brought her knees up, reacting to his touch, opening her legs wide for the primal mating ritual to begin.

Realizing that she was ready for his entry, Magnus could no longer refrain from claiming her. Lifting himself up, Magnus's lips found Diantha's mouth once again as he carefully guided his manhood into her tender, virginal walls.

Thrusting gently with his hips, he seated himself halfway on the first thrust and completely on the second. Beneath him, Diantha gasped softly at the sensation of his enormous member inside her, but was so distracted by his sweet kisses and the feel of his body that all she could do was encourage him. It was the most natural of things, his body buried deeply within her as it was always meant to be.

Diantha was so highly aroused by Magnus's touch that by the third or fourth thrust, she cried out at the thrill of a climax. Magnus could feel her wet heat throbbing around him, milking him for his seed, and it was a struggle not to answer.

He would, but not now.

At the moment, he simply wanted to savor their first coupling.

It was more than he had ever dreamed of, her heated, wet body responding to his as he'd never known a woman to respond in his entire life. He wanted to experience her, just a little, before succumbing to the inevitable.

His thrusts were measured and deep as he held Diantha's pelvis against his, his mouth on her lips. As he continued making love to her, he could feel another climax wash over her and still another. Diantha was gasping beneath him as if she couldn't breathe, her body stiffening as wave after wave of rapture coursed through her.

Finally, Magnus allowed himself to climax, filling her womb with his hot seed. Even after he released himself, he continued to grind his pelvis against hers and felt her ripple with climaxes. He'd lost count after the first few. His hands and mouth were all over her flesh, her breasts and shoulders, and anything else he could manage to touch.

As he lay on top of her, still joined to her body, he knew that this had been the most miraculous experience of his life. He'd had women before. But until now, he'd never really understood what it was like to experience the act as it was meant to be. Before, it was simply about satisfying an urge.

But now…now, it was about expressing love.

Nothing he had ever sampled had ever come close.

"I love ye, Sweet Bee," he whispered. "Ye're my everything, sweetheart. Never forget that."

Exhausted and overwhelmed, Diantha opened her mouth to reply but ended up dissolving into tears. Concerned, Magnus lifted his head to look at her, but she covered her face with her hands. Worried, he held her close.

"What is wrong?" he whispered. "Did I hurt ye?"

She wept softly, wrapping her arms around his neck as he pulled her closer. "Nay," she said, kissing his chin. "You did not hurt me. Not at all. I just never knew this would be so beautiful. You are everything to me, too, Magnus. You always will be."

Her words filled him. Such simple words, but of tremendous impact. It was a moment he wanted to live in forever, a world where he was loved and wanted. A world away from the halls of Culroy and the Fields of Mars.

This was *his* world, with Diantha, and he would never leave it.

They slept.

CHAPTER TWENTY

"They departed and I saw them head down the hill, but they'll be back. I can feel it."

Clegg was standing with Axel at the gatehouse of Caelian Hill, listening to the man's report as the sun began to rise in the east. The clouds from the night's storm had rolled out, leaving a pastel sky and a glorious landscape.

A new day was coming.

So was a new challenge.

"We have had times when guests and patrons have become a nuisance," Clegg said. "But I agree with you, Axel. Ayr and his son will return. At first, I felt it for Magnus, but now I feel it for Diantha. I told Magnus to marry the woman and he did."

"Just now?"

"Just now," Clegg confirmed. "He has asked to be moved south with his new wife, and I have decided to move him to the Tri at Berwick, as far away as possible from Ambrose Stewart and his appalling son."

Axel nodded. "I will prepare an escort if that is your wish," he said. "But I would suggest we move them out quickly."

Clegg nodded. "Agreed," he said. "This morning, in fact. But until they are clear of the Cal, it is my sense that they must be protected. Axel, I want you to tell Lor and Bane what we are doing. Have them create a group of elite warriors willing to protect Magnus and Diantha while they remain here and until we can move them out of Scotland. I suspect Ayr is only after Diantha at this point, and if he is able to get his hands on her, we will lose Magnus. And I do not want to lose him, because where he goes, his friends will go, and we will have a mess on our hands."

"Understood, my lord."

"You would go with him, too, would you not?"

The corners of Axel's mouth twitched. "I greatly respect the Eagle. He is as fine a warrior as I have ever known."

"That was not the question. He is also your friend, and you would follow him were he to leave here to reclaim his wife."

"I would go."

Clegg chuckled. "I knew this," he said. "You are too sentimental for your own good, my friend. But everyone likes Magnus and Diantha and a great many men would rush to Magnus's side, so we must make sure this does not happen."

"Agreed, my lord."

"Rouse our elite. Keep them in and around the village because that is where I feel the Stewarts will go. And Axel?"

"My lord?"

"Do not let Magnus know. Tell the men to stay out of sight. I do not want Magnus to know that we are watching out for him because it might injure his pride."

Axel cocked his head. "Why would he think that? He knows we will fight for him."

Clegg smiled humorlessly. "He knows, but a man does not want to realize he needs others to protect his wife in moments like these. Leave his pride intact. Move to help him only if it is absolutely necessary."

As Axel headed off to do his bidding, Clegg retreated into the keep of Caelian Hill, but it was not to sleep or eat. He, too, was determined to help Magnus and Diantha until the storm passed, even more than he already had, so he went into a seldomly used chamber where he kept things of value to him.

The chamber was sparsely furnished, an oilcloth over the single window in the chamber having been in place for a good many years. In fact, Clegg couldn't remember the last time he'd come to this chamber. The latch on the wardrobe door was nearly rusted into one position, and he had to fight to open it. But once it opened, it revealed exactly what he had come for.

His old armor.

This was the stuff he'd worn when he'd made a name for himself as the best mercenary money could buy, long ago. It was exquisitely crafted armor, and even as he fingered it, he could see that it had barely aged since the last time he'd worn it. It was a little dusty, perhaps even a little rusty, but it was still functional. And then he saw the tool of his trade from those years ago.

His sword.

Clegg could see his sword at the bottom of the wardrobe, a magnificent piece of equipment that had been forged in Toledo by the finest Castilian swordsmith. He hadn't seen it in a long while but when he picked it up, he couldn't remember it ever being out of his hand.

Et Victor.

That was what he had named it—The Conqueror.

It seemed that *Et Victor* was being called forth one last time.

Clegg was ready.

PART FOUR

An Inopinatum Finis

(An Unexpected Ending)

CHAPTER TWENTY-ONE

STANDING OUTSIDE HIS COTTAGE, MAGNUS HAD AN UNOB-structed view of the sunrise in all its magnificence. Everything seemed brighter this morning, smelled headier, a world that was beautiful and new. Even the birds in the trees had his attention, something he wouldn't have normally noticed.

But this morning, he was noticing everything.

The beauty of life.

It had everything to do with the magnificent woman in the cottage behind him. Diantha was packing for their journey while Magnus had gone to see Lor and Bane, but both of them were missing. Isabail didn't know where her husband had gone and nei-ther did Lucia, so Magnus found himself looking over the warriors' village and to the arena beyond, wondering where they could have gone. He didn't want to leave without saying goodbye, but he also didn't want to leave Diantha alone.

It seemed strange that his friends should be gone so early in the morning. He knew there wasn't any training going on at this hour. In the warriors' village below, he kept an eye out for Tay or Aurelius, watching the few men that were stirring at this hour, but he did not see them. Given that they had not gone to bed until just before sunrise, he could not imagine they were up at this hour.

But then again, he couldn't imagine Lor or Bane up, either.

It was all a strange mystery.

He could have gone back inside to help Diantha, but he didn't feel comfortable doing that. He could feel the same tension this morning that he felt last night, wondering if Ambrose and Conan had left the Ludus Caledonia for good. Until he received confirmation that they had left, he was on his guard. That meant that he was going to patrol around the cottage to protect the precious cargo inside.

His wife.

A smile spread across his lips as he realized that, as of a couple of hours ago, he had a wife. That was never anything he'd ever imagined for himself. It was a strange realization, but it was also a wonderful one. It was surprising how he felt complete this morning, as if an unknown missing piece inside of him had been found.

Diantha was that piece he had been missing all along and never knew it.

Magnus thought back on all of the women he had toyed with over the years, of all of the females he had admitted to his bed. There had been times when he'd had more than one woman a night. On some nights, if he was feeling particularly randy, there had been a constant stream of women in and out of his bed, two or three at a time to satisfy his voracious appetite.

But it occurred to Magnus that even with all of those women, he had always felt empty the next day. He had always felt just as lonely as he ever had, and he realized in hindsight that all of those women represented something he could never satisfy—the missing piece that only one woman, the *right* woman, had filled so easily.

He wasn't alone any longer.

That was perhaps the most joyous realization of all.

With a sword in hand, one he kept in his cottage for self-protection, he wandered circles around his cabin, hearing Diantha speaking sweetly to her little bee, who had died while they had been sleeping. The bee, which had meant so much to her, had died on the day of her marriage and there was something poignant about that. It had filled a need in Diantha, too, as she'd mentioned, but with the advent of Magnus, the need had been filled. The little bee had done his duty and now his time was over.

But they'd always remember that little bee.

There was a line of trees a few feet away from his cottage and then a clearing after that which was sometimes used as a traveling path from the village up to the community garden and the kitchens. Magnus was over in the clearing, watching the warriors' village come alive as the morning deepened, when he heard something behind him.

Whirling around, sword leveled, he came face-to-face with a man he'd never seen before.

It was an older man, about his height, whose wet, dark hair had a good deal of gray in it. He was well built and healthy, and from what Magnus could see, he didn't have any weapons on him.

Magnus frowned.

"Who are ye?" he demanded. "I've not seen ye here before."

The man's behavior seemed timid, uncertain. "I've not been here before," he said. "My first visit tae the Ludus Caledonia was last night."

Magnus didn't think the man was much of a threat, so he lowered his sword. "What are ye doing near the village?" he asked. "'Tis forbidden tae visitors."

The man nodded with resignation. "I thought so," he said. "But I had tae come. I am looking for my son."

Magnus frowned. "If yer son ran off, then ye should tell the sentries. I canna help ye."

The man didn't say anything for a moment. He kept his gaze fixed on Magnus. "Ye're the man they call the Eagle?" he asked.

Magnus scratched his head, growing bored with the conversation and a patron who had evidently not left when he was supposed to.

"If ye saw me fight last night, then ye know I am."

The man nodded. "I did," he said. "Ye were magnificent."

"I know."

The man grinned, amused with the reply. No thanks, no gratitude. Simply *I know*. "I heard that yer name is Magnus Stewart," he said.

"It is."

"My name is Hugh Stewart. Ye're the son I am looking for."

It took Magnus a moment to realize what the man said. He was so busy being bored with the conversation and thinking on

Diantha in the cottage a few feet away that several seconds ticked by before the statement registered. Then he looked at the man sharply, his entire face contorted with shock and disbelief.

"Ye're *who*?" he gasped. "Hugh Stewart?"

Hugh put up his hands because he could see that Magnus was about to erupt. "I am, and if ye'll give me a moment, I'll tell ye why I've come," he said quickly. "Agnes came tae see me, Magnus. Lady Ayr came all the way tae Blackridge House tae see me and tell me that Ambrose has been lying tae ye all of these years. Magnus, no matter what the man has told ye, I dunna hate ye. I've not disowned ye. It's been Ambrose trying tae keep us separated for his own selfish gain. Agnes told me all of it."

He was blurting out the words so quickly that it was difficult to understand him, and Magnus was quivering so that he could hardly breathe. He heard the man's words, trying to absorb them, but fifteen years of being told the opposite blocked out nearly everything he was hearing.

"Nay," he finally said weakly. "Nay, 'tis not true. Ye canna be my father."

"I am, I swear it."

"My father is the Duke of Kintyre and Lorne."

Hugh put his hands on his chest. "I *am* the Duke of Kintyre and Lorne," he said. Then he pulled out a dagger he had with his crest on the handle. It was a fabulous piece, well crafted, and he tossed it to the ground at Magnus's feet. "See for yerself. *Look*, Magnus."

Magnus wanted to walk away. He really did. But it was out of disbelief and agony: disbelief that the man was who he said he was and agony if it was all true. Everything in his body was telling him to walk away.

But his heart was telling him to stay.

With his gaze on the man, he bent over to pick up the dagger, taking a brief moment to inspect it. The hilt had a gorgeous crest carved into it, inlaid with gold and the family motto.

Si rex vult.

If the king wills it.

The ground started rocking unsteadily. Magnus stared at the crest and the motto, knowing that was indeed the motto of the Duke of Kintyre and Lorne. He'd known that from his childhood. After a moment, he looked at the man standing a few feet away.

"Ye're truly Hugh?" he asked.

Hugh nodded. "I swear tae ye on my father's grave," he said with quiet sincerity. "I am Hugh and ye are my son. I swear by all that is holy."

Magnus was calming down, but only marginally. The disbelief was fading in lieu of monumental confusion. He just stood there with the dagger in one hand and his sword in the other, trying to process everything Hugh had said to him.

"I canna believe it's ye," he finally said. "I always imagined the things I'd say tae ye if I ever saw ye, but now...now, I canna remember anything."

Hugh understood. "And I always thought that I'd tell ye I loved ye even if ye dinna want tae hear it," he said. "I never thought my first words tae ye would be of Ambrose."

Ambrose. That hated, horrific name. The one that churned Magnus's insides, the reason he was outside at this very moment. He was starting to focus on what his father had told him.

"Ye said...ye said that Agnes told ye that Ambrose has been lying?"

Hugh nodded. "She did," he said. "Magnus, there is nothing I can do tae make up for years of estrangement, of ye thinking I dinna want ye around. But it was a lie orchestrated by Ambrose Stewart. When ye were at Culroy, I would send ye missives, but I never heard anything in return. Agnes told me it was because Ambrose burned the missives and told ye that I hated ye. That wasna the truth, lad, I swear it."

Magnus was beginning to understand what Hugh was telling

him. In truth, it was a simple thing to believe because he'd spent years with Ambrose and his deceit. He knew what the man was capable of. It absolutely made sense that Ambrose had burned any missives from Hugh meant for Magnus.

The realization hit him like a hammer.

"My God," he finally muttered. "He burned them and told me ye wanted nothing tae do with me. That's all I ever knew."

Hugh looked at him sadly. "I know," he said. "But it isna true, lad. It was never true. Why do ye think he held ye hostage? Because ye meant something tae me and he knew he could use ye against me. Did ye ever realize that?"

Magnus hadn't, but he understood what his father was saying. It made a good deal of sense. But there was so much more he didn't understand.

"But…but ye sent me away when I was born," he said. "Why did ye send me away?"

"Because I had no choice," Hugh said, lines of anguish on his face. "Ye see…I loved yer mother. She was a lady-in-waiting tae my wife, whom I dinna love. I married her because I was tricked intae it by Ambrose. I married his sister."

Magnus hadn't known that in the least. He'd never even heard a hint of it.

The revelation was shattering.

"The Duchess of Kintyre and Lorne is Ambrose Stewart's *sister*?" he gasped.

Hugh nodded. "Ambrose promised me a great alliance should I marry her," he said. "But he lied. He lied about so many things. Marjorie wasna a wife, she was a dictator. She tried tae manipulate everything I did and told her brother everything that happened in my household. Ye must understand something, Magnus… I loved yer mother. Whatever ye think of yer birth, know that ye were conceived in love. Marjorie knew this, and when ye were born, it was she who sent ye and yer mother away. She could never be the wife

I wanted and she could never be the woman I would love, and she knew it. Marjorie was a bitter, nasty woman."

Magnus was coming to learn a great deal, more than he'd ever expected to know about himself or his origins. It was shocking and it was horrific, but as he looked at Hugh, he could see that Hugh was the one who had really taken the brunt of Ambrose and Marjorie Stewart's vitriol.

Hugh was the real victim in all of this.

"Bloody Christ," Magnus muttered. "Then it was Marjorie who made sure I was seized away from my mother's family when I was a wee lad and taken hostage by Ambrose."

"'Tis true," Hugh muttered, reliving those horrible memories. "By the time I found out about it, there was nothing I could do. They had ye. I tried everything I could tae get ye back—money, property—everything. But Ambrose kept ye. He said it was insurance against me. As the years went on and Ambrose told me that ye hated me, I just stopped trying tae contact ye."

Magnus could see it all so clearly, but there was still part of him that was wounded by it all, wounded that his father perhaps didn't fight harder for him.

Wounded because he had always felt unwanted.

"He told me ye wanted nothing tae do with me," he said. "That was all I ever knew of ye. And my mother's family told everyone that my father was a servant. Did ye know that?"

Hugh nodded. "I did," he said. "They said that tae protect ye because the brother of a king has many enemies."

"That was the only reason?"

"I swear tae God it was the only reason."

"What about my mother? Where is she now?"

For the first time in the conversation, Hugh didn't appear so distraught. "She is well," he said. "Ye've not had contact with her in many years, I'm told."

Magnus shook his head. "Nay," he said. "Once I was taken away from her and spent those years at Culroy, I never heard from her. I thought it was because she dinna want anything tae do with me, but now I'm coming tae think that Ambrose burned anything she might have sent me, also."

Hugh nodded at the sad realization. "I know yer mother wouldna have let ye go without a word. She loved ye deeply."

Magnus was feeling all kinds of turbulent emotions, more so when it came to his mother. "I've not forgotten her," he said. "I've fond memories of my childhood with her, and there were times when I missed her. But I dinna return tae her when Ambrose released me."

"Why?"

"Because I was free. I dinna want tae return tae my mother and her family and become their burden. I had tae find a life for myself." He shrugged. "And mayhap the fact that I hadna heard from her the entire time I was at Culroy had something tae do with it."

Hugh sighed faintly. "Magnus," he said quietly, "I know she sent missives tae ye, but ye never responded tae them, and much like me, she thought ye dinna want anything tae do with her."

Magnus's brow furrowed. "How would ye know that?"

"Because Marjorie died around the first of the year," Hugh said, watching Magnus closely for his reaction. "I married yer mother two months ago."

Magnus's eyes widened. "Ye *married* my mother?"

Hugh nodded. "Aye," he said. "That makes ye my legitimate heir."

Magnus's jaw dropped. "Are ye serious?"

Hugh dipped his head. "I swear I am," he said. "But no one could tell me where ye were, least of all Ambrose. But thanks tae Agnes, I found out, and here I am tae make sure ye know the truth. Even if ye never want tae see me again, I thought ye should know *everything*."

By now, Magnus had calmed down a good deal. He could recall a few momentous occasions in his life—when he was taken to Culroy Castle, when he was released from Culroy, when he was brought to the Ludus Antonine, and when he married his wife.

But this moment…this one ranked among the biggest events in his life. His very own father, a man he'd thought had hated and disowned him, was telling a dramatically different story than the one he had always believed, and Magnus could see that the root of all of his troubles, the seed of all his evils, was Ambrose Stewart. A man who was still trying to ruin him.

A man who had already ruined his father.

After a moment, he shook his head.

"I dunna even know what tae say," he said. "'Tis as if everything in my life has been a lie, and the anger I feel toward Ambrose threatens tae consume me. I dunna know if it's an anger I can control."

Hugh nodded. "I know it well," he said. "I've had the same anger since Agnes came tae tell me the truth. But…but I need tae ask ye one thing, Magnus."

"What is that?"

"Are…are ye glad tae see me?"

Magnus looked at the man, seeing the desperation in his eyes. A smile spread across his lips as he took a few steps toward him and handed him his dirk, hilt-first.

"Aye," he said hoarsely. "I'm glad tae see ye, Da. I can hardly believe I'm saying it, but it's true. I am."

Hugh smiled timidly. "Are ye happy here, Magnus?"

Magnus nodded. "Verily," he said. "The Ludus Caledonia is my home and the warriors are my family. But that doesna mean I dunna have room for my real family. It's simply something I never thought I would know. I've been alone my entire life, but now… now I have more family than I ever realized."

Hugh was vastly relieved to hear that. "Good," he said. He meant it. "I want ye tae do what makes ye happy, but I also want ye tae know that ye're my heir. What exactly that means is up tae ye. Ye may not want the responsibility. But I hope ye'll at least think about it. And me, also. I'd like tae know my only son, on whatever terms he wishes."

Magnus smiled at the man. He could feel the genuine emotion, the hope and the fear, radiating from him. Truth be told, he had enough hope and fear of his own—hope for the future, and fear for it as well. He still could hardly believe any of this. But there would be no future at all if Ambrose was still a threat.

"I'd like tae know ye, too," he said. "I'm glad ye came tae find me, I truly am. But ye should know that Ambrose isna finished with me yet."

Hugh's smile faded. "I've heard," he said. "Agnes told me he was trying tae turn ye against me one last time."

Magnus sighed heavily, turning to look at his cottage, still quiet and peaceful. "Strangely enough, he hasna tried—yet," he said. "My wife and I are leaving today because Ambrose is after *her*. She was a hostage at Culroy like I was, but Ambrose cheated her father and intended tae marry her tae Conan. She ran away from them, and by accident, they located her. In fact, that's why I am out here this morning. I'm protecting her until we are escorted away from here."

Hugh was quite concerned. "Where are ye going?"

Magnus gestured to the south. "England," he said. He looked at his father again. "But I will admit that it concerns me that ye're here, because the perimeter of the Ludus Caledonia is well protected, yet ye managed tae slip past them. How did ye do it?"

Hugh sighed heavily. "The truth is that I never left," he said. "I came tae watch the games last night and never left. When everyone was leaving, I found a gully tae hide in and then I ventured back out when all was quiet. Finding ye here was just a coincidence."

"Finding ye here is a coincidence, too."

The reply didn't come from Magnus.

Startled, both Hugh and Magnus turned in the direction of a heavy cluster of trees that was between the warriors' village and the gardens to the northwest. Emerging from those trees was something they had hoped not to see.

Ambrose Stewart was heading straight toward them.

And he wasn't alone.

CHAPTER TWENTY-TWO

MAGNUS'S SWORD CAME UP.

"Stop right there, Ambrose," he said, forgoing any formal title of address. "Ye've come as close as I'm going tae allow."

Ambrose came to a halt, his gaze moving between Hugh and Magnus. There was some amusement in his expression, as if this were all just a lighthearted reunion, when the fact was that he had at least six or eight armed men with him, including Conan. They were fanned out behind him, waiting for the command to move.

Magnus could sense that there was a rush waiting to happen. Reaching out, he grabbed his father, pulling the man behind him so he could protect him. He then swung his short sword in a skilled, flashy movement that showed his comfort and skill with the weapon. Wordlessly, he was stating that he knew how to use it.

Ambrose put up his hands to show he was unarmed.

"I've not come for ye, Magnus," he said. "Nor have I come for Hugh, though I dinna know the man was even here. When did ye arrive, dear cousin?"

Hugh was behind Magnus, his dirk in hand. It was all he had, unfortunately, and he could see that he and Magnus were outnumbered. He'd purposely come unarmed to the Ludus Caledonia because he hadn't wanted to be perceived as a threat.

He hoped that decision didn't cost him.

"Dunna worry over me, Ambrose," Magnus said steadily. "What matters most is that ye brought armed men intae the Ludus Caledonia and I dunna think they'll take kindly tae it. Why on earth would ye do such a thing?"

Ambrose started looking around. Specifically, he was looking at the cottages several yards behind Magnus.

"I've come for something that belongs tae me," he said. Then, he turned to Conan. "Is this where ye saw Diantha?"

Conan was well back and away from Magnus. Considering he was afraid of the man after seeing him fight in the arena the night before, he made sure that he was far away from him.

The bully was cowering.

"Aye," he told his father. "She went intae the second cottage, over there."

He was pointing to Lor's cottage, and Magnus was listening to it all very carefully. It was clear that Ambrose wasn't interested in him at all, only in Diantha. Magnus already knew that the pair had spotted her, but here they were, extremely close to her, having sneaked into the Ludus Caledonia without even being seen. Clegg had been certain they would not leave completely, and he'd been correct, unfortunately.

Damn...

Magnus had a very big problem on his hands.

He was the best warrior the Ludus Caledonia had to offer, but even he was mortal. He could take on a group of armed men, but he wasn't certain for how long before they overwhelmed him. Things like kicking them in the head and clubbing them in the groin were part of his tactics in the arena where they weren't allowed to use real weapons, but these men had swords. They'd come to kill anyone who stood in their way.

That man was Magnus.

"Ye're not going intae the warriors' village," he said evenly. "If ye do, ye'll be walking intae an encampment of armed men, and there are many more of them than there are of ye."

Ambrose didn't seem to be bothered by that. "I told ye I am here tae retrieve what belongs tae me," he said. "Diantha de Mora is here. She's Conan's betrothed and I want her back."

Magnus debated his next move. He could try to keep the situation calm until someone in the warriors' village saw what was going on and told the sentries, or he could posture aggressively and hope it was enough to drive Ambrose back. He needed help because he didn't want Ambrose's armed guards getting around him and to the cottages.

To Diantha.

He found himself praying that Lor and Bane would make an appearance.

He needed help.

"Do ye even want tae know why Hugh is here?" he said, trying to shift the subject. "He came tae tell me that he sent me missives during my time at Culroy, missives ye burned. Ye told me he hated me, but that wasna the truth. Ye lied tae me, Ambrose. What else have ye lied about?"

As he'd hoped, Ambrose's focus moved to Hugh, still standing behind Magnus. He stared at him a moment before snorting.

"Is that why ye're here?" he said. "Tae mend ties with yer son?"

Hugh nodded slowly. "Ties ye tried tae sever, I hear."

Ambrose didn't deny it. After a moment, he simply shrugged. "Ye married my sister and fathered a bastard," he said. "Ye dinna think I would retaliate?"

Hugh scowled. "Ye're the last person in the world tae judge a man," he said. "The sins ye've committed far outweigh anything I've ever done. Ye had no right tae keep Magnus from me."

Ambrose's eyes flashed with rage. "Ye shamed my sister and ye dinna expect me tae do all I could tae keep the lad from ye?"

"Ye're a damned fool," Hugh growled. "Ye forced me tae marry yer sister with promises of an alliance, but ye went back on yer word."

Ambrose's eyes narrowed. "Ye werena worthy of my word, Hugh."

"Why?" he snapped. "Because I'm the brother of the king and ye're not? That was always at the root of this, wasna it? Yer petty jealousies caused ye tae lie and cheat and try tae control me and my family, and when ye couldna do that, ye spread rumors about me. Ye tell everyone I'm allied with the Laird of the Isles."

"It's true!"

Hugh took a deep breath so he wouldn't fly at Ambrose with his fists. "The only thing that's true about that is that Magnus's mother is a daughter of John McDonald, Laird of the Isles," he said. "I wasna allied with them until I married her. She's now my wife and Magnus is now my rightful heir. It's a bond ye canna break and we'll tolerate yer lies no longer."

Ambrose was starting to lose some of his confidence. He considered the separation of Hugh and Magnus some of his finest work, but now he could see it had been ruined. Somehow, the two of them had connected in spite of his attempts to keep them apart, and that realization was beginning to shake him. But that understanding also swung his focus back on Diantha, something he *could* control.

"Get out of my way," he snarled. "If ye dunna move, I'll kill ye."

Magnus took a defensive stance, the sword leveled. "Ye've seen me fight in the arena," he said. "Are ye sure ye want tae tangle with me? Because the first man I'm going tae cut down is Conan."

"Not if I get tae ye first."

"Ye'll never make it," Magnus said. "Yer son will die right before yer eyes if ye make another move."

Ambrose's jaw was twitching furiously, his anger having reached the tipping point from control to chaos. He yelled a command to his men, who started to move, and Magnus prepared for the onslaught, his sword arcing in the morning light.

But then a strange thing happened.

Suddenly, men were bolting out of the trees, pouncing on Ambrose's armed men. Startled, Magnus realized that he was seeing Axel, Wendell, and Milo, heavily armed. His shock grew when he watched as a large figure in heavy armor moved out of the trees and took down Conan, cutting through the man's neck and sending his head spinning to the cold, wet earth.

Clegg made the first kill.

Men were rushing past Magnus from behind. Lor, Bane, Tay, Aurelius, and Galan charged headlong into the remaining armed soldiers, including Ambrose, who started to scream when he realized they were being overrun by armed men.

Life and death were being played out before Magnus's eyes as his friends descended on Ambrose's men. But hearing Ambrose scream at the sight of his headless son propelled Magnus into action.

The Eagle attacked.

His target was, in fact, Ambrose, who was trying to run. Magnus ran past Lor, who was wrestling with a particularly large soldier, and Magnus went airborne as he rushed by, using a tree as leverage. He kicked off of the tree trunk, propelled himself through the air, and kicked Lor's opponent in the head so hard that he broke the man's neck.

As the soldier went down, Magnus landed on the ground, but his feet were still moving. They never stopped. He closed in on Ambrose as the man scrambled to get away, but Clegg was suddenly between them. Magnus had to sidestep Clegg or risk running into the man as Clegg used *Et Victor* to slice through Ambrose's chest.

In a heartbeat, Ambrose Stewart was dead.

It was over before it barely began.

In the sudden stillness, Magnus stood over Ambrose and watched the man bleed out all over the sweet Scottish earth. When he turned to look at Clegg questioningly, to ask him why he had killed Ambrose, Clegg removed his helm and looked Magnus in the eyes.

"You'll not have this on your conscience, Magnus," he said quietly, knowing what the man was thinking. "This way, your path to heaven will be easier for not having killed a member of your own family."

Magnus looked at the man in shock and perhaps some gratitude. "But *ye* killed him."

Clegg pondered that statement, looking over to the son he'd also killed. As Axel and Lor and Bane and the others made sure everyone else was dead, Clegg considered his response.

"This is not something you need to be burdened with on your wedding day," he said. "Let this be the first day of the rest of your life with your new bride, Magnus. Do not let it be the day you killed a cousin because he threatened you. Let that be my privilege… Let it be the privilege for all of us. Magnus, this man has been making your life hell since you were a child. You have finally found happiness and he was intent on ruining it. I am an old warrior, my path to hell is already set. One or two more dead men on my soul will not matter, but you…you deserved better than what you received. This is our gift to you, lad…the gift of peace."

Magnus was stunned. He looked around at the men of the Ludus Caledonia: Axel, the stern manager, Wendell and Milo who were long-time trainers, Aurelius and Tay and Galan who were his dear friends. And finally Lor and Bane, the best friends a man could ever have. Magnus had wondered where they'd gone to that morning and now he knew.

They had gone to protect him.

There was a lump in his throat at the realization.

"I should have known," he said, looking to the men who had just saved his life. "I should have known that I was not alone, but it is the first time in my life when I can say that with confidence. As a man who never had friends until I came tae the Cal… Nay, as a man who never had *brothers* until I came tae the Cal. We are indeed a clan of brothers. Ye just proved it."

Clegg put a meaty hand on Magnus's shoulder. "In my case, it was purely selfish," he said, handing his sword over to Axel because he was already exhausted having swung the thing. "Now, I will not have to send you to Berwick. You can remain here as my top warrior and continue to make me money. But for the rest of these men… Aye, they are your brothers. You are most fortunate, Magnus."

As Magnus came to grips with what had happened, Axel approached Clegg. "And the bodies, my lord?" he asked. "What will you have me do with them?"

Clegg's silver eyes surveyed the carnage. As a man of numerous battles, of negotiations, contracts, sieges, and surrenders, he knew better than anyone else what had to be done in a case like this.

It was a coldhearted but necessary command.

"Burn them," he said quietly. "Burn everything and sink the ashes in the lake to the north. Find the carriage, for it must be nearby, and burn that, too. No trace, Axel."

Axel understood. "No trace, my lord."

With that, Axel, Wendell, and Milo headed off to summon some soldiers to help as Magnus went over to Lor, Bane, Galan, Tay, and Aurelius. They were all standing in a semicircle, surveying the ruins of their short-lived fight.

Magnus was feeling particularly emotional as he looked at them. They all meant a great deal to him even if they hadn't saved his life and the life of Diantha.

His wife.

It occurred to him that they probably didn't know that.

"Though we spend our nights fighting for money, it never occurred tae me that I'd actually be in a fight for my life here at the Cal," he said, looking over at a headless Conan. "Certainly not like this."

Lor was standing next to him. "Ye're sure ye're well?"

"I'm well. Why do ye ask?"

"I want tae make sure ye werena insulted by this," he said. "Magnus, we all know ye are a legendary fighter, but even legendary fighters need help now and then. Ambrose was going tae go through ye tae get tae Diantha. Ye know that."

Magnus nodded. "I know that," he said. "I was prepared tae take him on alone, but even I knew the odds of me emerging from that unscathed werena good. I'm not offended by yer help, believe me. But ye should know something."

"What?"

"I married Diantha last night. 'Tis my wife ye're speaking of now."

The congratulations came. Magnus was patted on the head, the shoulder, and someone slapped him on the rear hard enough to jolt him. He thought that might have been Aurelius, the big brute. He rubbed his arse, grinning at the men who were very happy for his good fortune. But as the congratulations went around, Magnus caught sight of Hugh, standing several feet away.

His smile faded as he locked gazes with the man, realizing Hugh had just seen his friends cut down Ambrose, Conan, and several armed guards with little effort. It had been a brutal takedown, but a necessary one.

He was certain that no one understood that better than Hugh.

At least, he hoped so.

Ambrose had tortured Hugh most of all.

"I'd like all of ye tae meet my da," Magnus said, a smile spreading across his face. "I never thought I'd have the privilege of introducing ye tae him, but this is Hugh Stewart, Duke of Kintyre and Lorne."

Attention turned to the older man who faintly resembled Magnus. It was Lor and Bane who first greeted him, followed by the rest. It wasn't often that a duke was in their midst, Scottish royalty, but mostly they greeted the man warmly because he was Magnus's father. He could have been a pauper for all they cared. But he was Magnus's father and worthy of their respect, regardless of his lot in life.

Clegg greeted him as well, inviting him to Caelian Hill for food and refreshments. Ever the gracious host, Clegg insisted even when Hugh tried to beg off. Magnus simply laughed, waving his father on and assuring him he would join him soon. It was the only way Hugh would go.

He didn't want to leave his son.

But Magnus wasn't going anywhere.

Never again would they be separated. As he assured his father that he would join him as soon as Clegg dragged him away, he heard a shaken voice behind him.

"Magnus?"

Diantha was standing a few feet away, her eyes wide with terror at the carnage spread out. She wasn't close enough to really see who the dead were, and Magnus quickly went to her, trying to block her view. He put his arms around her, turning her back for the cottage.

"Magnus, what happened?" she said, trying to look over her shoulder at the mess. "I heard voices and then I heard the fight. Are you well, *querido*? Were you hurt?"

"I'm not hurt," he said. "Everything is fine now."

Magnus managed to get her back to the front door of the cottage but she wouldn't go any further. She dug her heels in, refusing to move.

"Magnus, *please*," she begged softly. "Tell me what happened. Who are those men? Are they all dead?"

He cupped her face, forcing her to look at him. "Ambrose is among the dead," he said steadily. "So is Conan. They were coming for ye, Bee. We had tae stop them."

Diantha closed her eyes as the news settled in. She'd heard the skirmish from the cottage and she'd been absolutely terrified, knowing Magnus was in the middle of it. She was beyond relieved to know that he hadn't been injured, but more than that, she realized that their troubles were over. Ambrose and Conan were dead. They'd come for her, as Magnus and everyone else knew they would, and they'd been punished for it.

We had tae stop them.

Tears streamed from her eyes.

"Dead?" she whispered. "They're dead?"

"They are, sweet."

"Truly?"

"Truly."

"We will never have to fear them again?"

"Never."

She broke down at the realization, weeping softly as Magnus held her. Her relief was too great for words. Years of captivity, of anguish and heartache, had just been ended.

For good.

She could hardly believe it.

Wiping at her eyes, Diantha struggled to reclaim her composure as her gaze fell on a group of men several feet away. They were all looking at her. Lor even raised his hand and gave her a brief wave.

It took Diantha a moment to realize that Magnus hadn't been alone in his fight against Ambrose and Conan.

He'd had help.

"They…they helped you," she said. "All of them… They *helped* you?"

Magnus turned to look at the group, smiling wearily. "They helped *us*," he said. "They're our family, Bee, and like any family, they'll kill and die for ye. They werena going tae let Ambrose get tae ye."

The impact of the situation sank deep and Diantha shook her head in wonder. "I can hardly believe it."

He looked at her. "Why? Ye know they love us. Why should ye be surprised?"

Diantha shook her head, trying to put it into words. "I've been alone most of my life until now," she said. "I've heard of other women having great friends and big families, but I never understood that until now. I never understood what the bonds of friendship and family could mean, but I do now. At least, I am learning."

"We're *both* learning," Magnus said. "We have each other and we always will, but we also have a company of the greatest champions the world has ever seen. *Our* family, Bee. The Ludus Caledonia is many things, but the bond of warriors is its greatest strength. We saw that this morning."

Those were among the greatest words Diantha had ever heard. As Magnus led her over to the group of men who had saved their very lives, all Diantha could see within them were the hearts and souls of true champions.

True brothers.

With an Eagle to lead them all.

EPILOGUE

The Month of April
Year of Our Lord 1489

"FIGHT, MAMA! *FIGHT!*"

Nikki was straining against his mother, wanting very much to go onto the field where his father was training with a new group of recruits and some of the Ludus Caledonia's elite fighters. Magnus, Bane, Galan, Tay, and Aurelius were on the arena floor, demonstrating technique.

But Nikki wanted to join them—badly.

Isabail was having a difficult time holding on to him as Diantha and Lucia sat together, each with a twin. They were starting to walk now, so it was imperative to have a good grip, as Diantha had learned. It was excellent practice for her, considering her own baby was due in about three months.

As Isabail struggled with Nikki, in a basket beside her an infant let out a cry. Her newborn, Knox, had the lungs of a bear, or so his father said. Named after Isabail's great-grandfather, he had a crown of dark-red hair. Isabail had two big, healthy boys on her hands and Lor could not have been prouder.

But Isabail was exhausted.

"I'm taking the bairns back tae the cottage," she said, trying to hang on to Nikki while picking up her infant basket. "I'll be—"

She was cut off when Nikki burst free and began rushing down the steps of the lists toward his father. Isabail knew she couldn't catch him, so she didn't even try. She shouted down to Lor on the arena floor, warning him of the incoming child.

Lor, seeing his firstborn charging toward him, went to intercept the boy. But Nikki didn't want his father; he wanted Bane's sword. He always wanted Bane's sword. Bane dutifully handed over the heavy, dull *gladius* and the child dragged it away, happy.

Even from the lists, the women could see the men down below, smiling at the child who very much wanted to do what his father and his father's friends were doing. Nikki was becoming the mascot for the warriors with his unbridled enthusiasm and glee, and he was well loved by all.

As Diantha watched the little boy among the warriors, Lucia tapped her on the arm.

"Bee," she said. "Look… 'Tis Hugh."

Diantha turned around to see Hugh entering the lists with his wife in tow, the lovely and sweet Fia. Diantha immediately stood up, with the baby on her hip, and made her way up the stairs to them.

"Good morn," she called, waving at them.

Hugh and Fia caught sight of her and quickly headed in her direction. "Good morn, Bee," he said. "'Tis a lovely day. How is my grandson?"

Diantha beamed. She had truly come to love Hugh and Fia over the past several months, generous and kind people who traveled from Edinburgh at least three times a week to watch Magnus fight.

Never had they pressured Magnus to be anything other than what he wanted to be, even though he was heir to a substantial dukedom now. They had only expressed their pride in what he was—a great warrior—and they had gone out of the way to support him. It was as if they were making up for lost time, something that had overwhelmed Magnus at first because he wasn't used to having his father around, or any parents for that matter. But both he and Diantha had grown to love the pair.

Nowadays, it was as if there had never been any separation at all.

"Your grandson is well." Diantha rubbed her rounded belly. "He keeps me up at night, however. He likes to kick."

Hugh burst out laughing. "Like his father," he said. "He is already practicing kicking people in the head."

Diantha giggled. "That is true," she said, turning her attention to Fia. "Good morn to you, Fia."

Fia McDonald Stewart, Duchess of Kintyre and Lorne, was a genuinely sweet and docile creature, beautiful to a fault. She looked very much like her son with her dark-green eyes and wavy hair, and it was clear where Magnus had gotten his comely looks. They were the proudest parents in Scotland these days, and Diantha had been thrilled with their addition to their lives.

It was as marvelous as she could have hoped for.

As she sat with Fia and Hugh, Magnus was down below on the arena floor, watching the trio with pride. Every time he saw the three of them, he could hardly believe how rich his life had become.

Rich with love, rich with family.

But he was forced to look away when Lor had him demonstrate an advanced technique to subdue a man without using a weapon, and in this case, it was Galan. After he shoved Galan's face into the dirt to finish the move, Lor sent his *novicius* back into the holding area with Tay and Aurelius.

For today, the lesson was over.

"The duke has returned," Bane said, coming up behind Magnus as he looked up to the stands. "The man has barely missed a night in all these months."

Magnus pulled Galan up into a sitting position as the man brushed dirt off his face. "He's making up for lost time," he said. "But I dunna mind. We've had many long, meaningful discussions and I feel as if I know him well. He's a good man."

Bane nodded. He, too, had engaged in a few discussions with Hugh over the past several months and he genuinely liked the man. "I'm curious," he said. "Does he ever bring up Ambrose?"

Magnus shook his head. "Nay," he said. "He only brought up Ambrose's widow once, tae say she's living a good life now. Her wicked husband and son have vanished without a trace, and she's evidently grateful for it."

Bane chuckled softly, removing a piece of leather protection he had on his forearm. But his gaze returned to the duke, up in the lists and chatting amiably with Diantha.

"Ye told me once that yer da was a rebel," he said after a moment. "The man doesna look like a rebel tae me."

Magnus grinned. "What does a rebel look like?"

Bane shrugged. "I dunna know," he said. "I always imagined them tae look like us—barbarians."

Magnus laughed softly. "Sometimes rebels are in sheep's clothing," he said. "Though my da hasna actually discussed his relationship with the king with me, in the few comments he has made, I get the sense that he's very much in the constant state of rebellion I was always told of. There are things he doesna approve of."

"He's not tried tae pull ye intae it?"

Magnus shook his head. "Nay," he said. "But something tells me it will come up at some point."

"What are ye going tae tell him if he wants ye tae side with him?"

Magnus shrugged, unfastening his gloves. "I'm not sure," he said. "I never planned tae stay at the Cal forever, even before I knew my da. When he passes on, I'll become the Duke of Kintyre and Lorne, and responsibilities come with that. Will I side with my uncle, the king? I canna say, but that's a long way off. I'm happy where I am, at this moment."

Bane's gaze moved to Diantha, sitting beside Fia. "But what about yer wife?" he asked Magnus. "Is she happy?"

"Of course she is. Why do ye ask?"

Bane shrugged. "Something Lucia said," he replied. "She mentioned that Diantha still wants tae return tae Santacara. Ye married her, so it's yer property now, too. I've always wanted tae go tae Navarre. Mayhap when ye go, I'll go with ye."

Magnus looked at him. "Ye think Clegg is going tae let ye? What are ye going tae tell him?"

"That I must go because ye need looking after."

Magnus grinned. "And ye would, too," he said. But he sobered quickly. "I still intend tae take her back tae her homeland, but not now. Not until the bairn is old enough tae travel. She's sent a couple of missives tae Santacara since she's been at the Cal, but she's not received a reply. I know she's hurting because of it. Something tells me that her father is long dead and I think she knows it, but now that she's safe from Conan, there's no great sense of urgency. Simply...curiosity."

Their conversation was cut off when a chain, with a shackle on each end, landed a few feet away. They looked over to see Lor standing a few yards away with Tay and Aurelius. They were both holding the same chains and shackles, and Lor pointed to the restraint in the dirt.

"Pick it up," he commanded. "We're going tae run through some team exercises. Choose yer partner."

Magnus, Bane, and Galan groaned. "I'm not fighting with the Beastly Bastard again," Magnus said, pointing to Tay. "That big ox trips over his own feet."

Tay bared his teeth at him. "It's the Beast from the East," he said. "But I wouldna expect the Chicken tae remember that."

Magnus guffawed. "Ha!" he said. "Go trip up someone else, ye big ox. Aurelius is a good choice. The Irish Fart can lug ye around when ye fall."

Everyone started to laugh. "It's the Celtic Storm tae ye, Chicken," Aurelius said indignantly, shaking his fist at him. "I'm going tae pluck yer feathers when I catch ye."

Bane darted over toward Lor. "I'll partner with Lor, thank ye," he said. "At least I'll have a fighting chance."

Magnus shook his head at the man. "He's perfect for ye,

coward," he said wryly. "The Highland Dimwit and the Kitty from the Hills have teamed up."

That brought more laughter since Lor's nickname, during his fighting days, had been Lion of the Highlands. They all had slanderous versions of their fighting monikers and no one was spared. Not even Galan, the Sapphire Dragon.

Lor pointed at Magnus and Galan, standing a couple of feet apart.

"Ye've insulted everyone, so that leaves ye with Blue Lizard Guts over there," he said. "Good luck, Chicken. Ye're going tae need it."

Everyone was laughing, putting on their shackles, getting ready to fight to the last man standing as a group of *novicius* watched from the sidelines. This happened often and it was meant to show the newcomers how teamwork and tactics blended together, but with the six of them—Magnus, Lor, Bane, Galan, Tay, and Aurelius—it was usually a battle of insults and humor, and a great treat for the spectators.

But the truth was that it was a bonding of brothers.

Magnus looked forward to these moments more than the games themselves. He loved harassing Lor and Bane and Galan, and they loved harassing him in return. As he'd said once, that was how they showed their love for one another. He remembered something Lor had said to him once:

We're all part of the same clan. Ye're my brothers and I'd fight tae the death for ye, so that makes us family.

It was so very true.

On the day that Magnus had first come to the Ludus Caledonia, he could never have imagined how his life was about to change. The massive fight guild buried in the hills south of Edinburgh was to become all things to him—a place where he found his family, a place where he married his wife, and on a warm evening in late July, the place where his son, Cortez, was born. The Ludus Caledonia, to Magnus, wasn't just any place.

It was *the* place.

It was his home.

In the years to come, when his duties as the Duke of Kintyre and Lorne would take him away from the Ludus Caledonia, Magnus would always remember the lessons he learned there and the men who had left such a lasting impact. They would always remain fresh in his mind, as if he had only just left them, and wherever he went, they were never far from his heart.

Many years later, when Clegg de Lave finally passed away, Magnus kept his promise and, along with his Ludus Caledonia brothers, made the trek with Clegg's body back to Italy where he was buried next to Benedetta in a tiny church in the hills overlooking Rome. The ring Clegg had given to her and loaned to Diantha had been tucked into his closed palm.

Our time will come.

For Clegg and Benedetta, it finally had.

For Magnus and his brothers at the Ludus Caledonia, it would continue to be their time, until the end of all things. A family to treasure for always, and a love for his wife that would endure throughout eternity. Though Magnus had returned Clegg's ring, he'd replaced it with one decorated with bees.

His Sweet Bee.

The Eagle, and his legacy, would live into legend.

AUTHOR'S NOTE

I sincerely hope you enjoyed Magnus and Diantha's tale. It's quite a story!

As an author, I do a lot of research whenever I write a historical romance and this story was no exception. But there are a couple of things I'd like to mention about information incorporated into this book.

The first thing of note is the Spanish language. At this time, there was no Spain as a country, but several kingdoms in what is now modern-day Spain. As you know, our heroine is from the Kingdom of Navarre. Spanish, as a language, was spoken, however, and what Diantha speaks is Castilian Spanish, although she would have also possibly spoken Basque, depending on where she was living in Navarre. Most of the Spanish languages are similar, having all derived from Vulgar Latin, and having developed particular nuances of their own over the centuries.

The second thing of note is the marriage between Magnus and Diantha. Clegg told them to speak the words that would make them married, and they did. Believe it or not, this was perfectly legal. The Catholic Church encouraged marriage, of course, but a couple didn't have to be married by a priest. In fact, they weren't even married inside churches. Usually, it was done outside the church, but a priest wasn't even required. There is documentation of people marrying in homes or even taverns by simply speaking the words "I do." What sealed the deal, of course, was the consummation. Once that took place, the marriage was binding. You can find more information about medieval marriages online or at your local library.

For those you who enjoy family trees, here is a list of Magnus and Diantha's future children. Notice how Diantha made sure they had strong Spanish names. Spanish Highlanders are definitely something to be explored in a future book!

- Cortez
- Paloma
- Stephen
- Matias
- Catalina

Thank you for reading Magnus and Diantha's story!

Hugs,
Kathryn

Acknowledgments

This is one of the more humorous books I've written (and I hope you, as the reader got a kick out of the jokes and taunts from the gladiators), but I'd like to acknowledge where some of that humor comes from—my very own children, two of the funniest people I've ever known. To my son, James Le Veque, who inspired some of this hilarious male banter, and to my daughter, Dr. Mollie Le Veque, who takes witty remarks and humor to a whole new level. To say I'm proud of them is an understatement. They inspire me every single day.

Of course, I would be remiss if I didn't mention my husband, Rob, and his constant support. Without him, I couldn't do what I do, and my gratitude is endless.

I would also like to acknowledge my readers, without whom none of this would be possible.

And lastly, a shout-out to the team at Sourcebooks Casablanca for their expertise, diligence, and guidance, and to my agent, Sarah Elizabeth Younger. You are all amazing!

About the Author

With over one hundred published novels, Kathryn Le Veque is a critically acclaimed *USA Today* bestselling author, a charter Amazon All-Star author, and a #1 bestselling, award-winning, multipublished author in medieval historical romance.

Kathryn is a multiple award nominee and winner, including the winner of *Uncaged Book Reviews* magazine's "Raven Award" for Favorite Medieval Romance and Favorite Cover. Kathryn is also a multiple RONE nominee for *InD'Tale Magazine*, holding the record for the number of nominations. In 2018, her novel *Warwolfe* was the winner in the Romance category of the Book Excellence Award and was also a finalist for several other awards. Kathryn's books have hit the *USA Today* bestseller list more than fifteen times.

In addition to her own published works, Kathryn is the president/CEO of Dragonblade Publishing, a boutique publishing house specializing in historical romance, and the president/CEO of DragonMedia Publishing, a publishing house that publishes the Pirates of Britannia Connected World series. In July 2018, Kathryn launched yet another publishing house, WolfeBane Publishing, which publishes the World of de Wolfe Pack Connected series (formerly Kindle Worlds).

Kathryn is considered one of the top indie authors in the world with over two million copies in circulation, and her novels have been translated into several languages.